Look for *Desperate Remedy* and *Fatal Diagnosis*,
featuring Edwina Crusoe.

Coming soon in Bantam paperback!

KILL
OR
CURE

An Edwina Crusoe
Mystery

MARY KITTREDGE

BANTAM BOOKS
NEW YORK TORONTO LONDON SYDNEY AUCKLAND

This edition contains the complete text
of the original hardcover edition.
NOT ONE WORD HAS BEEN OMITTED

Kill or Cure
A Bantam Crime Line Book / published by arrangement
with St. Martin's Press

PUBLISHING HISTORY
St. Martin's hardcover edition / May 1995
Bantam paperback edition / August 1996

ISBN 0–553–57585–6

Published simultaneously in the United States and Canada

PRINTED IN THE UNITED STATES OF AMERICA
RAD 0 9 8 7 6 5 4 3 2 1

KILL OR CURE

B*eware*, Marion Bailey wanted to whisper to the two women entering the suburban coffee shop together.

The older woman, her white hair elaborately arranged, wore a plaid pleated skirt and a cream boiled-wool jacket from beneath which peeped a rope of pearls too huge and perfect to be real; her manner, though, hinted that they were real. The younger one, perhaps thirty-five, was wearing wheat-colored slacks and a black raw-silk tunic that draped her tall frame elegantly; her best feature was her mouth, which looked as if it laughed easily and didn't lie very often. Both women carried big paper shopping bags bearing the names of upscale department stores from the nearby mall.

Beware, Marion wanted to say; *all this, the coffee shop with its tables of light, polished wood and its waitresses in frilly uniforms; the good clothes you wear so carelessly, as if you were entitled to them; all your unthinking happiness:*

It is an illusion. It can be swept away in an instant.

She smoothed the papers beside her coffee cup. They were copies of the love letters her husband, Gerrald, had been sending to another woman. What kind of man, she wondered, made copies of his love letters?

She had known of the letters since the day before, when the woman from the telephone company had called. Were the Baileys having a family emergency, the woman had asked? If so, special arrangements could of course be made about the bill.

Startled, Marion had answered sharply. No, there was no family emergency, she said. Meanwhile in her mind she

1

seemed to hear a small, bright sound, as of some fragile object shattering.

Sorry, the woman from the telephone company had replied; it was only that the long-distance charges were so numerous and large, they'd been red-flagged by the billing computer. But if no special payment arrangements were needed—

There would be no trouble about the bill, Marion had told the woman, and hung up swiftly. Gerrald was away on business in Chicago (he'd said it was business; he'd said Chicago), and Gerry Junior was off camping with a friend. Marion herself was due at work very soon, as a nurse at Chelsea Memorial Hospital. Thoughtfully, she had picked up the telephone again and used it to call in sick.

All the rest of that day she had moved slowly and carefully, as if she really were an invalid, but this morning she had gone straight from bed into Gerrald's home office. Neither the phone bills nor the letters had been difficult to find, once she knew what she was looking for. Sitting on the floor in her nightgown, Marion had read them all from beginning to end.

Now she was miles from home, after driving for hours with no particular destination. Unfamiliar surroundings were comforting, somehow; it was easier, feeling so alien and strange, to be in a place she did not know.

Still, she would have to go back and decide what to do.

♦ ♦ ♦

Getting shot *hurt*. It hurt a *lot*, not like on TV where the guys just yelled and grabbed themselves, made a face and kept on running or driving or shooting back. But the pain was not the worst of it.

Gerry Bailey, thirteen years old, leaned his bike against the steps of the two-story frame house on Gillette Street where he lived with his parents, leaving his backpack strapped to the bike's aluminum rat trap in case he needed to make a quick getaway. Then he scrutinized the house, starting with the attic windows and carefully working his way down.

It was four in the afternoon; his mother was at work, and his father was in Chicago, which meant that the house was empty. *Should* be empty: Gerry finished his examination of it with a check of the innocent-looking back door. It was closed, and no twitch of the curtain betrayed anyone lying in wait behind it.

But then, it *would* look okay, wouldn't it? If someone sneaky was waiting for him, in there.

His legs made his decision for him, trembling so hard as he climbed the back steps that he thought he was going to fall. He had to get inside before old Mrs. Washington from next door saw him and came tottering over to find out what was wrong.

Gasping, he flung himself in and locked the door. No one jumped him, but the familiar smells hit him hard: clean laundry, tuna casserole, and lemon furniture polish, all the safe, silent ordinariness of home threatening suddenly to overwhelm him. Then without warning came the memory he must not, *must* not have:

The woods. Tad Conway digging in his backpack, bringing out his father's gun. And then . . .

No. Gerry's chest thumped with renewed fright, setting off bombshells of pain in his wounded ear. Nearly fainting, he made his way down the hall, staggered and caught himself on the corner of the kitchen counter.

Steady. No one was going to help him. He was thirteen years old, not some dumb little kid, and he had to get control of himself, to think and plan like the guys on TV did. Most of all, he had to get away. Otherwise the cops would catch him and *throw the book at him.* That was what his father said would happen if Gerry was ever caught for committing a crime: the cops would come and his father would tell them to *throw the book at him.*

Or maybe it wouldn't be the cops . . . but what would happen in *that* case didn't bear thinking about. Gerry grasped the banister of the hall stairs, pulling himself up. Money; he had to have money and he had to have medicine, and through the rising tide of rich, red pain foaming and hammering in his head, he was pretty sure he knew where he could find both.

In the medicine chest in his parents' bathroom were bottles of leftover prescription painkillers and antibiotics. Gerry knew they were there because his mother had told him about them, and warned him never to touch them. He'd felt like saying *she* wasn't supposed to have them, either; he'd learned in health class to throw old medicines away. But now as he got a look at himself in the bathroom mirror, he was glad he hadn't said it.

His ear was so red that it was almost purple, swollen to twice its normal size. Crumbs of blood edged the spot where the bullet had punched out a chunk of cartilage. The swelling had closed the hole, but the would was still leaking something extremely unpleasant, and the puffiness had spread into his cheek, giving him the appearance of a sick chipmunk.

Seeing it made it hurt a whole lot worse, and he didn't have to be a nurse like his mom to know that it was already getting infected. Desperately, he rummaged among the medicine bottles in the cabinet, frowning at the names on the labels.

Percodan, read one; *for pain*. Gerry shoved two of the small tablets into his mouth and swallowed them with a handful of tap water. *Amoxicillin*. It sounded like penicillin so he swallowed two of those, too. Then he took all the other bottles that said *for pain* or whose names ended in anything like *cillin* and shoved them into his pockets.

A wave of faintness washed over him; what if the pills had gone bad, or simply didn't work? Would he die? What was going to happen to him? His own eyes stared out of the mirror at him, bright and glassy the way they had been that time he'd caught the flu and had a high fever.

Okay. Chill out, now; just chill out. He steeled himself for what came next. He had to wash the ear, and apply ointment: what his mother had called *oinkment* to make him laugh, back when he was a little kid and was always falling off his tricycle or something. Blinking away tears, he reached for the necessary supplies: Mercurochrome, a tube of Bacitracin, a washcloth, and soap. This was going to hurt; still, he *had* to do it.

His hand hovered over a package of gauze squares and a roll of adhesive tape; after you cleaned a wound and applied ointment, you were supposed to put on a dressing. He was puzzling over how he could tape a gauze square to his ear and keep it there when a car pulled into the driveway.

The car door slammed. The back door of the house opened and closed. But I locked it, he thought; *how can it be opening when I locked it?*

Footsteps crossed the hallway and started up the stairs.

◆ ◆ ◆

"Gerry? What are you . . . oh, my God." Marion stopped in the bedroom doorway. Her son's face was swollen and tear-stained, filled with fear and with a kind of grief that only belonged on the face of an adult. Leaves and twigs were woven into his sweater, as if he'd fallen hard and not bothered brushing them off.

Because he was running, something was chasing him and he was running. And his ear . . . she took a step, tentatively, the way she might approach a frightened animal. A whistling sound was coming from somewhere nearby, but it couldn't be important; not now.

"Gerry. It's okay, honey, I'm not going to be mad. You can tell me. Did you have some sort of an accident?"

He nodded, his gaze darting past her into the bedroom, to the table on her side of the bed. She usually kept money in the drawer; had he been planning to steal it? To run away? But it wasn't there now; she had taken it when she left the house this morning, half-planning to run away herself. Then she noticed the prescription vials scattered across the vanity, and an even worse suspicion seized her.

"Honey, you didn't take any of those pills, did you?" There were enough drugs there to kill a horse, but he wouldn't, he didn't have any *reason*.

"Mom?" His voice came out a croak. "I don't feel so good."

The whistling grew louder. It was coming from Gerry; he was wheezing. A bolt of real fear shot through her, bracing her. "Come on," Marion said in her best I'm-your-mother-and-let's-not-have-any-more-of-this-nonsense voice. "We're going to get in the car and go see Dr. Schneider."

His eyes rolled back. The Mercurochrome bottle slipped from his hand and shattered, and he dropped as if shot.

◆   ◆   ◆

Miraculously, the kid hadn't cracked his head open or knocked a tooth down his throat when he hit the floor, and now that he had an airway, a bolus of steroids, and an IV loaded with aminophylline running into him, the pediatrician in Chelsea Memorial's emergency room that evening thought he was probably going to be all right.

The pediatrician, Roberta Glass, glanced at the cardiac monitor behind the boy's gurney, noted that his vital signs were stable, and scribbled two more consult requests into his chart. General surgery had better have a look at that ear, and pharmacy could figure out which pills he'd been allergic to.

That, of course, was the cause of his respiratory distress: a medication-induced allergic reaction. But what had he been doing in the first place, swallowing pills? With a final check of his IV line, which had been a bitch to put in but was running smoothly now, Roberta went out to talk to the kid's mom again.

Marion Bailey wore a neat sweater and skirt, stockings, and low-heeled shoes. Her hair was combed and her pocketbook was unscuffed; her features were lightly touched with makeup. She looked like a normal mom, quite normally anxious about her son. But the boy had also suffered a gunshot wound, sixteen hours or so ago by the look of it, and enough pills had been found stuffed into his pockets to stock a small drugstore.

"Dr. Glass," Mrs. Bailey said. "Is he all right?"

Telling people that their kids were going to be okay was one of the pleasanter aspects of practicing pediatrics; at least it beat hell out of telling them they weren't.

"He's doing nicely, thanks to you," Roberta said. "That was good thinking, injecting him with the bee-sting kit. But why did you have one, and how did you know you should use it?"

Mrs. Bailey smiled weakly. "His dad's allergic to bees, and I'm a nurse; I work here. So when I saw the pills and realized Gerry was wheezing . . . well, I had to do something, and I thought it might help. You're sure he's all right, now?"

"Pretty sure. We're going to keep him overnight. After that, we'll see." Roberta guided Mrs. Bailey from the waiting area into a small conference room. "Please, sit down."

Mrs. Bailey complied, frowning in confusion. "I thought you were taking me to see Gerry."

"I am. But first I need to know how Gerry was shot. I'll have to put it in my report, when I notify the police. It's the law, whenever a gunshot wound comes in. And we'll need to talk about all those pills."

"Shot? You mean . . . that's what's wrong with his ear? Someone *shot* Gerry?"

"I'm afraid so. Even with all the bruising and swelling you can still see the powder marks around the wound. Someone shot him. Or," Roberta added carefully, "he might have shot himself, accidentally. Mrs. Bailey, do you keep a gun in your home?"

She sagged. "No. Oh, my God."

"What about his father? Maybe," Roberta probed gingerly, aware from the deepening of Mrs. Bailey's frown that this was an unhappy topic, "maybe he knows something about all this."

"Mr. Bailey is in Chicago. On business. I called his hotel a little while ago, but they'd never heard of him. I suppose he must have changed his mind about where to stay."

Pain roughened the woman's voice. "I see," Roberta said, deciding not to press. "So all you know is that you came home and found Gerry in your bathroom, just before he began wheezing?"

"Yes. He'd been camping with another boy last night, out in West Park. There are teachers' conferences this week, so they didn't have school. He must have thought I'd be at work when he got home, but I . . . I took the day off. I had an errand."

She looked up defensively. "I know it might seem like too much freedom, but they've done it before, and they've always been all right."

"Perhaps if you speak to the other boy," Roberta suggested.

Mrs. Bailey jumped up. "Of course. I was so worried about Gerry, I didn't think. I'll call Tad Conway's mother right now and find out what he says happened." She left to use the phone.

Roberta felt sure that Mrs. Bailey was telling all the truth she knew. But if Gerry's friend had been there when Gerry was shot, where was the friend now? Why didn't he go with Gerry, to help him, and why hadn't the boys sought medical care, or indeed the assistance of any adults, for at least twelve hours?

Mrs. Bailey appeared in the doorway. "Janet Conway's been trying to call me," she said. "Tad hasn't come home."

◆ ◆ ◆

Working security in a big-city emergency room was no picnic. For one thing, the people who visited emergency rooms were often in bad moods; for another, they were generally drunks, dopers, pimps, punks, loonies, stumblebums, and a whole Heinz variety of other human toxic-waste situations whose moods security guard Rick Bixby didn't really give a good goddamn about, except that he had to stand there and put up with them, eight hours a shift.

What he really liked was when one of them got belligerent, which these kinds of people tended to do pretty often; they seemed to have as little control over their own emotions as they did over anything else. Then Rick got to seize the offender and march him out, or if it was a patient, lock his arms and legs in leather restraints. Rick got a charge out of the struggling and cursing that went on then, especially if the cursing was in a foreign language; Christ, Rick thought, couldn't they even learn to curse in English?

And tonight would really be a horror show, because it was a full moon *and* today was welfare-check day. That meant the loonies would all be out doing the things they did (jumping from windows or off of bridges, setting fires, sewing buttons on themselves) while the rest were busy doing what *they* did (buying pint bottles of Night Train with Rick's hard-earned tax dollars, then smashing the necks off the bottles and trying to carve one another's hearts out with them, a project at which Rick fervently wished more of them would succeed).

Sighing, he leaned against the wall of the emergency trauma admitting area. If only he could carry a gun, he would like the job better. But the hospital administration geeks didn't allow guards to carry, so all he had was a night stick, handcuffs, and a walkie-talkie in case he needed to call for help.

Right; like he was going to need help. Even without a gun he could take any jerk-off moron dumb enough to try taking him. At the moment it was quiet, though, all the people home gobbling up their rice and beans, pigs' feet, and foreign messes that who could tell what was in them: chopped-up stray cats and dogs for all Rick knew, the disgusting things those people liked to eat.

In one of the treatment rooms, a kid lay on a gurney, great big cold pack on his ear, moaning like he was trying to wake up. Tough luck, Rick thought at the kid. Shouldn't have done whatever it was you did, got you in this fix.

A woman in a wheelchair gave Rick a shaky smile; he let his eyes go blank, as if he were Superman and she were on the other side of a wall of kryptonite. Not only was she black, but she was old; another category of person Rick had absolutely no use for. The kid moaned louder, trying to sit up, but no one paid any attention and he collapsed back onto the gurney.

Then Dr. Granger came in. Rather, he didn't exactly come in; he looked in, from the waiting area.

Of everyone Rick had met in the emergency room, he liked Granger the best. Good-looking, smart, and not the least bit stuck-up despite all his money and education (even the medical students, Rick was resentfully aware, thought they were better than he was), tonight Granger wore a green scrub shirt, faded Levi's, and running shoes. Granger, Rick thought, was cool.

At the nursing desk, Granger's wife glanced up. She was pie-faced, with red hair, freckles, and a mole like a big, brown bug perched at the corner of her eyelid; in her nurse's dress she looked like a sausage wrapped in white butcher's paper. But when she smiled at Granger, she was almost pretty.

Granger nodded back at her, then resumed scanning the trauma corridor. Something was strange about Granger tonight, Rick thought with the beginnings of unease, the way the surgeon kept looking around like he was measuring the place for wallpaper or something. What the hell, Rick wondered; the guy was acting weird. Still, as a surgical staffer, Granger had just come off a thirty-six hour shift, and after a stint like that, Rick supposed Granger was entitled to act weird if he wanted to.

A lab runner hurried by, carrying a clanking metal basket of blood tubes. An X-ray machine rumbled halfway out of the elevator, got stuck, and stood there as the elevator door banged against it, trying to close. Somebody laughed, or sobbed; Rick couldn't tell which. The kid on the gurney sat up all the way this time, emitting a low groan.

And Dr. Granger produced a small, silvery handgun, placing his first shot squarely into Rick's forehead before Rick could even register the idea that his final, dying moment had arrived.

◆ ◆ ◆

"What did Granger do then?" Edwina Crusoe asked.

It was two days later, nearly forty-eight hours since one of Chelsea Memorial Hospital's brightest young physicians had walked into the emergency room and attacked three people, killing two of them.

"According to witnesses," Ed Chernoff replied, "he shot his wife at close range, at the nursing desk."

Chernoff made a pistol of his hand and fired it: boom. "She died instantly. Next, he shot at the kid."

Edwina closed her eyes. Just this morning, one of her two-year-old twins had stumbled in the midst of a temper tantrum and bumped his head on the coffee table. The injury only raised a lump, but to think of that perfect pink flesh being *shot* at. . . .

Chernoff stood at his office window, gazing out at the New Haven Green. He was a tall, slightly stoop-shouldered man with pale blue eyes, dark hair going rapidly to salt-and-pepper, and a long, deeply wrinkled face tanned the color of an old boot by years of solitary weekend sailing.

"He missed the kid, somehow," Chernoff said. "Then a couple of city cops grabbed him and rushed him out of there. I got the call from Whitelaw about two hours later."

As an attorney, Chernoff was neither as imposing-looking nor as impressive-sounding as some of the other partners in the old, highly regarded law firm that Chernoff had established. But he had one trait the other partners lacked: if he believed in you, he would bloody his arms for you, even if privately he thought that your case was hopeless and that you were going to jail.

"Tom Whitelaw," said Edwina. "President and CEO of Whitelaw Enterprises, calling in the cavalry for William

Granger." That was odd, seeing as Granger's dead wife was also Whitelaw's dead daughter. But then, Tom Whitelaw was pretty odd himself, as in Edwina's experience billionaires tended to be.

Chernoff nodded. "Whitelaw says it was obviously temporary insanity, he wants everything done to get his son-in-law freed. Says he wants Granger declared unfit to stand trial, and if that doesn't work, he wants an NGRI plea, whatever it costs."

"A not guilty by reason of insanity defense in the shooting of his daughter." Edwina didn't bother remarking on the oddness of that; Chernoff knew.

"You'd think Granger was the blood relative, instead of the girl," he agreed. "But that's Tom. Once he decides something, the rest of the world falls into line, or so he fondly believes."

"And you agreed to take it. But you don't like it."

Chernoff shrugged. "My feelings aren't at issue here. My obligations are. Whitelaw's been our firm's client a long time, personally and through his business."

"So Granger gets the defense his father-in-law is demanding, or your firm loses what, maybe a quarter of its billings?"

Chernoff grimaced. "More like half, though I'll deny I said so. What with corporate, contracts, liability, and the family's personal work . . . it goes on and on. I've told the partners we shouldn't be so dependent on one client, that someday the tail was going to want to start wagging the dog. But nobody listened, and now there's not a lawyer in the house without a nice, hot lunch, courtesy of Whitelaw Enterprises, sitting on his plate."

He sighed. "The partners would take me out and hang me if the Whitelaw billings went south. Which they would; Tom's used to getting what he wants, and what he wants is that kid off the hook, one way or another."

"Can it be done?"

Chernoff paced the carpet. "I've talked with young Granger, set up the formal interviews with the psychiatrists so we can get an initial ruling at an early competency hearing. But I'm no virgin at this stuff, Edwina; I know what they're going to find."

"He's fit to stand trial."

Ed picked up the antique cut-crystal inkwell he used for a paperweight, turning it unhappily in his hands. "He understood what was going on and was able to consult with me. He can participate in his defense."

"So you'll need to go to trial and show that although he may be competent now, he wasn't responsible for his actions at the time of the shootings."

And that, as they both knew, was a dicey proposition, since juries tended to believe in what they saw, and in their own preconceptions. Thus an alert, well-groomed, well-oriented defendant started out with three strikes against him; how could he be so normal-appearing in court, juries tended to ask themselves; if he was insane when the offense was committed?

"There's one other thing that may help us," said Chernoff. "Whitelaw's got a private psychiatrist, name of Frieda Schreiber, on Granger's case. She's not on Chelsea's staff, but she has admitting privileges there. Well thought of, a bit unorthodox, reputable as far as I've been able to learn. And she's a friend of the family; she's seen Granger several times already."

"And?" Naturally Granger would have enlisted the help of a private psychiatrist. "What's the punch line?"

Chernoff smiled thinly. "The punch line is, she specializes in multiple personality disorder; MPD, for short."

"Oh-ho, the old 'blame-it-on-my-evil-twin' routine. What do you suppose gave Whitelaw that idea?"

"The psychiatrist did, after seeing Granger. Apparently it was she, not Whitelaw, who suggested that she visit Granger, merely as a courtesy. Once she saw him, she got interested; she asked Whitelaw to hire her on, and he agreed."

"I see. You've spoken with Dr. Schreiber?"

Ed nodded. "She says MPD takes time to diagnose properly,

and devising a treatment plan can take even longer. After that, therapy may go on for years. But if Granger turns out to have it and a jury buys it, Whitelaw gets his wish; it's possible grounds for an NGRI."

"Well, then, I guess my first stop is the medical library, to read up on it. But other than that, I can't help wondering why you need me," Edwina said. "You've got investigators on your staff. And this sort of thing isn't really my line, you know; I usually snoop for victims of unscrupulous medical practitioners, not for medical practitioners themselves."

After twenty years as a registered nurse at Chelsea Memorial Hospital, Edwina had switched to investigating medical fraud. The number of outright phonies preying regularly on the fears and hopes of sick people could populate a fair-sized prison, and, she thought, ought to; her specialty was identifying medical slime toads and presenting them, along with evidence, to the Slime Toad Division of the appropriate law enforcement agency.

"I'll need somebody who's familiar with Chelsea Memorial," Chernoff said. "A lot of the information we want will come from there. And then there's the Whitelaw situation; most of my investigators couldn't get past the gatehouse, much less through the front door."

Edwina didn't like being chosen for things on the basis of her ability to get past snooty butlers, even though she had been getting past them since her mother had laced on her first pair of little white baby shoes. "You don't care about my investigating talent," she said. "You just want my social connections."

Chernoff smiled tiredly. "Not true. But you do have more than a nodding acquaintance with the Whitelaws. You knew Charity Anne, for instance."

Edwina nodded, remembering the girl that William Granger had married despite his being a poor nobody and her having what seemed like all the money in the world. Their unlikely match had been the talk of Litchfield County, until

Tom Whitelaw pulled all his household trade from the local businesses for a month to silence the gossip.

"Charity Anne was younger than I am," she said. "But their summer house is next door to ours, in Newport, and in Litchfield their year-round place is near my mother's. They even blamed me at first, when she became a nurse. Some idea of following in my footsteps, I suppose they thought."

"But she wasn't imitating you?"

"I don't think so. As I say, she was quite young when I was around. I doubt she even knew much about anything I was doing."

A clumsy little girl with thick horn-rimmed glasses, carrot-colored hair, and a habit of falling off whatever she was perched on, Charity Anne Whitelaw had had enough trouble putting her own feet one in front of the other, never mind following in anyone else's footsteps. She had spent summers clomping stubbornly after the other children, trying and failing to be included by them, until at last she had given up the pathetic effort and retreated behind a pile of books. Then, as if to add insult to injury, a little sister came along: blonde, pretty, and charming as the older girl was not. Poor Charity Anne; never an ounce of luck.

"I suppose I could talk to them," Edwina conceded. "You'll let them know I'm there on your behalf?"

"Yes, yes." Chernoff seemed relieved. "Don't worry, I'll let Whitelaw know I'm sending you, all absolutely on the up-and-up. And don't worry about what you *don't* find out; it's your own special slant I'm looking for. Along, naturally, with any little nuggets my other investigators don't happen to run into."

He got up. "And thanks for coming by on such short notice, Edwina. How are Martin and Harriet, and the little boys?"

But Edwina was not about to be hurried. "What is it, Ed? There's something else going on with this, I can tell."

Chernoff looked uncomfortable. "Well. There is one other

small thing. The boy Granger shot at, in the emergency room."

"You said Granger missed."

"Yes. But the boy's involved in another situation, one I don't completely understand. Something about a gun and a missing playmate. He's in Chelsea's adolescent psychiatric unit right now, no visitors allowed but family. And that's a problem, because Granger said something to the boy before he shot him."

Chernoff gazed levelly at Edwina. "Granger says he doesn't remember any such thing, but the witnesses all agree, so you can see why I'm curious about any remarks that Granger may have made to the young man."

"The boy's testimony could make an insanity defense."

"Or break one. And I like to know in advance whether I'm going to be presenting evidence myself or having it handed to me like my own head on a bloody platter."

Edwina looked around Chernoff's office, with its mahogany-paneled walls, its bookcases filled with gold-stamped bindings, its gleaming, green-shaded brass lamps. He still wasn't telling her the whole turth.

"What will happen if you can't do what Whitelaw wants? If it turns out an insanity plea won't hold up? Or you end up not believing in it yourself?"

That was the other thing about Ed: If he *didn't* believe in you, he would drop you like a hot rock. He could afford to, and he had the guts to do it, even if it meant leaving the firm. But now the rock seemed glued to his fingers, and she wondered why.

"I have . . . a problem," he replied quietly. "Whitelaw knows about it, don't ask me how. And please," he added, in a tone of appeal she found frightening, coming from him, "don't ask what."

It wasn't like Ed not to be forthcoming with her; they had been friends for a long time, which was why she did not press him, or not as hard as she might have.

"All right," she said at last. "I'll get any information I can to help support an insanity defense for Granger, and any that doesn't support one, so you'll know what you're up against. But I've got to know the stakes, Ed. What if this case doesn't turn out the way Tom Whitelaw wants it to?"

"Then," Chernoff answered simply, "he'll ruin me."

* * *

Edwina could never resist the medical library's display of antique surgical instruments: pincers, bonesaws, and a trephining tool from the days when the cure really was worse than the disease. In the slate-floored rotunda beneath the library dome, she gazed into the brightly lit glass case of medical relics, then signed the log book at the security desk and took one of the clip-on badges that identified her as a visitor.

Turning toward the reference area, she ignored the arched passageway opening in the direction of the historical collection. Another day, she would browse through old literature debating the benefits of smallpox immunization, extolling the wonders of antisepsis, and arguing whether or not anesthesia for childbirth pain was morally defensible, in view of Genesis 3:16. Today she went on past the checkout desk, where instead of the thump-thump of books being stamped as patrons removed them from the premises, she heard a computer-generated beep as a bar code wand passed over a coded library card, then over the bar code in each book.

In the reference room, a similarly modern information highway had been paved; Edwina stopped at one of the many CD-ROM machines lined up on the counters and typed in several key words, along with a recent date delimiter. The antiquated charms of the card catalog, she thought, were less compelling since the advent of the CD-ROM; only the oldest handwritten catalog cards, with spidery, fading script and a lingering air of having been labored over by a fussy clerk in spectacles, could deliver a pleasure equivalent to that of having a list of twenty books delivered in twenty seconds. Pressing another key, she waited while a printer whirred over a roll of form-feed paper; then she tore off the list of volumes the machine had compiled for her.

Two hours later, she had not read twenty books, but she had examined each one; in particular, she had scanned their indexes. Seated in one of the study carrels in the part of the library basement that had not yet been remodeled, surrounded by shelves filled with bound medical periodicals, she listened to the steam clinking distantly in the old pipes and radiators, and thought about what she had read.

Multiple personality disorder would not have been mentioned in the older books, which she had asked the CD-ROM machine to eliminate from its search. Sigmund Freud had recognized and described the disorder, but most psychiatrists had accepted it only recently; some still did not accept it. Until about 1980, an MPD sufferer with access to the best modern psychiatric treatment—say, in Boston or New York—might have been diagnosed instead as having schizophrenia. One who lived in a less sophisticated place or an earlier era would have been thought to be possessed by demons, and either locked in a cellar or burned at the stake, depending upon local custom.

Whitelaw's psychiatrist friend Frieda Schreiber turned out to be an authority on MPD; there was a great deal of material by and about her in the collection Edwina had assembled, including a basic monograph that Schreiber had written. According to her, one in a hundred adults had multiple personality disorder, a condition in which two or more personalities shared one body. The original personality was usually unaware of the "alternates"; the symptoms included hallucinations, depression, anxiety, and confusion over "lost" time ranging from moments to years.

The victim could not remember any time during which an "alternate" was in control, since for all practical purposes the original did not exist then, and an alternate could be law-abiding or an amoral monster. But people with MPD in a sense "created" alternate personalities to suffer in their place and to be angry or vengeful. Thus at least one alternate in a set might turn out to be a most unpleasant character, indeed.

Interestingly, one of the books also contained an article discussing the proper public persona for a psychiatrist, with examples of the kinds of popular recognition that some, including Schreiber, had garnered. Schreiber, it seemed, was not esteemed by some of her colleagues; they felt her appearances on TV talk shows, among experts consulted for sensational crime trials, and in the pages of *People* magazine, for instance, were less than perfectly dignified.

When she had read this final article, Edwina placed the books on a cart for reshelving and returned to the main floor, where the antique trephining tool still glittered in its glass case. A printed card inside the case offered the information that trephining, the process of drilling a hole into the skull, was among the earliest of surgical procedures, first practiced by prehistoric peoples. Later, trephining was done to relieve pressure on the brain, as it still was today, and in some parts of the world was performed to create an exit for demons.

At the security desk, Edwina gave back her visitor's badge and went out into the bright day. The sidewalk was crowded with purposeful-looking people hurrying to complete their well-planned tasks; a medical center attracted clear thinkers, high achievers, and serious, goal-oriented individuals with no time for demons.

What must it be like, she wondered, to discover that demons were real, and that a flock of them was hiding in one's own head?

◆ ◆ ◆

"What do you mean, he won't talk? You're his mother; tell him to talk!"

Gerrald Bailey's angry commands erupted from the earpiece of the pay phone in the waiting area of the adolescent psychiatric unit at Chelsea Memorial Hospital. The waiting area was done up in shades of mauve and blue, with chairs upholstered in a fabric specially treated, Marion imagined, to repel tears.

"How'd you get this number, anyway?" he demanded. "I don't want you calling all over the place, Marion, trying to find me."

"I got it from your secretary," said Marion. "At first, she told me she didn't know where you were and didn't have your phone number. So finally I went down there."

"You went down there," he repeated. "To my office."

His voice was low and dangerous, the way it always got when she was, as he put it, making him do something they would both regret. Usually, Marion ended up regretting it more; he rarely struck her, but the things he said could be more bruising than punches, more hurtful than pulled hair or a twisted arm.

"Yes, I did," she replied, emboldened by the thousand miles between them, and by another feeling she did not bother examining closely. "She's pretty, Gerrald. You never said how pretty your secretary was."

"And you told her what?" he grated out.

"Well, I told her that Gerry Junior had been shot, and that he was in the hospital, and that Tad Conway hadn't come home. I said the police found the spot where they were camping, and they found blood but they can't tell yet if it's Gerry's or Tad's, and that they're still looking for Tad's father's gun."

She took a deep breath. "And then I told her that if she didn't give me your phone number that very instant, I was going to kill her. And I guess she believed me, because she did. Give me your number, I mean. I had the feeling she wanted to tell me something else, too, but she didn't. What could that have been, Gerrald?"

There was a brief, charged silence. Then:

"What could that have been, Gerrald," he mimicked nastily. "Listen, I'll be home in a couple of days, and when I get there I'd better not hear any more of this kind of crap out of

you. This is all your fault, Marion, I hope you know that, the
mess you've made."

"What about Gerry?" Marion relaxed in the phone cubicle. Something about the decorating scheme of the waiting
area really did tend to soothe a person, or maybe it was only
that Gerrald *was* so far away, his voice buzzing furiously from
the telephone, as impotent as a fly battering itself against
a windowpane.

". . . tell him he'd *better* talk," Gerrald ranted, "or when I
get home I'll whip his butt for him, too. Tell him to
straighten up, unless he wants to be a weakling like you,
Marion. You *tell* him, you stupid . . ."

Gerrald himself sounded weak: terrified, in fact. *You ain't seen
nothing yet,* Marion thought, surprised at her own anger, her own
calm as he went on haranguing and threatening. Distantly she
listened to his words, which seemed as irrelevant as an overheard conversation spoken in a foreign language.

Stupid. Weakling. What had made such words so compelling, she wondered, so believably that she had taken them to
heart and trusted them all these years?

Until now. God help me, until now. Quietly, she hung up.

◆ ◆ ◆

"Dear heart," said Harriet Crusoe, "you know I am not in the
habit of bullying you." But this was exactly the habit Harriet
was in; claiming otherwise was merely her opening gambit.

"Yes, Mother," Edwina replied, wondering which of her
own habits was to be attacked. Still, she couldn't help smiling as she said it, for at eight-six, Harriet remained so vig-
orously opinionated on such a variety of subjects that she
quite gave Edwina hope for her own old age.

"Emeralinda Whitelaw," Harriet pronounced, "is one of
my oldest friends. If you propose to go snooping into the
Whitelaws' affairs, you might at least have had the courtesy
to inform me."

"Mother, I am not snooping into their affairs. I've merely
been asked to assist, by their attorney, I might add, in—"

Then she stopped. Harriet's tone *was* forbidding; only not quite forbidding enough. Edwina relaxed, deliciously aware that Harriet knew all the good gossip from Boston to Philadelphia.

"Come on, Mother; give."

"Well," Harriet drawled, gratified by Edwina's interest, "Emeralinda did telephone me this afternoon to tell me that Ed Chernoff had spoken with you. Is the poor boy still languishing in dreary bachelorhood?"

Edwina suspected that the attorney's bachelorhood was not dreary, or at least had not been so in the past, but she was not about to tell Harriet that. "Cut to the chase, will you, please, Mother? Rita's bringing the twins back any minute."

"Oh, the darling boys," Harriet enthused, beginning to list their virtues; trying to get Harriet to stick to any one subject was like trying to make a cat learn parlor tricks: it could, but it wouldn't.

"Mother," Edwina put in, "what did Emeralinda say?"

Harriet huffed exasperatedly. "I'm trying to tell you, if you'd quit interrupting me. First of all, she's devastated over Charity Anne."

"Of course," Edwina repeated, not troubling to point out the unlikeliness of this. Emeralinda Whitelaw had taken her daughter's homeliness, clumsiness, and inability to learn the social graces as deliberate personal affronts, for which no amount of good-heartedness could atone. Only marrying a doctor had raised the girl's stock from the family-standing equivalent of junk bonds, and at that the marriage had raised the young surgeon's more; Tom Whitelaw, it was well-known, had longed for a boy and had gotten instead two girls.

"And," Harriet went on, "she wants to give that child some money. The boy who was involved in the incident."

Now, that sounded more like Emeralinda. Pay them off, hush them up, hide them away: all the little inconveniences of life. Make sure, by whatever means necessary, that they did not become Emeralinda's inconveniences.

"Really," Edwina said evenly after a moment. "What do you suppose it's worth, anyway? Being shot at, at point-blank range; being terrified. Knowing you're about to die."

"Now, dear, don't be cynical." But Harriet knew the truth as well as Edwina did: Emeralinda Whitelaw was about as prone to spontaneous charity as asbestos was to spontaneous combustion. "The boy will still have medical bills," Harriet added.

"Mother, you tell Emeralinda that under no circumstances is she to offer any money to anybody. Tell her to shut up and sit tight unless she wants to be prosecuted for witness tampering or something. I mean it, now; this is serious."

"Yes, dear," Harriet replied, sounding happy about having gotten what she wanted: the pleasure of dropping this little bombshell on Edwina, and the chance to tell Emeralinda Whitelaw what to do. "And give my regards to Ed Chernoff when you see him, won't you? Such a treasure; I can't imagine why foolish old Emeralinda would want to do anything without consulting him."

But Edwina could. *Granger said something to the boy,* Ed Chernoff had reported. Perhaps Emeralinda suspected what that something was, and didn't want it repeated. Or perhaps she knew.

◆ ◆ ◆

When Edwina decided to hire a mother's helper for the two-year-old identical twins, Jonathan and Francis, she began by carefully interviewing twenty-eight applicants and ended by employing the first one. Rita Famularo was a tough, wiry-looking girl whose black hair was spiky with styling gel. Dime-store rhinestones studded her triple-pierced earlobes, and her costume for the interview had been a man's white T-shirt, baggy green shorts, and black high-top sneakers over socks the exact same pink as Pepto-Bismol.

The twins had adored her, climbing onto her lap and peering with interest at the butterfly tattoo on her left forearm. "Hey, guys," she had addressed them affectionately around her chewing gum, "wanna see me blow a bubble?"

Whereupon a pale, purple sphere had begun growing out of Rita's mouth, inexorable as some science-fiction parasite, until with a quick, deliberate inrush of her breath Rita had made it vanish again. Then she'd let them ride horsey, one on each knee, while she sang them a nonsense song that started with "Hokey-pokey winkey-wonk," and ended with something that sounded like, ". . . the king of the cannibal island!"

"Canah Eye!" Francis had shouted, entranced.

"Poka wah!" Jonathan happily agreed, climbing down at Rita's request to play with his brother.

All through the rest of the interview, the boys had murmured to one another in soft, confidential baby talk, crawling around the legs of Rita's chair and patting at her high-tops as if to make sure she was still there.

But Rita was . . . well, not particularly refined, Edwina had told her husband. Too much eye makeup, and that hair, and good heavens, the tattoo. And those clothes, as though when Rita woke up in the morning the first thing she wondered was what to put on in order to look as little as possible like anyone else.

Rita wouldn't do, Edwina decided regretfully, and besides, Harriet would have a fit. But twenty-seven interviews later, exhausted by a parade of grim disciplinarians, New Age fanatics, macrobiotic vegetarians, and garden-variety dimwits, Edwina had called Rita back. Could she, Edwina asked, start in the morning?

Rita could; now the sight of her coming into the apartment, wearing an oversized green flannel shirt, purple leggings, and silver-studded cowboy boots, merely alerted Edwina to the fact that the twins could not be far behind. In another moment, they hurled themselves at Edwina's legs, babbling excitedly about the park and the little red wagon in which Rita never seemed to tire of pulling them.

Francis opened his fist to display his newest treasure: a smooth white pebble. Jonathan offered a flattened bottle top.

"Oh, thank you," Edwina told them. "Shall we put these in the collection?"

Nodding together, they watched her with narrowed eyes, alert for any deviation in routine (lately, anything they did two days in a row had also to be done on the third, while on the fourth day they rejected it with equal vehemence). Carefully, she positioned the stone and bottle top in the perfectly straight line formed by the other treasures; a clear green marble, a penny with a hole in it, a bluejay feather, and a leather button. Next, ritual demanded that they count the objects.

"One, one, one, one, one, one," Francis numbered them, for he was the detail-oriented of the twins.

"One!" Jonathan shouted, sweeping his hand out to include them all, for he was the generalist of the pair.

"Rita," Edwina asked later, as the boys ate a supper of fish sticks and brussels sprouts (Francis eating each sprout in small, equal bites; Jonathan popping in whole ones and chewing them with expansive gusto). "Do you think you could come up to Litchfield with me for a week or so? Starting, say, tomorrow?"

Rita poured milk into each boy's plastic cup; blue with stars for Francis, red with clowns for Jonathan. She wiped the bottle and placed it in the refrigerator as Maxie the black cat meowed at her, twining around her ankles and agitating for a fish stick.

"Don't see why not," she replied, mincing a fish stick onto a plate and setting it on the floor. She would have fed Maxie caviar if Edwina had let her. "Your ma all right?"

Rita had at first been afraid of Harriet, and then in awe of her. Recently, Harriet had begun taking advantage of this, making sharp little remarks about Rita's appearance and indicating that she still did not particularly trust the girl. Rita took these comments with fairly good grace, mostly because she so idolized Harriet, but Edwina did not care for them. She hoped their spending a little time together might reconcile her mother to

Rita, and at the same time show Rita that Harriet was not always the paragon that Rita supposed.

"She ought to slow down," Rita went on now. "I told her, I said, 'All this gallivantin' around ain't healthy for an old lady like you. Can't you knit or something'?' "

"Indeed," replied Edwina, noticing that Francis had dropped one of his brussels sprouts on the floor, and rescuing it before Maxie pounced on it. Which, she wondered, had made Harriet more apoplectic: the word 'ain't,' or the suggestion that she take up knitting? "And what did she say?"

"Oh, she said I was an impertinent baggage, whatever that means, and started in on my clothes again. I think she'd like it if I wore one of those uniforms, you know? Like maids in the old movies. Frankie and Johnny, eat up your fish sticks, hey, you wanna get big and strong. So, *is* she all right? Your ma?"

Edwina rinsed the fallen brussels sprout and ate it, under Maxie's disapproving glare. "She's fine. But I have some things to take care of there, and she hasn't seen the boys in quite a while, so I thought we'd all go. If it's not inconvenient for you."

"Hey, nothin's inconvenient for me. Free as a bird, I am," Rita said, without apparent irony. She wiped the boys' hands and faces with a dampened washcloth—a maneuver which if Edwina had tried it would have triggered stereophonic howls of protest—and lifted them from their chairs.

"Now," she told them, kneeling, "gimme a kiss an' go on in an' watch that video I got for you, about the dinosaurs. When am I gonna see you again?"

"Ay em!" Francis replied stoutly.

"Ih maw!" Jonathan agreed, as they trooped off.

Edwina had once asked Rita why she spent so much time and energy on somebody else's family when she might be off getting an education or starting a family of her own, but Rita had only shrugged in the vague way she did whenever she was asked about herself. Rita seemed to have no life other than the one she led with Edwina's children, and that had worried Edwina at first.

But Rita was reliable, energetic, and clean, had plenty of common sense despite her lack of schooling, and would cheerfully have stepped in front of a truck for the boys. Hearing Francis and Jonathan called "Frankie and Johnny" like characters out of an old blues song was a small price to pay, Edwina reckoned, for such a domestic paragon. Nowadays, it hardly bothered her at all that she did not know precisely where Rita lived, what she did on her days off, or where, when the girl let herself quietly out of the apartment every evening, she was going.

◆   ◆   ◆

"How could Emeralinda even be thinking of any other kid, when her own daughter has just been killed?" Edwina's husband, Martin McIntyre, asked a few hours later as he got ready for dinner.

"That's Emeralinda," Edwina replied. "Stiff upper lip all the way. Oh, I suppose she *cares*. But Charity Anne was never exactly the object of Emeralinda's whole affection. The poor kid started boarding school when she was five, and the highlight of Emeralinda's life was when Charity Anne got to be a teenager and could be packed off to Switzerland for finishing school with the other rich young ladies. And, of course, when Charity Anne got married."

Edwina pulled the boys' bedroom door partly closed. Francis was out for the count, but Jonathan murmured a sleepy protest; sighing, she reopened the door the requisite additional inch.

When they were infants she had enjoyed being alone with the twins, but now that they were toddlers, her solitary presence provoked them into tantrums and refusals, pitched battles and impossible demands. It was as if only by defying her could they develop their own wills, an idea she found less than comforting when Francis flung himself about, red-faced and incoherent with rage, or Jonathan lay rigid, holding his breath until he turned blue. Carefully, she tiptoed from the bedroom door.

"Anyway," she went on to Martin in the dining room, "I hope that money idea of Emeralinda's was only a trial balloon. No pun intended."

He opened the cartons of Chinese takeout: moo goo gai pan for himself, shrimp and vegetables for Edwina. "I'd guess she just wanted Harriet to run the plan past you, see if you'd go along like a good little girl scout or go screaming to Chernoff. Or," he added, "to me."

"Blast, that's right. I shouldn't be talking to you about this, should I? Who's prosecuting?" she added, unrepentantly.

McIntyre gave her an amused version of what his old police colleagues would have called the hairy eyeball. A tall, dark-haired man with a lean, intelligent face, he was a prosecuting attorney himself, after an early career as a homicide detective.

"Ginny Fowler," he replied, opening another carton. "And Chernoff had better have his thinking cap on for this one; she's angry about it, and insanity's a can of worms, anyway."

"Wait a minute, how do you know Ed's going for NGRI?"

McIntyre grinned. "Doesn't take Einstein. Bright young doctor, whole future in front of him, starts blowing people away. What would your first thought be? Except for one thing."

He dipped into the cardboard carton. "And don't worry about telling me any secrets, or vice versa. If Chernoff doesn't want something getting around, he just won't tell you; he won't tell anyone, and Ginny likewise. The NGRI's on the grapevine already, though. Ginny says Ed must have a death wish."

"Really. Is an NGRI that hard to win?"

"A bitch. Used to be, the state had to prove you weren't nuts. Now, you've got to prove you were. Well," he amended, "the courts are leaning hard that way. And since Hinckley, the atmosphere is more and more that it's not enough not to be able to resist the impulse; now you've got to be so nuts that you didn't know what you were doing or couldn't comprehend that your action was wrong. Which," he concluded, "let out a lot of nuts."

Edwina chewed a snow pea. "Past behavior? Demeanor before, during, and after the act? History of drug or alcohol abuse? Prior violence or psychosis? History of institutionalization, a record of treatment for mental or emotional problems?"

McIntyre took a swallow of his beer. "All that. If Ed can get any of that, he'll use it for background. But the main thing is the guy's state of mind while he was doing the deed, and the state presumes him sane at the critical moment unless the defense can show otherwise, very convincingly."

He crossed his plastic knife and fork on his paper plate, dropped his paper napkin on top of them, and folded the plate to put into the trash. Since the twins, china and crystal were distant memories, as were bedtimes later than eleven o'clock; the nursery day began at five.

"Does he need restraining, reforming, rehabilitating, or to have retribution exacted upon him, or not?" McIntyre recited in his best law-school manner. "Retribution meaning old-fashioned punishment, a trip to the woodshed. That's all the state wants to know, not if he howls at the moon or thinks aliens send messages to him out of his electrical appliances."

"So he can be legally sane and still have a mental illness, medically speaking?"

"You got it. Classic case is the guy who was squeezing his wife's neck, but he thought he was squeezing lemons. Legally, he was insane. Guy squeezing his wife's neck because God's telling him to do it, he thinks it's right, not wrong. So *he's* legally insane, too. Probably," he added.

Edwina let McIntyre clear her place; now that she was a mother, she was barely allowed to rinse a teaspoon, much less handle trash. Martin said pregnancy and childbirth had put her so far ahead in the chores department, she wouldn't be doing any housework until after the boys grew up and went off to college.

"What was the one thing?" she asked. "You said insanity was the first approach you'd think of here, except for one thing."

"Well, first of all, the guy's been functioning on a pretty high level. I mean, he's a surgeon, not some guy who spends his time collecting cans alongside the highways, right? But what I meant was, he didn't walk into just any hospital. He walked into Chelsea Memorial. And not just into any part of it, either; he went to the emergency room."

"But he worked at Chelsea, sometimes in the emergency room. It seems natural, doesn't it, that he would . . . oh. I get it."

"Right. When he got there, he didn't just shoot anybody. He killed his wife. The whole progression implies some fairly well-organized thinking, and *that* implies he knew what he was doing, maybe even premeditation. If you look at it from that angle, shooting the guard and trying to shoot the kid just shows he knew his action was wrong and wanted to cover up. With, for instance, an insanity story."

"Oh, dear. I suppose you could see it that way."

He nodded. "What I want to know is, how come her family is on his side, financing his defense?"

"You do have a good grapevine," Edwina said. "I guess the Whitelaws must think of him as part of the family."

"Right," he said skeptically. "Harriet thinks I'm part of the family, too, but the day a hand of mine harms a hair on your head, that's the day I start tying my shoelaces with my teeth. And think of what we'd do if someone hurt Francis or Jonathan."

"We'd tear the person apart," she agreed, and stopped. Sometimes she saw each day as a sort of board game, the object being to move two toddling markers past a variety of dangers, into bonus areas of milk and cookies, through penalty boxes in which they were deliberately naughty or declared they hated her, until at last they reached the winners' squares: their own little beds.

"As for anyone killing Charity Anne," she added, "I'd have

thought Emeralinda would personally go out and grind their bones to make her bread. After all, however emotionally distant Emeralinda was, she still thought of Charity Anne as her possession, and Emeralinda doesn't take well to being deprived of her possessions."

"So," McIntyre said, "there's something wrong, and Chernoff doesn't know what but he smells a rat."

"Which is the real reason why he wants me asking questions. He wants the rat scared out now, so it doesn't surprise him, later. I'm seeing Granger in the morning," she added.

McIntyre's eyebrows went up. He had become resigned to her interest in medical mayhem, but this was different. In fact, the one thing that had encouraged Ed Chernoff about the whole case, Ed had told her as she was leaving his office, was his interview with his client.

Granger was able to cooperate with his defense, and if he stayed able to, he would be judged fit to stand trial. But according to Chernoff, even though Granger didn't hear voices or eat imaginary flies, there was something very seriously amiss in his mental status; a realization that Chernoff had come to only slowly, after talking with Granger for a while.

Edwina supposed that she was going to realize it also, and she was not looking forward to the experience.

"I'll be fine," she told McIntyre, hoping that it was true.

◆ ◆ ◆

"I don't understand. *Why* won't Gerry say what happened? Why won't he tell us where Tad is?"

Standing in the waiting area outside the psychiatric unit, Janet Conway gripped an embroidered handkerchief in both her well-manicured hands. Tiny and dark-haired, she wore trim slacks and a cashmere sweater; diamonds twinkled in her earlobes and on her left hand. "Why?" she demanded again petulantly.

The police had been looking for Tad Conway for two days but had found no sign of the boy, and a pistol was missing from his father's closet. Marion's own son was sick, but she knew where he was; she knew, at least, what was happening to him. Janet didn't even have that much, Marion reminded herself.

"The doctors think Gerry could snap out of it," Marion said, "once he gets over being so scared. He had a high fever from the ear infection, and combined with the shock . . ."

But Janet wasn't listening. "Gerry did something to Tad," she said venomously. "That's why he won't talk, and why they've got him in this place: because he's crazy and he *did something to my son*!"

Marion felt, suddenly, not at all sorry for Janet. *Your* son, she wanted to say, stole a pistol from his father. *Your* son shot Gerry and nearly killed him in that park and that's why *your* son hasn't come home: because he knows that if he does, he'll be arrested and put in jail. That's what will happen to *your* son.

But she didn't say these things. She had learned a lot about silence recently; when Gerry's doctors wanted to try a new medication, or change the dosage of an old one, Marion listened. When they tied Gerry's arms, or tried to make him walk, or sat him in a chair with a bedsheet around his waist so he wouldn't slide onto the floor, she let them do whatever they wanted.

Gerry just sat there, or lay there, or collapsed when they tried walking him. Marion sat, too, reading or watching the TV. No one else realized what Gerry was doing, but she did. He was saying no: saying it completely, with his whole self. When he got finished saying it, she thought, he would stop. If he finished.

Janet's diamonds flashed as she kneaded her handkerchief; an hour earlier, Marion had visited the ladies' room adjacent to the waiting area and flushed her own wedding and engagement rings down the toilet. Now her hand felt light, as if it might float up on its own, possibly even to slap Janet, and the absence of rings between her fingers was like a familiar itch she had suddenly discovered how to scratch.

"I'm sorry Tad's not home," she said, but she wasn't. Janet

sounded, Marion decided, just like Gerrald: everything was somebody else's fault. Meanwhile, it was nearly eleven o'clock and the nurses had promised to let her in one last time tonight. Any minute would come the voice over the intercom, the buzzing of the electronic interlock.

"You call me," Janet Conway demanded. "If he says anything about Tad, you call me, and you'd better tell the police."

"I will," Marion promised, hearing the tiny, premonitory sputter of the intercom, turning toward the door with its small square of reinforced glass.

Thinking, *I'll do as I please.*

* * *

Shortly after he was taken into custody, William Granger had received a complete physical examination and a preliminary mental health evaluation. Through Ed Chernoff, Edwina had received permission to read the notes of these examinations. The chief psychiatrist on the locked ward had been notified, and an order allowing Edwina access to the records had been written and placed in Granger's chart.

At the nursing desk, Edwina asked for and was given the dark blue three-ring binder containing Granger's history and progress notes. Also in his chart was a printed form stating that he had been involuntarily committed for a period not to exceed seventy-two hours, a second from lengthening the allowed period to thirty days, hearing to be held for confinement contemplated beyond that time, and a judge's order requiring Granger to be released, if at all, into the custody of the court; this, in effect, was a Go Directly to Jail card, and the trump card of the bunch.

Edwina took the chart to a conference room near the ward's pharmacy area, closed the door, and opened the curtain of the window looking out onto the ward itself. From here she could see the entire ward, including the length of the two corridors, the central supply area, the utility room, and the doors that were the ward's only entrances and exits: the main door, operated by a buzzer-controlled electrical inter-lock, and the fire doors at the end of each corridor. For safety reasons the fire doors were unlocked, but beyond them was a closed stairwell with no access to anything except, seven flights down, a roofed outdoor area surrounded by a chain-link fence.

At the nursing desk, a young woman with greasy brown hair stood waiting until a nurse emerged from the medication room with a paper cup. The woman, who wore a blue-striped hospital-issue robe and paper slippers, swallowed the cup's contents in a gulp and shuffled away, passing within a few feet of the conference room window. As she went by, she glanced toward Edwina, made a grotesque face, and stuck her tongue out.

Edwina flinched, then seated herself at the conference room table and busied herself with Granger's chart, begin-ning with the admission notes. Physical exam had shown Granger to be a young white male, alert and cooperative, without obvious symptoms of any organic ailment and in no apparent distress. His reflexes and vital signs were normal ex-cept for a heart rate elevated to 125; this, the physician felt, was due to situational anxiety. A large, discolored swelling on Granger's left temple was ascribed to recent blunt trauma; questioning revealed that Granger had been struck by a policeman's baton while being apprehended. The remainder of the physical exam was unremarkable.

The preliminary psychiatric workup consisted of an inter-view and several brief tests designed to elicit gross signs of mental or emotional disorder. During these, Granger re-mained alert, cooperative, and without complaints. He cor-rectly named the president of the United States, the capital of North Dakota, and himself, and he counted back by sevens from 100 to nine without a single error. He knew where he was, and the date; when asked if he knew why he was being examined, he said that it was to make sure he was physically and mentally healthy. When asked if he knew what had hap-pened before the interview, he said that he did not.

At this point, he was noted to be oriented times three and without obvious thought disorder, except for his claim of amnesia concerning events preceding the interview. But during the next portion of the exam he did not fare so well.

Granger's interpretation of familiar proverbs was abnormally concrete and revealed some fairly violent ideation; when asked to explain the phrase, "People who live in glass houses shouldn't throw stones," he said that glass could break and cut people's throats. To "Let sleeping dogs lie," he replied that a dog might bite if woken suddenly. He denied auditory hallucinations, but said he sometimes did things in response to urgings from "forces inside himself." When asked for an example, he seemed not to have heard the question; when asked if he thought "forces" might cause him to do harm, he shrugged and said, "Things happen," but did not elaborate. Asked again to recall events just prior to the examination, he remained silent, but denied other memory lapses, blackouts, or difficulty with long- or short-term memory. He vehemently denied drug use or alcohol abuse, and toxicological screens done during his physical exam confirmed his statement.

Finally, Granger's affect was inappropriate; only when asked specifically about his wife did his cheerful expression falter. Then he looked bewildered and upset, asking the examiner if she would "survive her injuries." When the examiner replied that he did not know, Granger frowned and was briefly tearful, then seemed to forget about the subject. Otherwise he appeared upbeat and confident, seeming to enjoy all the attention he was getting; at the conclusion of the interview, he thanked the examiner and prepared to leave. When told that he was being placed on a seventy-two-hour mental health hold, he made no comment but said that he was hungry and wanted to eat "a snack." He was given a plate of saltines with peanut butter and jelly and a cup of orange juice, all of which he consumed.

As Edwina was turning the final page of the notes, a tall, middle-aged woman appeared in the conference room doorway.

The woman wore a black wool cape, black leather opera gloves, and very red lipstick; her auburn hair was held back by tortoise-shell combs. Placing her briefcase on the table, she shut the door behind her and sat across from Edwina.

"Good morning," the woman began, "I'm Dr. Frieda Schreiber. Mr. Chernoff told me you would be here today, so I thought I'd better have a word with you. I see you've already familiarized yourself with Dr. Granger's history."

She frowned at the blue chart folder. "I must tell you that I do not approve of your involvement; I believe that my patient's interests are best served by professionals. No offense meant."

"None taken," Edwina replied, and of course she did not go on to tell the psychiatrist that her lipstick was the wrong shade for her complexion, that her hairstyle was unbecoming to a woman of her age, emphasizing as it did the beginnings of a double chin, and that her cape resembled part of a costume that had originally included a broomstick and a tall, pointy hat.

"However," Schreiber said, "Mr. Chernoff wishes you to be informed, and I can comply up to a point."

"What point is that?" Edwina asked, thinking that if Granger turned out to need a cure whose ingredients included eye of newt, toe of frog, and three turns around an unconsecrated grave under a full moon at midnight, he had found the right practitioner.

"The point at which I decide it would be better to maintain his confidentiality," Schreiber replied, glancing at her watch. "I have an appointment in fifteen minutes."

Edwina sat up; two could do the businesslike routine. "Ed says you've seen Dr. Granger four times since his admission. What do you think of him? What's your impression?"

Schreiber smiled patronizingly; she had a little scrap of salad lodged between her front teeth, Edwina noticed with quiet pleasure.

"My impression is of an intelligent young man with a great deal of superficial charm, which he uses to manipulate others. I had known him socially, before the incident; I've been friendly with the Whitelaw family for several years. Still, he spent our first session trying to discover precisely the degree to which he could manipulate me."

"And how far could he?"

That smile again; the tooth scrap had disappeared. "Not far, and he didn't like it, but the issue soon became inconsequential. During our next sessions he exhibited emotional lability; he was guarded and suspicious, whiny and demanding, or withdrawn and silent. Then without warning he became manic, full of grandiose plans. I found him confusing until I began to see the obvious: the organizing principle behind his presentation."

"And when did that happen?" Edwina asked. "I mean, when did he start suggesting to you that he might be a multiple? Your very presence must have suggested it to him; as a physician, he must be aware of your reputation."

Schreiber looked up quickly. "He didn't suggest it. And I haven't mentioned it to him. Really, Miss Crusoe, what do you think I am?"

Studiously ignoring the question, Edwina went on. "I ask because the medical literature suggests that a diagnosis of MPD can take years. Yet you seem to have arrived at one in only a few sessions, over a couple of days. I was wondering why."

"A *correct* diagnosis can take years if the therapist is not familiar with the disorder," Schreiber replied crisply. "During that time, the patient may be repeatedly misdiagnosed, until he or she finds an appropriate therapist who accepts the reality of the disorder and is acquainted with its symptoms and treatment."

"A therapist, in short, such as yourself. Your practice, I believe, is devoted to the treatment of multiples."

"Not exclusively. I am interested also in the mind-body connection: the manner in which physical disorders may produce mental or emotional difficulties, and vice versa. That part of my practice is located in Litchfield County, which is how I met the Whitelaws. But I doubt Dr. Granger knows anything about me, professionally; he's a surgeon, not a psychiatrist."

"But you've published very extensively on the topic of MPD. You're well thought of in the field, and you've received popular attention, too—*People* magazine, wasn't it? I think I even read something about a private clinic you want to establish, a sort of Mayo for multiples. But for that you'd need support. Money, and influence."

Schreiber got up. "I fail to see what any of this has to do with Dr. Granger. Now, if that is all you have to say—"

"And now here's a case that's sure to make news," Edwina went on. "A handsome young doctor, a rich dead wife, and an unusual mental illness. It'll make the Menendez brothers look like Wally and Beaver Cleaver. And it could make you a star; it could get you the publicity you need to build that clinic."

"This is outrageous. How dare you imply such things. How dare you say I would fake a diagnosis, just to get something I might want."

"I'm not implying that at all, Dr. Schreiber; I'm stating facts. This case could make you even more famous than you are, and that could help you raise money. But your patient could end up on trial for his life, because he's killed two people. Now, if he's sick, he's sick, and I have no problem with that, but if he isn't and we don't find it out until he *is* on trial . . ."

Schreiber eyed Edwina coldly. "Come to the point, please. I'm late for my appointment."

"My point is that you say he is cunning, manipulative, and intelligent. But considering what he's done, I don't need a psychiatrist to tell me he's also got a serious screw loose, if you'll forgive my abandoning the technical jargon for a minute; I didn't come here to dazzle you with science."

"How convenient for you, because you haven't. Miss Crusoe, just what is it that you want to know?"

"Two things. First, I want to know if he could be fooling

you, not necessarily medically, but for legal purposes. Let's say he does have a legitimate mental illness; some people would say he must have, based simply upon his recent actions."

"The 'evil-as-illness' theory of human nature? Really, Miss Crusoe, I'm surprised at you."

"I only said I'd grant it, not that I believe in it," Edwina replied. "And whether I believe it or not, it won't get him off the hook in a court of law. Could he be faking the elements of illness that he needs in order to get an NGRI verdict? That's what I want to know, because if his defense attorney doesn't find it out until he *is* in court, it'll be too late for Granger."

Schreiber looked impatient. "There is no foolproof litmus test for mental competence; that's why courts and juries are charged with deciding it. But I don't see why he would fake that sort of thing; after all, an insanity verdict could mean he would end up hospitalized for even longer than the jail term he would receive if he were found guilty."

"Maybe, but it could also be less. I grant you, an institution for the criminally insane is not a good place to try to get well, but if he's not really sick when he goes in, it won't be long until he's out, will it? Say, a couple of years before he's certified free of mental defect or disease. Then, bingo: he passes Go and gets a great big inheritance. Charity Anne was a rich woman, you know."

Schreiber frowned. "I didn't think a person could inherit from someone he'd killed."

"Common belief, but it isn't quite that simple. If you are a named beneficiary in a person's will, and convicted of killing the person, then you cannot inherit under the terms of the will."

"Would such a young woman even have had a will?"

"Oh, yes. Charity Anne would have had a will drawn in anticipation of her marriage; all rich girls do. She would have named her husband in it, too; it prevents unseemly complications. Surviving husbands suing for more than the dearly departed wives meant to leave them, and other unedifying spectacles."

Schreiber looked nonplussed. "Do wealthy people fight over money that way?" she asked, and of course Edwina did not laugh out loud.

"Sometimes a disagreement does arise," she said, struggling to keep a straight face, "even among well-off people. A matter of principle, of course."

In Edwina's experience, the disagreement often resembled a cat fight, the cause of it might be as little as fifty cents, and the principle involved, very simply, was *That's mine*! But there was no sense in disillusioning Frieda Schreiber, who apparently believed good behavior had something to do with having money.

"At any rate," Edwina went on, "to be disinherited, Granger has to be criminally convicted of causing her death. Otherwise, he'll inherit all she left him, which I happen to know is rather a lot."

"My, my. You have been doing your homework." Schreiber's expression softened slightly. "I can't help admiring that. But you've missed two things. First, Dr. Granger's presentation so far is entirely consistent with my preliminary diagnosis. And although, as you mentioned, my opinion on such matters is well-respected, any other clinician experienced with MPD would tell you the same. Not only that, but he's going to require years of treatment, another drawback for him if we accept your suggested view of the matter: that he might be faking."

She took a breath. "If he wanted to fake something, the thing to fake would be an acute psychotic break, possibly precipitated by stress. It's easier, it requires less treatment, and Dr. Granger tells me his wife was planning to divorce him; that could provide a plausible trigger for a breakdown. And of course, if he had been planning to fake something, he would know that. He would have done his homework, too."

"I didn't realize the marriage was unhappy." A divorce could indeed precipitate a breakdown, but it could also trigger a change in Charity Anne's will, unless something happened to her before she *could* change it.

"And," Schreiber went on, "even in the best possible outcome consistent with your theory, Dr. Granger would never practice medicine again. I doubt that's a sacrifice any physician would deliberately make."

She picked up her briefcase. "So, the short answer to your question is: no. I don't think he's fooling me. I don't think he even knows he's a multiple; they hardly ever do, at first. It can take years of intensive therapy for a person even to begin to accept the idea, much less know that it is true in any but the most theoretical way. You must understand, I've seen a great many of these patients."

"Have any of them killed two victims in cold blood and tried for a third?"

Schreiber's glance flickered uncomfortably. "No. But that brings me to the final defect in your argument: your worst-case scenario. You see, Miss Crusoe, although I haven't had patients involved in situations like this one before, I have surveyed the literature extensively and testified as an expert witness in several cases. I've found that an insanity plea, when it fails, almost always results in conviction on the most serious of the charges. Juries don't like defendants who they think are trying to fool them by acting crazy. And people know that intuitively; Dr. Granger, for example, would know it."

She glanced at her watch. "He is quite an arrogant young man; in my experience, surgeons often are. He might think he could fake a mental illness; he might even think he could fool me. But I doubt he'd bet his life on his ability to fool a jury; the consequences could be too devastating, and even he is not so arrogant as that. Now, I really must go. What was your other question?"

"I want to see him. Talk with him, get a sense of him. Ed Chernoff's cleared it with the district attorney's office and the ward's chief psychiatrist, but I see by the order sheet that any visitors also have to receive clearance from you."

The doctor looked long-suffering. "You know, Miss Crusoe, you are really quite annoying."

"I'll take that as a yes, then, shall I?"

Schreiber sighed. "All right. I don't see the need for it, but I doubt it can do any harm. He's not to discuss the details of the incident at all. He hasn't done anything untoward since he's been admitted, but if he should, summon a nurse. Don't try to psychoanalyze him, and limit your visit to twenty minutes or so; he's exhausted. Good day, Miss Crusoe; it's been interesting speaking with you."

"Likewise, I'm sure," Edwina replied, and watched Frieda Schreiber go in a swirl of black cape and auburn curls. Behind her, the sad-faced girl with the greasy brown hair clicked the heels of her paper slippers together three times mockingly, and began to weep.

◆ ◆ ◆

"Hi. Ed Chernoff said you'd be coming in. Have a seat."

Edwina entered the small, single-bed hospital room and sat in the straight chair near Granger's bedside table. Granger lay on the bed, which was neatly made except for the heap of pillows he was propped on. Wearing hospital pajamas, socks, and a robe that closed with velcro instead of a belt, he looked comfortable and at ease, as if enjoying a well-deserved rest.

"So," said Granger, "what would you like to talk about?"

"Well, since I'm working for Ed on your behalf, I thought it would be a good idea to meet you. Put a face to the name, so to speak."

Granger glanced at the television, which was mounted on a pair of brackets near the room's ceiling. Phil Donahue was introducing a guest.

"And my story," Granger said. "Don't forget my story."

On the screen, a man in bright makeup had begun modeling a gauze tutu. Donahue tipped his head, as if marveling at his own good fortune in learning so much about the human condition every day.

"Yes, your story," Edwina repeated; no wonder Donahue's hair had turned prematurely white.

"I'll bet Donahue would have me on, don't you think?"

"Yes. Yes, I suppose he would."

He was trying to get a rise out of her, although she could not imagine why; she was on his team. Deliberately, she began gathering the details of his looks and mannerisms into a mental snapshot she could refer to later. He was about five-ten and 160 pounds, neither skinny nor over-muscled. He had curly brown hair and a short brown beard, and was handsome in a nothing-special way; only his eyes were unusual-looking. Hazel flecked with green, they appeared at once dreamy and alert, as if he were doing the assessing; as if he were in control.

"Are they treating you well?" she asked.

"Yes. I don't remember what happened, you know," he said. "You could say it's all that's left of my life, in the sense of it being all that matters. And I don't even remember it."

Edwina thought it interesting that he should establish that point immediately, without her having inquired about it.

"What about your family? Parents, brothers, or sisters," she added at his puzzled look. "Have they been in touch?"

He shrugged. "No. I lost contact with them when I went to college. They're very ignorant people and they felt threatened by me, so once I left, I just never went back."

"I see." She wondered which his family would feel more threatened by, his superior intelligence or his having killed two innocent victims. "And your friends? You must have friends here at the hospital, being on staff, and I suppose you and Charity Anne had friends together, too. Are they sticking by you?"

"All of them," he said confidently. "They're all my friends, anyway, not hers. She was always kind of a wet blanket."

He looked up and saw Edwina noticing the barrenness of his room; even here on a secure ward, he would have been allowed to keep cards or letters, even fruit or candy, had he received any.

"But I put the word out not to write or call," he went on. "And I sure don't want them seeing me like this. Later, when I can wear real clothes, have pass privileges and so on, then I'll see them. But right now, it's better if they stay away."

Remarkable; far from feeling sorry, he was looking forward to being allowed out on his own, and having clothing items like shoelaces and belts. It was as if once he had all the freedoms and things that he wanted, everything would be fine.

Piled on his bedside table were a half dozen paperbacks, mostly science fiction and horror novels, and a spiral notebook but no pen. He saw her looking at them.

"Say, could you lend me a felt-tip? Or a ballpoint? I'd like to start writing down my impressions, see, my ideas and the experiences I have here. I think it would make great material for a book. I keep asking for something to write with, but the girls keep forgetting about me."

Smooth, very smooth, even his calling psychiatric nurses "girls," as if they were his casual pals; probably when they came in to check on him every half hour, he told himself they were enjoying his company, not observing him as if he were some strange insect.

"You're not allowed to have anything sharp," Edwina said. Let him rationalize his way out of that one.

"Right. Sorry. I keep forgetting." He put his fingers to his temples. "It's not easy getting used to all this." He let his hands fall to his sides. "Is she . . . is she really dead? What they're saying happened . . . did it?"

"Yes, it did," she replied, "but Ed Chernoff and your doctor have specifically asked me not to discuss the details with you. Also, there's a police officer sitting outside who can hear every word you say; his testimony will be admissible in court."

Granger sighed, rubbing fretfully at his wrists, as Edwina began planning what in the world she would say to Chernoff; how had he come to the conclusion that Granger was ill in

any obvious manner? The guy was very odd, but Chernoff
had made it sound as if she would find Granger perched on
a windowsill, flapping his wings. And if Ed thought Granger's behavior was going to impress a judge or a jury, the attorney was in for a disappointment.

"Just one more thing," she said, preparing to go; there was
no sense staying any longer. "Why do you think Tom
Whitelaw is taking such good care of you? I mean, finding
you a lawyer and keeping you out of jail, and getting you
into the hospital. Why do you suppose that is?"

It was Whitelaw who had parlayed a bump on the head
into a potentially life-threatening injury; otherwise, Granger
would be in a state facility, where mental health observation
was carried out in considerably less luxurious surroundings.
The DA, not wanting to risk a lawsuit, had gone along with
Whitelaw's demand for a battery of high-tech diagnostic
tests, most of which could only be performed at the medical
center.

Granger frowned, his fingers moving under his sleeves,
and winced as if contemplating some particularly difficult
problem. "I guess Tom loves me," he said, tears welling in
his eyes. "Hey, I'm a lovable guy. Aren't I? Aren't I a lovable
guy?"

A sound of visceral pain escaped his lips as spots of blood
began spreading on the blue-striped bathrobe fabric. Edwina
slammed her fist onto the red emergency call button on the
wall beside the bed.

Dreamily, Granger withdrew his hands from his bathrobe
sleeves; smiling, he held them out to her. Bright red blood
was flowing briskly down his arms, and from between each
hideously painted thumb and forefinger dangled a strip of his
flesh.

◆　◆　◆

"Tad?"

It was dark in the crawl space. And cold, terribly cold. At
one end of the space, a small square of light shone onto the

dirt floor; the hole was big enough for a boy to wiggle through, and for the light to come through. Not big enough for an adult; not quite. But the voice came through.

"I know you're in there, Tad. I can't get you out yet, but I will. Oh, I will. You can depend on it."

He forced himself farther back into the darkness.

"There are *things* in there with you, Tad, did you know that? Things. Rats, spiders. Centipedes."

The voice lingered lovingly over the words. "Big ones; big, hungry ones. Hungry for you."

Something sharp jabbed his back. The crawl space was filled with old building materials somebody had shoved there a long time ago: lumber, bricks, a roll of tarpaper, some bags of concrete. Hunkering down among them, he blundered face-first into a nest of cobwebs.

Biting his cheeks, he tasted blood, and didn't scream.

And the voice kept coming through the hole.

♦ ♦ ♦

The old Crusoe place in Litchfield County was the kind of authentic New England colonial mansion that tourists would have loved getting the chance to ooh and ah at, only they never did because they never found out about it. Facing southwest so that its back was turned against the nor'easters of Litchfield County's famously frigid winters, the house overlooked several hundred acres of prime, unspoiled New England real estate without itself ever being visible at all, except perhaps by a determined person with a telescope. Harriet complained that it could also be viewed from a helicopter, and from the hot-air balloons that sometimes floated, miragelike, over the landscape in summer. But that, Edwina thought, was only Harriet, who secretly enjoyed the idea of people troubling to spy on her from helicopters and hot-air balloons.

At the wheel of the old Volvo station wagon she had taken to driving since the twins were born (an unsatisfactory substitute for her beloved Fiat two-seater, it had the advantage of being—so far, at least—indestructible), Edwina turned off the main road onto a familiar dirt track that was muddy in summer and treacherously rutted in winter, flanked by thickets whose blooms in spring hid thorns large and sharp enough to put an eye out. Now in early winter a carpet of poison ivy spread beneath the brambles, three-lobed leaves slowly turning the color of old wine.

Home again, Edwina thought happily, for the pleasures of home seemed to multiply the longer she lived away from it. In the back, Francis and Jonathan slept, slumped like sacks of flour in their identical car seats; between them, Rita turned the pages of a magazine whose cover featured a full-color photograph of a man with a safety pin fastened through his cheek.

Musing on the question of where such magazines got the money to produce full-color photographs in the first place, and on just what sort of statement a man with a safety pin stuck through his cheek was supposed to be making anyway, Edwina muscled the Volvo on up the dirt road until she reached an iron gate. Here she got out, pressed a button on one of the pillars at either side of the gate, and waited under the silent gaze of two huge stone lions, one atop each pillar, until a familiar figure appeared.

"'Allo, Miss," the figure called. "Awfully good to 'ave you back. Brought the little nippers along, then, 'ave you? 'Ang on, we'll 'ave this gate open for you in a jiff."

"Hello, Mr. Watkins," Edwina replied, pleased at the sight of the old man stumping as reliably as ever down the lane, wearing his chilly-weather uniform of red buffalo-plaid jacket, corduroy pants, and Wellington boots. "Won't Mother have some kind of an automatic release put on that gate for you? It's a shame, your having to walk down all this way."

Watkins turned an iron key in the box-lock that fastened the gates. "Already done it. But I can't see what's what through an electrical contraption, can I? Could be anybody, mashin' on that button. B'sides, it keeps me spry, then, don't it?"

He swung the gates wide and she ran to him as she always had, feeling his arms wrap around her and burying her face in his jacket. The smells of bay rum, pipe tobacco, and wood smoke sent her back to the days when the limousine driver would collect her from the private nursery school she attended and let her out between the big iron gates where Watkins always waited for her.

"There, now," he said, holding her away. "Don't you look a treat. Go on up, she isn't 'alf excited about your coming. I'll close 'ere."

At the house, Rita took charge of the twins, flinging their bags from the Volvo's cargo area and herding the two toddlers across the pea gravel to the kitchen door, into the care of the cook. Inside, they would be stuffed with cookies and have their thirst slaked with root beer, get their greedy little hands crammed full of new toys, and in general be pampered unmercifully, that being Harriet's method of subduing twin two-year-old boys; Harriet was nothing if not efficient.

"Dear heart," she enthused, emerging from the potting shed with a pair of secateurs in one hand and a slip of midnight blue cineraria in the other, "how glad I am to see you. Leave the car; Watkins's boy will get it, and I've asked one of the upstairs girls to unpack for you. I hope that's all right?"

Harriet accompanied this remark with an acute little glance, for on past occasions Edwina had made it clear that she was not only capable of carrying and emptying her own bags, but of ironing and mending any items that happened to be found lacking in them, too; if she'd liked being waited on hand and foot, she could have remained in Litchfield. But in Harriet's household, one did as was deemed proper by Harriet; besides, it was much easier on the help if they were allowed to do for all and sundry, instead of having to remember who wanted waiting on and who did not.

"Yes, Mother," Edwina said, having conveyed her unchanged opinion on the subject with a quick little glance of her own; one of the delights of having an elderly mother, and of being on easy terms with her, was the amount of repetitive talk that could be dispensed with, so as to get straight to the good parts.

"How," she asked, "are the Whitelaws doing? I might take a ride over there tomorrow and have a chat with them. Unless you think that plan inadvisable?" She followed Harriet into the potting shed.

"I think it's a very good idea, and the sooner the better." Harriet snipped the florets from the cineraria, dipped the stem into a heap of rooting powder, and gave the cutting a brisk, businesslike shake. "Emeralinda is bearing up well, but I wish I could say the same for that horrid man she married. He drinks now more than he ever did. Lorelei, of course, just goes on as always."

She plunged the cineraria into a pot of rooting medium, tamped the rich, black mixture of soil and vermiculite firmly about its stem, and gave it a judicious watering.

"There," she told it, setting it into the warming tray under the grow lights to make up its mind: would it become a vigorous young plant, or an addition to the compost heap?

Harriet stripped off her gardening gloves. "Tom Whitelaw," she pronounced, "may be stubborn and rich, but he's also a fool. An old fool who never got the son he was hoping for, perish the thought, and spent his life fiddling around with those silly companies of his. To hear him talk, you'd think he built that pile of capital he's sitting on, clucking like the fat old hen he is, as if he were going to hatch something out of it."

She wiped the secateurs with antiseptic and dried them before putting them away; Harriet's potting shed, like the rest of her very extensive establishment, was as clean and well-organized as an operating room. Edwina glanced with appreciation at the rock maple potting benches, the quarry-tile floor, and the clay pots from thumb-sized to gigantic all scrubbed and arranged on their shelves. At the back of the shed was a sliding glass door leading to a greenhouse where, if it behaved well now, Harriet's cineraria might hope to live out its more mature days in temperature-controlled luxury; in the center of the greenhouse sparkled a pool in which Harriet still swam fifty laps every day.

Glancing at the pool, Harriet veered off into a report of what her doctor had said: that at her age, she might be overdoing things. But she loved the pool and would just as soon be found floating in it as giving up swimming in it; besides, if she let one thing slip, another would surely follow, and *then* where would she be?

"Perish the thought?" asked Edwina, who was used to catching onto a thread of her mother's conversation and holding it while the rest of the skein spun out. "Why shouldn't Tom Whitelaw have had a son? And why shouldn't he be pleased with himself for getting so rich? He made a fortune, and you must admit that's *almost* as good as inheriting one."

Harriet scowled, pulling off her gardening apron. "I," she replied, "must admit no such thing."

Edwina suppressed a grin. In Harriet's opinion, new money was almost as bad as none, and was often worse, since having it in no way guaranteed knowing what to do with it. Harriet's idea of decent, respectable money was money from which the grime of commerce had long been rubbed, preferably by jostling against a lot of other old money in some enormous old trust fund somewhere.

"Besides," Harriet added, "he didn't make it. He married it." She paused for Edwina to absorb the implications of this. "And then he expected Emeralinda to deliver him an heir to the fortune, a male heir, mind you, on top of the fortune itself."

"Ah," said Edwina, beginning to be enlightened. "I never knew it was Emeralinda's money." She followed her mother from the potting shed into the champagne-colored light of an early December afternoon, her footsteps crunching loudly in the bright, white pea-gravel of the dirt.

"That was part of the deal," Harriet said. "Emeralinda behaved as if it were his money, so that within a few years there was hardly anyone who remembered that it wasn't, and she let him manage it, too. Not," Harriet added grudgingly, "that he's done such a bad job of that. But he's been a dreadful father to those two girls, and with a son, he'd have been worse. Girls are more resilient."

"Indeed," said Edwina. "And what did Emeralinda get out of the deal? She must have been madly in love with him; otherwise I can't imagine her not putting him in his place at every step. Or are his people some fine old family I've never heard of?"

This was so unlikely that Harriet did not bother to reply; owing to her ancestors and upbringing, there were hardly any fine old families Edwina had never heard of. Emeralinda had done a magician's job of inserting Tom Whitelaw into the tight, xenophobic little enclave that was old-monied Litchfield society, so that now, just a generation later, only a few elderly folk remained who remembered that he hadn't been there all along.

"Love?" Harriet's laugh tinkled thinly as she opened the door of the big house, her gaze raking the paneled entry area in case anything in it had been dirtied, or moved and not put back exactly in its place, since last she had inspected it.

Edwina followed, inhaling the smells of home: beeswax, lemon oil, lavender and cloves, and something delicious roasting out in the kitchen. From the hall came the measured ticking of the clock her great-great-grandfather Crusoe had brought back from one of his trips to Germany; upstairs, faint creakings and patterings were doubtless the sounds of a new maid who had not yet learned to go about silently.

"That girl," Harriet sighed, confirming Edwina's guess. "She used to belong to Beatrice Olderman, who finally had to give up and go into a home, and I promised I'd take her."

Not for the first time, Edwina regretted her mother's turn of phrase; on matters to do with class, Harriet's outlook might accurately be described as prehistoric. Still, Harriet paid her employees exorbitantly, lavished medical and pension benefits on them, and in several cases had educated their children, or if the children turned out (in her opinion) to be

ineducable, found work for them; more than one incorrigible
Litchfield lout, Edwina happened to know, had set his foot at
last on the straight and narrow after a stint as one of
Watkins's boys.

"Why did she marry him, then," Edwina asked, "if it
wasn't for love?"

By now she had hung her coat in the cloakroom, checked
on the boys, who were happily munching cake, and seated
herself in the dining room. Lunch was she-crab bisque
thinned with a splash of sherry, split Vermont milk crackers
toasted and spread with Brie, and a salad of artichoke hearts
dressed in olive oil and balsamic vinegar. To wash down this
simple repast, Harriet had chosen an unassuming little *premier cru* that tasted like heaven and did not quite cost the
earth; Edwina raised her glass to her own good fortune, and
prepared to be edified.

"Emeralinda Kent was the only child," began Harriet, "of
the two worst drunks you have ever seen in your life. Charming, but hopeless at anything but flitting about the social
scene. And of course, at producing Emeralinda."

She applied herself to her bisque. "Your father used to say
they'd have been better off as golden retrievers. Beautiful,
you know, but stupid."

Mother, Edwina was about to say, will you get to the
point? Harriet silenced her with a look.

"At any rate," she continued, "one morning the pair of
them were coming home in their sports car, after a night on
the town. They got all the way from Manhattan to Washington Depot, don't ask me how, when they ran off the road,
through a hayfield, and straight into an oak tree."

Harriet took a sip of her wine, and then another. "Well,"
she went on at last, "Martin Fryer, whose oak tree it was,
heard the crash and got to the car while the acorns were still
falling on it. He said it was the neatest double beheading
he'd ever seen, not that he'd seen many, but you get the
picture."

Unfortunately, Edwina did.

"Which left Emeralinda alone. A convent-school girl, just seventeen years old, and rich as sin. Naturally, she was at once surrounded by lawyers, one of whom was Thomas Whitelaw."

"Oh," said Edwina, seeing now how Emeralinda and Whitelaw had formed their alliance. "She married him for her money."

"Precisely. Even at that age she knew a shark pool when she saw one, some wanting a bite of this, some a bite of that. And she knew better than to bloody the waters with a lot of piecemeal fish food, too."

"They'd get her," Edwina said. "The lawyers would all get together, and divvy her up among themselves. So she married one of them, to help her hold the rest off."

Harried nodded. "And that's how Thomas Whitelaw became the second-richest man in Litchfield County, second only to your father. He soon gave up his practice and spent his time managing the family fortune."

A thought struck Edwina. "Was Ed Chernoff one of them? One of the lawyer sharks?"

Harriet eyed Edwina. "Why, yes," she replied. "I believe he was." She picked up the small silver bell by her plate; at its summons a woman in a uniform appeared to clear the table.

"Come along," Harried told Edwina, "I'll show you the new gloxinias from White Flower Farm. They're spectacular and I have high hopes for them. Unless you need to cross-examine your poor old mother any further?"

"Well, I do have one more question. I can see why a man might want a son, and take a son-in-law as next best. And I can understand why a man like Thomas Whitelaw would want to marry off his daughters, too; after all, they would inherit hugely someday. He would assume that married women were less vulnerable to the sort of fortune hunter he had been, wouldn't he?"

"I told you he was a fool," Harriet commented.

"But," Edwina went on, "it was Charity Anne who married Billy Granger, not Lorelei. And I can't help wondering . . ."

"Lorelei is pretty and as rich as Charity Anne was, so why not marry Lorelei off first?"

"Exactly." Edwina followed Harriet into the sun room where the gloxinias waited. "And Charity Anne was bright; she might even have been able to manage a fortune on her own."

Harriet began undoing the brown paper parcel with the White Flower Farm insignia on the label. "And Lorelei is stupid? Tut-tut, mustn't underestimate. There's a brain beneath all that yellow hair. And you forget: even among the rich, marriages are not arranged with the same coldhearted efficiency as they once were, back in the good old days."

She lifted the gloxinia bulbs from the wood shavings packed around them. "In fact I believe Granger courted both girls for a while, but Lorelei wouldn't marry him. Wouldn't have anything to do with him. Charity Anne got him on the rebound and didn't even care, she was just so happy to have made the catch."

Harriet looked up, her pale old eyes knowing and amused. A lifetime of writing romance novels had made her, if not quite a cynic, then a realist, and having more money than God had finished the job; she could afford never to be deceived.

"So," she queried, "who turned out to be the stupid one, in the end?"

◆　◆　◆

"I don't understand," Marion Bailey said. "What do you mean, his hospital stay isn't covered by insurance? My husband's insurance policy covers all our medical expenses."

The hospital billing clerk faced her across a counter, in a little booth designed for this sort of interview: plenty of space on the clerk's side, hardly any on Marion's, and between them a sliding window that could be closed, should the conversation turn nasty.

Which it was about to; the clerk's voice was apologetic but firm. "I'm sorry to have to tell you this, Mrs. Bailey, but that policy has been canceled. I've checked, and I'm certain there's no mistake."

"Canceled? But my husband, through his company . . ."

Gerrald's medical insurance was free, as a job benefit, and it covered the whole family. So she had elected not to sign on for coverage at the hospital; why pay when you didn't have to?

"Mrs. Bailey," the billing clerk said gently, "your husband is no longer employed by that company. The policy was canceled when he left the position, about three weeks ago."

"Oh," Marion said, stunned. So it wasn't only a girlfriend Gerrald had been hiding; he'd quit his job without telling her, then left town and even tried to keep her from finding out where he was. But the enormity of Gerrald's betrayal paled against the immediate implications of it. What would happen to Gerry Junior?

The clerk's voice brought Marion back to the present. "I'm sorry," the clerk said, "but your son will have to be transferred to anther facility. Chelsea Memorial doesn't provide uncovered custodial care. There isn't any funding for it."

Marion stared. "But Gerry isn't receiving custodial care. He's acutely ill. Ask his doctors. They're trying everything, trying to find something that will . . ."

Snap him out of it, said a cruel voice in her head. *Turn him back into the boy he was last week, instead of a slack-faced, drooling lump that can't keep food in its mouth and has to have its diapers changed. Something to undo what's been done to him: a brain transplant, maybe. Or a time machine. God knows they've tried everything else.*

The clerk looked regretful, but she was adamant. You walked into a hospital, you handed your fate to utilization-review boards, whose sole concern was that you not occupy a bed or receive treatment for an instant longer than was absolutely necessary, and to cost-containment specialists, whose job was to make sure somebody paid for every aspirin tablet you swallowed and bandage you bloodied.

"He's not a custodial patient," Marion whispered.

But he was. They'd tried everything; nothing was working. He could get his medications adjusted, his diapers changed and a sheet tied around his waist in a state facility just as well as he could here.

"When?" she asked, close to tears. All at once she knew how welfare patients felt, sick and beaten and impoverished, sitting across from clerks in booths like this one, listening to the way their lives were going to go.

"The doctors reassigned his status this morning," the clerk said. "The social worker's trying to line up a bed for him over at Briar Hill."

Marion's heart sank. "Isn't there anywhere else?"

Briar Hill was a warehouse with forty-bed wards, rows of beds with kids tied into them, staff so overworked that a child was lucky to be seen by a professional person once a week. Only the saintly or the decidedly unsaintly worked there; every year another awful story about the place came out in the newspapers.

"I'm sorry," the clerk said again, rustling her folderful of papers in a way that let Marion know the interview was over. "Meanwhile, you'll want to start thinking about how to pay your son's bill. I'm going to set up an appointment for you with one of the hospital's financial specialists."

"Financial specialists." The words shocked Marion out of the swamp of confusion she'd begun sinking into.

"Yes," the clerk said, "to set up a payment schedule. It would help if you could pay something right now. Based on what I've seen so far, the bill is going to be rather large, so the sooner you get started on it, the better." She glanced at her watch with ill-concealed impatience.

Probably, Marion thought, it was time for the clerk's break; God forbid anything should mess up her routine. First destroy a person's life, then head to the cafeteria for coffee and a piece of pastry.

She leaned over the counter. Her heart, she noticed, was beating fast. "Now, you listen to me," she said in a tone she had never heard coming out of her own mouth before. It was a tone that suggested mayhem, last-ditch acts of violence committed suddenly in public places by desperate people.

"My son was attacked in this hospital's emergency room," she said, "by a member of this hospital's medical staff. Gerry came in with a minor gunshot wound and an allergic reaction, and the emergency room incident *caused* his psychiatric condition."

Whatever that is, said the nasty little voice in her head.

"Mrs. Bailey," began the clerk, "I don't think——"

"I don't care what you think. He's not to be transferred. He's to stay where he is, for as long as I say. And as far as bills are concerned, I think this hospital owes *him* money, and I'll let you how *much* money after I've talked with my attorney."

Whoever that is, remarked the nasty voice in her head, but Marion told it to shut up.

◆ ◆ ◆

Anywhere strange but at Harriet's house, the boys refused to go to sleep, unless they were in the same bed as Edwina. Hotels were bad, and friends' houses were worse; at least in hotels, the beds were wide, so Edwina could lie down with one of the twins on either side of her and sneak out later, to slide in beside Martin in his big bed. At friends' homes, Francis would fling himself red-faced and shrieking to the floor, where he pounded his fists and kicked his little feet; Jonathan would hold his breath until he fainted. Edwina suspected that what they really wanted was to drink martinis and smoke cigars with other freakishly precocious infants; staying up late with their parents was only a symbol of the delights they were being deprived of. She suspected too that some of her friends thought seriously about tranquilizer darts.

But at Harriet's house, peace reigned supreme. By seven in

the evening, both boys were out cold; Edwina thought the amount of attention they received here, combined with all the mothering going on around the place, must make them feel extra-secure, or perhaps only exhausted. She turned out the light in the nursery next to Rita's room and tiptoed out.

"Crashed?" Rita asked, coming up the back stairway with a bottle of Coca-Cola in her hand.

Edwina nodded. "They're sound asleep, and probably they'll stay that way, they're both so tired. I'm sorry there's not much for you to do here in the evenings. You could go to a movie or something," she offered, "if you feel like taking the Volvo into Litchfield."

Rita shook her head. For her costume this evening she had chosen the top half of a pair of red long johns, partly covered by a hand-embroidered velvet vest; the embroiderer had been fond of sequins. The bottom half of the outfit was a pair of slim black leggings; alone, these would have been too plain, so Rita had accessorized them with a pair of purple boxer shorts, thick woolen socks the color of oatmeal, and hiking boots.

"That's okay," said Rita, cracking her gum. "I brought some magazines and tapes, and there's that big TV in my room. I'll stay here and listen for the boys so you can visit with your ma."

Edwina didn't even want to contemplate Rita's hair, or her remarkable makeup. Back in New Haven, Rita looked like a cross between a homeless person and a fashion model; here, against a backdrop of polished pine floors, antique heirlooms, and crystal chandeliers, she looked more like someone who had just dropped in from Mars.

Still, she was so good with the boys and so easy to be around. Edwina couldn't imagine giving anyone else run of the apartment, or letting anyone else take charge of Francis and Jonathan, but she trusted this mother's helper completely.

"Rita, has my mother been making you feel uncomfortable? She doesn't mean to, you know. She's just very . . . opinionated."

Rita laughed, heading for her room with her Coke. "She's that, all right. She said I ought to stand up straighter and take better care of my skin."

Edwina wondered if Rita's laugh sounded a little forced.

"Oh, an' watch how I talk around the boys," the girl went on, frowning as she fingered a blemish near her eyebrow, "on account of they could pick up my bad diction. An' not chew gum, she said, 'cause it looks gruesome, so I didn't while I was with her, but now I am again, just when I'm upstairs."

The girl grinned; was it, Edwina wondered, a perfectly happy grin? "She's right," Rita said. "Your ma gives good advice."

But too much of it, Edwina thought, exasperated.

"That all?" Rita asked cheerfully.

Anyone else could have made the question sound snotty, and with plenty of reason; after listening to one of Harriet's little lectures on the art of self-improvement, Edwina herself had been known to turn moderately snappish.

"Yes, Rita," Edwina said. "That's all. Thank you."

Rita closed her door; a moment later, Edwina heard the door into the boys' room opening quietly. She thought of asking Rita to keep the volume down on the television, but stopped herself. If the boys woke up, they could watch TV with Rita, or she would read them stories. They would be fine.

So Harriet's comment shocked Edwina, when she found her mother in the pantry counting up the silver before putting it away. Harriet said she did it for the insurance company, which otherwise would have made her keep the heavy old pieces in a box at the bank. Edwina thought the counting-up had become a ritual, like looking in all the closets and under the bed at night before going to sleep. Thinking this, she believed at first that she had misunderstood Harriet's words.

"I said, you'd better watch that girl," Harriet repeated,

slotting another butter knife into the silver chest. "Don't you notice how she looks at things? As if she's eating them up with her eyes. She hasn't got two pennies to rub together, but she wants to have. That one bears watching."

Suddenly, Harriet Crusoe's clear-eyed outlook seemed a good deal less clear, and a hundred times less attractive, than it had only a few hours earlier. "Mother," Edwina managed, "I trust Rita to take care of my children."

"Yes, you do. And I think it's a mistake. What do you know about her? Nothing, because nothing is what she's told you. Those ridiculous things she wears, and the way she behaves to me. Even when I criticize her, she practically curtsies. It isn't," she finished, "natural."

Edwina stared. Harriet was in high dudgeon. "Mother, what exactly do you think Rita might do? Steal things? Spray-paint grafitti? Kidnap the boys, maybe, and hold them for ransom?"

That was a hot one. Anyone but Rita who had them for more than a few hours would soon be paying Edwina to take them back. Harriet seemed to read Edwina's thought.

"They're not as wild as all that. They're upstairs asleep like two little angels right this minute," she pointed out.

"Because they're exhausted, and zonked out from metabolizing all the sugary things they've been eating all day. Which, by the way, Rita does not let them do at home because I've asked her not to, and unlike some people, Rita listens to what I say; sometimes she even behaves accordingly."

"Fine." Harriet lowered the top of the silver chest and locked it, and dropped the key ring into her apron pocket. "Just remember what I said, when the inevitable happens."

Softening, she turned in appeal. "Dear, I truly don't mean to interfere."

Then stop, Edwina thought. "Mother, why are you doing this? I know you don't much approve of Rita, but you've never seemed so against her before. Is something else wrong?"

Harriet frowned. "Of course not. What could be wrong?"

"Have you been feeling all right?"

"I feel fine, and do not patronize me, please. I've said what I have to say. What you do about it is your affair."

Edwina thought Harriet ought to needlepoint that last phrase onto a pillow, or cross-stitch it onto a sampler. *Or have it tattooed on her arm,* she thought, uncharitably. The idea that anything was strictly another person's affair and not her own to meddle in was one that could use some fastening into Harriet's consciousness, one way or another.

But Harriet had no spare time for needlework; what with the running of the big old house, gardening and swimming and social activities, and the production of the romance novels she wrote at the steady rate of five pages per day, Harriet had no spare time at all. Each book still sold copies mounting into the millions, too, so that when Harriet did have an extra moment, she dictated replies to her fan mail.

Which, Edwina thought, was beside the point; clearly, Harriet had something on her mind, and it was causing her to be even pickier and more meddling than usual. Just as clearly, she wanted Edwina to go away; not forever, but for a little while. Harriet required time to herself, lots of it, and at regular intervals; she always had.

"Maybe I'll see if the Whitelaws would like company this evening, instead of tomorrow," Edwina said. "It's only seven-thirty now. Do you think they'd mind?"

Harriet smiled gratefully. "I think that's a lovely plan, and I'm sure they'd enjoy seeing you."

She took off her apron and stepped into Edwina's embrace, smelling as always of Pear's soap, scented face powder, and Joy perfume. Against Edwina's shoulder her elaborately coiffed white head trembled slightly with early Parkinson's disease, and in Edwina's arms her body felt tiny and fragile, a bundle of frail sticks.

"You're sure you wouldn't rather I stay?" Edwina asked.

"Of course not. Give Emeralinda my love, and be careful on the road. That curve just before you get to Cornwall Bridge is a perfect horror."

Harriet smiled, composed and ready for her own evening. She was a good mother.

◆ ◆ ◆

With the sound turned down so it was nearly inaudible, Rita Famularo flipped the channels on the big color television until she found one that was broadcasting music videos. On the screen, the lead singer of Six Dead Cannibals screamed and flailed his arms while the other Cannibals pretended to be boiling him in a pot. The song, called "Eating Your Heart Out," was boring; all the Six Dead Cannibals' songs were, but Rita like the costumes.

On their thin, religiously exercised bodies the Cannibals wore ballet tights, leotard tops silk-screened in jungle designs, and red satin hearts positioned like targets on their chests. They wore necklaces that looked like real teeth and bones, and their lips were stained as if they really had been eating hearts.

Rita sat back and watched the video analytically. If she had been doing the Cannibals' design for this song, she would have given them tattoos, realistic native-looking ones across their foreheads and cheeks. She would not have put a bone in the lead singer's nose; that was corny. And she certainly wouldn't have used dark body makeup, since everybody knew the Cannibals were not black, but if they insisted on being dark she would have made them all get tans, then oiled them until they glistened.

Jonathan appeared at her elbow, his sleeping eyes wide at the sight of the men cavorting on the screen. "Bad," he murmured, getting the point of it all at once.

Rita changed the channel and lifted him up beside her, where he settled comfortably; moments later, Francis climbed into her lap. On the TV, *Masterpiece Theatre* was starting; the drama was Part One of a lavishly produced family saga that took place in a house nearly as big and luxurious as the one Rita was in now.

Frowning, Rita tried the channels again, but everything

else was either too violent for the boys or too foreign for her; sitcoms in which everyone seemed to have plenty of money, solid families, and lots of opportunities made Rita feel disoriented, as if the programs were being beamed from a distant planet. She switched back to *Masterpiece Theatre*, which was at least up-front about being a fantasy; in that way, it was like the music videos.

"Gamma," Francis chortled, pointing at the elegant old lady who was the matriarch of the family-saga clan. Rita knew she was a matriarch because Alistair Cooke had said so, introducing the drama.

She wished Francis hadn't mentioned his grandmother. Mrs. Crusoe had seemed angry with Rita, only Rita didn't know why. She didn't often react to other people's anger when she thought it was unfounded. But in some indefinable way she felt that Mrs. Crusoe must have a good reason for her anger, and that Rita herself was inadequate to understanding what it was. Mrs. Crusoe, with all her energy and talent, her indomitable vigor and purpose, was in essence all that Rita dreamed of being, and never could be, for the simple reason that Rita did not have any money.

It was all very well to have energy and talent, Rita thought; both of those she had in spades. But when you lived from paycheck to paycheck in a furnished room, where you'd moved to get away from your alcoholic mother and abusive stepfather, you needed more. What you needed was some kind of a break.

"Mine," said Jonathan, waving his chubby hand to indicate the expensively furnished room with its canopied bed and huge color TV, its plush carpeting and heavy draperies. He had begun saying "mine" about everything lately, but in a way, he was right: probably he and Francis would own all of this someday. Both boys would go to private schools and be put through college, have careers that fulfilled their talents and ambitions, and on top of that, they would always be rich.

Rita shifted between the boys in the big, soft chair. Old

Mrs. Crusoe had a sharp tongue, but she knew so many things that Rita didn't know: how to talk and behave so that people respected her, how to move through life in an orderly way so the things she wanted done got done. And the reason for it all was simple.

Mrs. Crusoe was tough, smart, and determined, and that plus a fifty-cent piece would get her a cup of coffee, but without the fifty-cent piece, it wouldn't. Rita sighed deeply, as the little boys drowsed against her.

Money. If only she could get some.

◆ ◆ ◆

Working the evening shift at the hospital, Jennifer dreaded the hours after eight most of all, because that was when the visitors went home. Psychiatric patients were on their best behavior for company, thinking that if they behaved "normally" enough for friends and family, they might be discharged sooner.

But when the visitors left, the atmosphere changed. Nobody was on their best behavior anymore; it was back to business as usual, and that scared Jennifer half to death, even though she was only a ward secretary and not really responsible for anything that went on. She was just terrified of mentally ill people.

Straightening in her chair behind the nursing desk with the telephone and the call-light console both blessedly silent for once, she forced herself to get on with the census report, which had to be sent to the admitting department. Based on it, the emergency room staff would know how many new patients they could send up during the night shift. On the census sheet, she listed each patient's name, room number, diagnosis, and condition, added up the number of beds filled, and totaled the number available.

Next, Jennifer divided the number of patients the ward had presently by the number of nurses scheduled for duty on the night shift to get the staff ratio: one nurse to every three patients, one to four, or one to five. Fewer than one to five meant the ward was closed, no matter how many beds it actually had vacant; anything more than one to three meant another, less well staffed ward could try to pull one of the extra nurses for its own needs during the night. Tonight, the ratio as usual was one to five, if no one called in sick; staffing was short on the night shift.

The ward's two corridors were known as A and B; A had even-numbered rooms, and B had odd. Jennifer finished the census and handed it to the head nurse to be initialed and sent off just as someone on the A corridor began screaming.

One of the nurses made a "help me, Lord" face, and got up from her own chair behind the nursing desk. "I wonder how long he'd keep at if it I just let him howl?" she remarked to nobody in particular, and ambled down the corridor toward the source of the commotion.

"Criminy," said the head nurse when Jennifer handed her the census sheet. "Three paranoid schizos, two new acute psychotic breaks, a half-dozen suicide risks, and Bill Granger. I hope the pharmacy remembered to send up enough Thorazine, or it's gonna be a hot time on the old ward tonight."

The screaming was hoarse and rhythmic, as if it were coming out of a machine. Jennifer reminded herself that she needed this job, that Personnel had promised a transfer to another department as soon as one became available, and that in only two hours and twenty-nine more minutes, she could get out of here.

"Who's Bill Granger?" she asked, more to be hearing something besides the screaming than because she really cared.

The head nurse looked up in surprise. She was a gray-haired old battle-axe with a gruff, no-nonsense manner, but Jennifer liked her; she made Jennifer feel safe.

"He's the guy who shot up the ER the other night, killed a guard and his own wife. In for psych-eval, meek as a little lamb, then this morning he starts on this self-mutilation kick."

The old nurse shook her head, scrutinizing the census sheet. "Scratched big gouges in his arms, they had to put mitts on him, keep him from doing it some more."

Jennifer was sorry she'd asked. The screaming intensified to frenzied howling, then suddenly shut off like a switch.

"Hmph. About time." The head nurse initialed the census sheet and handed it back to Jennifer. "Granger," she snorted. "I could evaluate *him*. He's got 'em running in circles, looking for a diagnosis. Nobody can get a handle on him."

"You could?" Jennifer asked. She didn't really want to know any more about Granger, but if there was something she did want, it was the idea that a person could get a handle on things.

Smiling, the nurse resembled an amiable bulldog Jennifer had seen once, dressed up in a nurse's costume with a lot of other trained dogs, doing tricks. Even the head nurse's hands were like big, clumsy paws; only when she was with a patient did you see how delicate they really were. She had become a nurse before Jennifer was born, Jennifer realized suddenly.

"Bill Granger," the nurse said flatly, "is a lying son of a bitch. If he's sick, I'm Emily Dickinson."

"You mean he's faking?" Jennifer struggled with the idea. Being here on purpose, wanting to be here at all: that *was* crazy.

The old nurse winked. "Don't tell anyone I said that. But you heard it here first. Believe me, when you've been around as long as I have, you can tell, not that anyone's going to ask me. Now, get that census report out of here before the ER sends us another batch."

Two hours and nineteen minutes later, Jennifer's shift was over; the electric interlock clicked shut behind her, and she was free. The lounge area was quiet, dim-lit by a single lamp; in her hurry, Jennifer nearly missed seeing the figure that sat in a dark corner. Startled, she quickened her step toward the corridor to the elevators, but changed her mind in midstride and snapped another lamp on instead. Darn it, she worked here, she belonged here, and if whoever that was *didn't* belong here, she was going to call security.

"Can I help you?" she demanded, in her best official ward-secretary voice. She could sound pretty brisk and business-like when she had to.

The figure looked up slowly; Jennifer recognized her. It was the mother of one of the patients on the teenage ward, whose visitors shared the lounge. Jennifer opened her mouth to say she was sorry, but the woman spoke first.

"No, you can't help me," she said. "I'm going to have to help myself." Then she laughed, as if at an amusing joke.

The sound chilled Jennifer; it resembled the mad laughter she had always been terrified to hear, and now heard too often. It was crazy-sounding, worse than screaming. She peered more closely at the woman, whose eyes were ringed with fatigue and who gazed back with perfect, passive lucidity.

"I'm trying to figure out what to do," the woman said, "and I've decided I'm going to sit here until I have figured it out."

Jennifer frowned. A person couldn't sit forever outside a psychiatric ward, figuring out what to do. What if there wasn't anything to do, or at least not anything good?

Still, there was something about the woman: a calmness, some kind of confidence, combined with the look of a person who had been driven into a corner and didn't have any choice. Jennifer thought the woman might actually do it: sit there.

Sit there and figure it out.

"I'm sorry about your son," Jennifer said.

"Thank you," the woman replied. "Good night."

Jennifer crossed the lounge, and looked back; the woman was gazing at a blank patch of wall, nodding as if in agreement with herself. Maybe I should call security, Jennifer thought.

The elevator door opened; Jennifer stepped in. The woman's face had taken on a slight frown of concentration.

No, Jennifer decided *Let her sit there. She's not hurting any-thing.*

And if she's sick, I'm Emily Dickinson.

◆   ◆   ◆

The Whitelaw mansion, called Merrivale, had been built at the turn of the century by the architect who created Marble House and The Breakers for the Vanderbilts in Newport. It had twenty bedrooms and almost as many baths, a grand entrance hall with a ceiling decorated in gold leaf, and a third-floor ballroom in which, it was rumored, a ghostly twenty-piece orchestra could still be heard playing fox trots on certain evenings.

Tonight, however, was not one of those evenings, and not only because of the temperature, which had plummeted to freezing. The house had been sided in Sing Sing marble, which was limestone quarried by prison inmates; some of its forbidding aspect was due to this circumstance, but not all. Merrivale, Edwina reflected as she pulled into the driveway circle, had rarely been less merry than it was tonight.

Picking her way in the moonlight between the box hedges, she found the front door and stood there while the sound of the big old iron knocker echoed within. Finally came footsteps crossing the tiled entry hall; the peephole cover in the heavy, old door slid aside, a bolt grated, and the door opened.

"Edwina, how wonderful to see you," Lorelei Whitelaw said, "and it's lovely of you to come. Mother and Daddy are so sad, they need someone to talk to. Come in, and give me your coat."

Edwina stepped into the hall, which was like some vast chamber of an enormous art museum, while Lorelei Whitelaw handed Edwina's coat to the uniformed black woman who appeared, looking anxious, behind Lorelei. At the Whitelaw mansion, black help was the rule; Edwina had long ago chosen not to ask why, because she knew she would so much dislike the answer.

"I'm sorry about Charity Anne," Edwina said. "Please accept my sympathies, and Martin's, too."

Lorelei's smile faltered. "Thank you. It's awful. I mean, everyone knows Charity Anne and I weren't close, but I can't seem to get my mind around it. Why he would do such a thing, I mean."

"I don't think anyone knows. Yet," Edwina added, thinking that this was not the first thing Lorelei had been unable to get her mind around, and was unlikely to be the last. Lorelei was a healthy-looking blonde with cornflower blue eyes, perfect skin, and a glow that came from plenty of vigorous daily exercise, plus about a zillion watts of sex appeal. But Lorelei was no mental giant, whatever Harriet said about her, and it occurred to Edwina that the girl's uncomplicated outlook ought not to be wasted, under the circumstances.

"Lorelei, wait," she said as Lorelei turned to lead the way across the vast hall; at this hour, the elder Whitelaws would be in the evening room at the other side of the house. "You and I could chat, before I see your parents. I'd like your own opinion on a few things."

Lorelei flushed, perhaps at the idea that anyone could be interested in her opinions. "All right. Let's go out in the kitchen. I haven't eaten my apple yet today. I'm so sick of apples."

"Then why do you eat them?" They passed through the pantry with its pair of walk-in freezers, double refrigerator, and rows of shelves filled with flour, salt, spices, and other culinary ingredients; Emeralinda was famous for the quality of her table, if not perhaps for its quantity.

From a room beyond the pantry came the sound of a cops-and-robbers TV show and a whiff of cigarette smoke. Edwina would very much have liked to enter this room and to talk to whomever she found in it, but questioning the kitchen help was probably not on Emeralinda's list of acceptable visiting activities. Besides, the servants were off duty now, and it would be too bad to catch them enjoying their forbidden cigarettes; Emeralinda was a terror on the topic of smoking.

"If I don't eat apples," Lorelei said morosely, "I'll eat cookies and potato chips. Three fruits, five vegetables, eight glasses of water; I'm a walking chart of the healthy food groups. But it's that or get as big as the Goodyear blimp." She plucked an apple from the bowl on the counter and crunched into it.

One of the charms of Lorelei's beauty was that it looked so effortless. But in the bright lights of the kitchen, Edwina saw Lorelei's eyebrows, plucked into soft, arched wings, and her nails, so regularly manicured that the cuticles barely existed; her makeup, of which there was actually quite a lot, had been artfully applied to look like none.

"You take a lot of trouble with your appearance. That is," Edwina said sincerely, "you look great. It's too bad Charity Anne never tried to . . . well. I probably shouldn't say that."

Leading into a potentially sensitive topic was tricky, especially with someone like Lorelei; a lifetime of being thought less than brilliant tended to instill a certain caution in people, except of course in those who truly were dim-witted.

Which Lorelei was not. "Too bad my sister never took a page out of my book? Believe me, I tried. Once I even got her to sit still for a make-over. I fixed her hair and face, did her nails, and gave her one of my outfits to put on. She took one look at herself and headed for the shower. After that I never bothered."

"Why? That is, why did she undo it all?"

Lorelei chewed her apple slowly. "Charity Anne thought I got the beauty," she said finally, "and she got the brains. And she was used to it. You know how things can be not the way you want them—they can hurt, even—but at least they're familiar? Charity Anne was like that."

She finished her apple, dropped the core into the garbage disposal, and turned it on briefly. Nothing as messily organic as composting occurred anywhere near the Whitelaw establishment.

"Sometimes I wonder, though," Lorelei said, "what it would have been like. If she'd . . . well, if she'd liked me."

She laughed sadly. "But I guess there's no point in wondering that, is there?"

"My mother says Billy Granger made a play for you. Before he and Charity Anne started dating, I mean."

Lorelei shrugged. She was wearing a sky blue jogging suit of some lusciously fleecy material and white moccasins, soft and comfortable-looking. But her answering look was sharp.

"I saw him a couple of times. We didn't hit it off, so I stopped seeing him. I wasn't mad at her for stealing him away, if that's what you mean. She was welcome to him."

And what a comfort that must have been, Edwina thought, that Charity Anne could have Billy Granger because Lorelei didn't want him. "What about him? He didn't mind when you dropped him?"

Lorelei looked impatient; for a moment, Edwina saw the hard edges underneath the soft exterior. Lorelei, when all was said and done, was a beautiful woman with a lot of money and a habit of getting just exactly what she wanted, most of the time.

"I don't know if he minded or not. It wasn't up to him." She frowned at her nails. "Look, this new polish is chipping, and I spent a fortune on it. I'm going to complain about it."

It wasn't that Lorelei was stupid, exactly; it was that she seemed interested exclusively in trivial things; for anything beyond the excruciatingly superficial, she had the attention span of a fruit fly.

Or so it seemed she wanted people to think. Edwina sensed a carefully guarded personality beneath Lorelei Whitelaw's beautifully groomed surface.

"Did Charity Anne ever mention any trouble between herself and Billy? Do you know if they quarreled? I've heard she was planning to get a divorce, but I don't know why. Did she ever say anything about him threatening her, or hitting her?"

Lorelei looked impatient. "How would I know? I told you, my sister and I weren't close." Her cornflower blue eyes clouded with petulance.

"I'm sorry. I know this is a difficult time for you."

The apology seemed to satisfy Lorelei, who tossed her yellow hair. For an instant the gesture reminded Edwina of a horse, preeningly accepting a sugar lump.

"Anyway," Lorelei said, "if they fought, she never mentioned it. That was her marriage made in heaven; it was supposed to be perfect. Maybe she did want a divorce, but she'd have killed herself before she said anything about it to me, or to Mother and Daddy."

Still, something must have hinted in advance that all was not well; people didn't just shoot one another out of a clear blue sky. Had Charity Anne been too proud, or too frightened, to admit that her marriage was deteriorating?

"What was he like?" Edwina asked.

Lorelei frowned, considering. "Intense. Hard-working. He was a first-year surgical resident, and they drive them like mules. He liked coming up here to get away from it all, he said, when he had any time off. Funny thing was, he didn't even want to be a doctor. He told me that when we were dating. He wanted to be a writer, but there's not much money in it; not enough. He felt bad about it, he said, but he'd made his decision and that was that."

Edwina recalled the notebooks on Granger's bedside table, and his request for a writing instrument. "Did he seem like the kind of person who could handle pressure? Being a surgeon, well, there are other specialties he could have picked. And then, when he married Charity Anne—"

"Then he was rich, and could have quit?" Lorelei laughed mirthlessly. "You don't know my father. Even Charity Anne wasn't allowed not to work, unless she wanted to live here, like I do. If Billy had gone that route he wouldn't have been sitting around writing anything. He'd have been digging a new dry well for the guest house, or breaking up rocks for the garden wall."

"I see." A life spent under Tom Whitelaw's thumb couldn't have looked attractive to Granger, especially if it was spent at manual labor. Still, a surgeon's life was slavery, too, unless it was the life a person wanted.

"Was Billy the sort of guy who always picked the hardest thing to do?" Lots of medical types were. "And found out too late, maybe, that he'd picked something he really disliked?"

Lorelei shook her head. "He felt trapped, I know that much. He felt he didn't have any choice. So I guess maybe he snapped."

"Maybe," Edwina repeated doubtfully. He hadn't lashed out at his work; he'd lashed out at his wife.

"Anyway, Daddy wants an insanity defense," Lorelei went on, "because he thinks then he might get Billy back someday, if he's in a hospital instead of jail. To Daddy, marrying Billy was the only good thing Charity Anne ever did; he wanted a son more than anything. And Mother wants it, I guess, because it's the best of a bad deal."

She looked up. "I mean, socially speaking, it's better to have a sick person than a convicted murderer in the family. Not that she approves of either one, naturally, but if it's a flat-out felony she can't put much of a spin on it, can she?"

Lorelei might not be too bright, Edwina thought, but there were some things she had absorbed with her mother's milk; one was *What does Daddy want?* and the other was *What will people think?*

The people in question were the chosen few whom Emeralinda thought fit to sit at her dinner table; the trouble was, in the wink of an eye they might decide her table wasn't fit for them. Rich people could be so fickle, Edwina though wryly; one little homicide conviction and suddenly you were persona non grata.

"And what do you want?" she asked, not that Lorelei's wishes were going to cut much ice. One Whitelaw wanting something was unstoppable; get them both going in the same direction, even if their motives differed, and you might as well step out in front of the Metroliner.

Lorelei picked polish off her fingernail. "Even if it was only temporary insanity, he'd have to be crazy to do what he did, wouldn't he? That's the only way I can figure it out."

She took a deep breath. "So what I want is for this to be

all over. Charity Anne is buried and now we can have the
memorial service. Mother's already arranged for the food and
drinks, and for extra help to serve and clean up for the reception, after the service. Once that's over, I can put it behind
me. To forget it; that's all I want."

For a moment the look in her wide blue eyes was defensive, but only for a moment.

"I told you, my sister and I were never close."

◆ ◆ ◆

"Well, well," Tom Whitelaw boomed, putting down his glass
of whiskey and soda. "Here's the little Crusoe girl, all grown
up."

He was a red-faced man with lanky white hair, big hands
that he waved when he was talking, and a bluff, hale-fellow-
well-met manner that was, as Harriet put it, all show and no
blow.

Across the room, Emeralinda Whitelaw winced in a way
guaranteed to be noticed by almost any woman and missed
by all but the most observant of men.

She hates him, Edwina realized, *and wants me to know it. Or
she wants me to think I know it.* Edwina smiled levelly back at
the old woman: *message received.*

"Forgive an old man for not getting out of his chair," Tom
Whitelaw said, gesturing at his cane. "Sit down. Have a
drink?"

"No, thank you. I can't stay long. I just wanted to stop in
and tell you how sorry I am about everything, and to let you
know I'll help in any way I can. Ed Chernoff sends his regards," she added, turning to Emeralinda.

The old woman's smile was acid. "Dear Edward. Thomas
has such great faith in his abilities, and in Frieda Schreiber's."

"The boy broke down," Whitelaw said. "There's no cause
for what he did. Obviously, he needs treatment. Freida's a
fine psychiatrist, and Chernoff's going to make sure the boy
gets all the care he needs."

Emeralinda's face expressed clearly the sort of treatment

she thought Billy Granger ought to receive. If a lynching party could have been assembled at that moment, she would have provided the refreshments.

The silence lengthened. Edwina wondered if she ought to plunge in; Ed Chernoff would have warned them that her visit was not purely a social call. But she was unsure, given the conflict apparently simmering, where to begin; anything that smoothed the way with one Whitelaw might rankle the other.

Emeralinda took pity on her, at last. "You want to know about him," she said. "Our son-in-law: what he was like, who his friends were, how he behaved. Whether or not we saw it coming."

As she had, her tone suggested, only nobody had listened to her. Edwina noted also Emeralinda's use of the past tense, and the way her husband bridled against it. If Granger expected to return to the bosom of this family, he would be about as welcome as an asp as far as Emeralinda was concerned, and the battle was escalating into a full-scale power struggle between the two old people.

"There was nothing to see," Whitelaw asserted truculently. "He was under more pressure than we knew; work, a new marriage, getting himself accepted as part of this family."

He shot a dark look at Emeralinda. "He should have talked to me about it, man to man. Possibly I could have done something to help him, before he broke down."

Like putting him to work in the garden, breaking up rocks, Edwina thought. "I wonder about his family," she said. "His relatives. He told me he's estranged from them, but surely you met them? You've spoken to them since the . . . the tragedy?"

"I talked to his mother on the telephone, soon after the children announced their plans," Emeralinda said. "She was dreadful, refusing to come to the wedding. She made it clear she wanted no part of me, and the feeling, I assure you, was mutual. The father, I hear, is an itinerant laborer of some kind; I got the clear impression he's a ne'er-do-well, and I doubt we'll hear any more from either of them."

"You've told them, though, about what's happened?"

"The number," Emeralinda replied significantly, "has been disconnected, no doubt for nonpayment of the bill. Unless they all moved back to the hills of West Virginia, or wherever it is they came from. I wash my hands of them; if William wants his parents to know his troubles, he can tell them himself. The same goes for his friends, if he has any; he didn't bring any of them to the wedding, either."

She bent forward, a lean, horse-faced woman with dark, heavy-lidded eyes and a long nose down which she peered intently. "Everyone was talking about it. It was as if he'd just dropped in from outer space."

Of course, that would be a sticking point with Emeralinda; as pedigrees went, Billy Granger was nothing more than a pound puppy, and she liked her genealogies gilded.

"But Charity Anne would do what she would do," the old woman went on with barely concealed wrath. "And Thomas, of course, was all in favor." She settled back, her thin, aristocratic nostrils flaring, to await what foolishness her husband would utter next.

"The boy's people were unfortunate," he conceded. "But not every girl marries a Vanderbilt," he added with pointed emphasis.

Pink spots appeared on Emeralinda's cheeks; she gripped her walking stick. That she herself had not married a Vanderbilt was clearly still a matter of some emotion for her. Quickly, Edwina put in a comment of her own, before another murder could occur in this unfortunate family.

"In other words, you don't know," she said.

She got up and walked around the room. "You don't know his family," she said, fingering the keys of the Steinway grand. A few sour notes told her that music was not among the consolations of the household. "And you don't know his friends."

She turned to the bookshelves, where morocco-bound volumes were arranged, punctuated here and there with recent dust jackets: Book-of-the-Month Club and Reader's Digest Condensed. Emeralinda read literary romance, apparently, while her husband preferred the new military thrillers. Unless, of course, it was the other way around.

"In short, you don't know much about the man your daughter married except what *you* think and feel about him. But what I need are facts, you see. Ones Ed Chernoff can assemble and present to the jury; ones that will support an insanity defense."

Whitelaw looked disgruntled at her tone. In his opinion, the facts were what *he* said they were, and woe betide the person who suggested otherwise. Emeralinda bridled, too, but her dark eyes glittered.

"You'll have to find the people who have the facts Ed needs so badly," she said. "What's the old saying, that the truth shall make you free?"

She laughed, a bitter sound that degenerated into a coughing spell. "Free us, my dear," she managed when she could catch her breath. "Free us from that awful young man. Losing our daughter is bad enough, but to have a convicted murderer in the family . . . I don't think I could bear it."

"It's not a matter of what you can bear," her husband said. "It's a matter of what's right. He had a mental breakdown and did something dreadful, something tragic. But if we're the only decent family he has, all the more reason we should help him. Dr. Schreiber agrees, and I'm sure the facts," he added, "will bear me out in my opinion."

Or *else*, his tone implied, causing Edwina to wonder again just what hold Whitelaw had over Ed Chernoff.

"I'll do my best to help," she said, preparing to go. As she crossed the vast tiled hall alone, the same black woman as before appeared, carrying Edwina's coat.

"Good night, ma'am," the woman said, letting Edwina out. "Be careful, it's dark."

The cold, fresh air was bracing after the suffocating air of

conflict and sorrow in the house, but as she crossed the driveway something continued troubling Edwina; reaching her car
with its litter of toys, books, and other little-boy items, she
realized what it was.

The Whitelaws' daughter had died a few days ago, and
they hadn't even held the service yet, but neither of the parents seemed particularly grief-stricken. Emeralinda was worried about salvaging her social standing, while Thomas
Whitelaw wanted to champion the young man for reasons of
his own.

They were upset, certainly, but mostly on account of their
own preoccupations, next to which their daughter's death
seemed almost beside the point. It was as if Merrivale itself
had closed seamlessly up to fill the place Charity Anne had
occupied.

Or as if she had never really had a place there at all.

◆ ◆ ◆

"Tad? I know you're in there, Tad, and I know you can hear
me."

He was hungry and thirsty and he had to go to the bathroom; he had to go badly. But the voice kept coming through
the hole, and he wasn't getting near it; not in a million years.

Once, the shape of a face had appeared in the hole, blocking the light so that Tad could not see its features. He'd
pitched a brick at it, and it had not appeared again.

That was good, because his arms were so cramped up now,
he wasn't sure he could even lift a brick. He'd been here for
hours, maybe even a whole day; maybe, he thought uncomfortably, for a whole lot longer. Time was getting kind of
weird, the difference between an hour and a minute getting
strangely blurry.

"Tad, I'm leaving for a while. There's food out here, and
soda. And you can use the john."

Tad came alert. Yeah, sure, he was stupid enough to fall
for that trick. He narrowed his eyes, wishing they could
shoot cosmic rays.

"Honest, Tad, I'm leaving. You can come out. Of course, you won't be able to get out of the house, and there's no phone. And the windows . . . well, you'll find out about that. But I want you to be able to eat and drink, and if I try to push anything in there, you'll probably clobber my hand with a board or something. Besides, I can't push the john in there."

Tad looked at the pile of jagged-ended boards, filing away the idea of their usefulness as weapons for future reference. From outside the hole he heard water running, a pan being filled, and the *whuff!* of a gas burner being lit. Keys jingled, shoes scraped the floor, and the door slammed. And then nothing.

Trick, it was a trick. He'd stick his head out through the hole and the trap would snap shut; no way was he going along with that.

But there was no other way out of the crawl space. Built of concrete blocks on three of its sides, it shared a wallboard partition with the rest of the house on the fourth side. Only the ragged hole, which Tad figured had been left to shove junk lumber and other building discards through, offered escape.

A smell came through the hole. For an instant he panicked, thinking it was smoke, but it wasn't: it was coffee. He could kill for a hot cup of coffee. Eyeing the lumber pile again, he decided that maybe he would.

◆ ◆ ◆

As the teaching hospital associated with a major university medical school, Chelsea Memorial was the stomping grounds of some of the country's most eminent physicians, as well as some of its prize jerks. Frederick Glosser, M.D., the Dean of Medical School Admissions, had promised Edwina an appointment at two-fifteen; it was now three-thirty, and even his secretary looked apologetic.

"He's often late for appointments, I'm afraid," she said. "Dr. Glosser is a very busy man."

And I, Edwina thought, am a busy woman, God forbid he should ever think of that. Fortunately, she had not driven all the way down here from Litchfield only to see him. She didn't really even need to talk with Glosser, only to get some files from him.

"I wonder," she said to the secretary, not feeling hopeful, "if possibly you could help me."

But almost before she finished describing what she wanted, the secretary handed over a file folder. "I made several copies of everything people were asking for when they began calling," she explained, "including the material on Dr. Granger. We've had so many calls: newspapers, the TV and radio stations, the police, district attorneys, attorneys for the estate of the guard who was killed, and Dr. Granger's attorney, too. Dr. Glosser finally told me just to give the material to anyone who asked for it."

Edwina flipped through the folder, which was very complete: transcripts, essay, résumé, references. "What about the boy?"

The secretary looked puzzled.

"There was a boy involved in the incident. In the emergency room. I should think his family would have quite a case."

"Now that you mention it, there was," the secretary said. "I read that part in the newspaper, myself. But I haven't heard from them yet. Oh, dear, perhaps I should make more copies of the files."

"Maybe you should. Unless his parents think lawsuits are against their religion, they're going to be suing the dickens out of the hospital right along with everybody else."

"Oh, dear," the secretary said again, and got up to turn the copying machine back on.

Outside, Edwina tucked the file folder into her bag and joined the hurrying throng: students lugging backpacks full of books and papers, clerks and secretaries leaving at the end of the day shift, interns and residents in scrub suits, headed for in-service lectures or to afternoon rounds. Crossing the street, she entered the hospital lobby and took the elevator upstairs.

Ed Chernoff had set up an appointment for her here, with one of the people Granger had named when asked to provide a list of his friends and acquaintances, persons who might vouch for his character; the one Chernoff wanted Edwina to meet was an ex-roommate and medical-school classmate of Granger's named Sheila Klainberg. But first, Edwina wanted the lowdown on Klainberg herself, and for the lowdown on anyone at Chelsea Memorial Hospital there was only one man to see: Michael Milliston Horton Hasbrouck III, M.D., Chief of Medical Staff at Chelsea.

She found him on the medical ward. "Don't hurt 'em, and don't scare 'em," he was saying to a group of interns and medical students gathered in the doorway of a treatment room. She stood on tiptoe to peer over their shoulders into the room, where a large, pleasant-appearing black woman sat on the examining table, wearing a rayon dress, a green felt hat, and an expression that looked doubtful in the extreme.

"Because if you hurt 'em, or scare 'em," said Dr. Hasbrouck, who was better known as Mickey Three, "their airways'll close up and you'll never get into 'em. Am I right, Mrs. Wilcox?"

"Oh, yes," Mrs. Wilcox said, eyeing the long, thin catheter Mickey Three was brandishing. "Where do you think you're going to put that thing, anyway?" she blurted.

"Now, Mrs. Wilcox," Mickey Three replied smoothly, "I think we both know the answer to that question, don't we?"

Edwina shook her head; if there was a foremost authority on not hurting 'em and not scaring 'em, Mickey Three was it. Some of his students said that if he could get you talking, Mickey could take your appendix out without your noticing; Edwina had once seen him get a blood-gas sample, put in an endotracheal tube, and catheterize a left subclavian artery before the patient even realized he had been admitted to the hospital.

Edwina owed her friendship with Mickey to a medical

school happy hour one evening when he was rip-roaring
drunk, just after his wife had left him for a housepainter.
Mickey said he should have figured it out earlier, because the
painter had been coming to the house every day for two
weeks, and the house had aluminum siding. Full of misery
and gin, he had poured out his sorrows, some of which concerned his father's stock-market manipulations; a day later
when he got over his hangover he had called to beg her not
to repeat the family secrets he had revealed to her. His father,
he said, was not a normal man.

This was an understatement: Mickey Two was the East
Coast's most successful crime boss since Don Corleone. The
difference was, his hit men were ones who could predict a
rise in the value of a penny stock twenty minutes before the
decimal point moved three places to the right. They knew
how to read a quarterly report; more important, they could
get one in timely fashion, which for their purposes was after
it arrived at the printer but before it was distributed to
stockholders.

Meanwhile, once he got over his wife and the housepainter, Mickey Three had become a fountain of useful, enter-
taining information; he adored gossip, it turned out, and
could dish it with the best of them once he knew that it
would not be repeated. So Edwina felt sure that if there was
anything interesting to report about Dr. Sheila Klainberg,
Mickey Three would report it. Patiently, she waited for the
students to finish questioning him, so she could ask him a
few questions of her own.

◆   ◆   ◆

"Edwina, you look like a million bucks," Mickey Three said.
"Mrs. Wilcox, this is Edwina Crusoe. She's a nurse. I hope
you don't mind having her in here with us? Good; open
wide."

At Mickey's insistence, the treatment room on Chelsea's
nonacute medical ward had been turned into an unofficial
outpatient clinic; so many of the ward's patients were poor,

and so many of their visitors had medical problems, that Mickey Three had simply begun treating them himself, saying he liked to keep his hand in.

"Uh-huh," he said, aiming a flashlight down Mrs. Wilcox's throat. He charged any treatments or prescriptions his clinic visitors needed to the accounts of patients they had come to see, a practice he justified by saying that if they waited until they were sick enough to go to the emergency room, they would get the same care but at five times the cost and with ten times the risk of complications, and they still wouldn't be able to pay the bill, so what difference did it make?

Edwina was pretty sure there was a flaw in that reasoning, but she didn't care. She sat down to wait, on a chair so rickety that it might have been intended to drum up business for the orthopedic clinic, in a twelve-foot treatment room with old green linoleum, battered walls, and a collection of medical equipment that had been brand-new right around the time the germ theory of disease was first being developed.

Fortunately, most of the cases Mickey saw there didn't need much in the way of cutting-edge medical paraphernalia, and this one was no exception. Seated on the edge of the examining table, Mrs. Wilcox opened her mouth again and without protest let Mickey put a long, cotton-tipped swab much farther down her throat than Edwina would have thought humanly possible to tolerate.

"Bingo, all done," he said, withdrawing the swab, whereupon Mrs. Wilcox swallowed hard and blinked; otherwise, she gave no sign that she had even noticed a procedure so unpleasant that, as Rita had once put it after being diagnosed with a throat infection, it was like being gagged with a backhoe.

Mickey popped the end of the swab into a test tube, corked it, and dusted his hands together. "Technique," he said, "it's all in the technique, and by God, I've got it."

Mrs. Wilcox rolled her eyes at Edwina. "He do think he's good, don't he?" she commented.

"Ah, but I am good," Mickey said. "I got that catheter right down into your left mainstem bronchus a little while ago, without your turning a hair, snagged up a truly interesting-looking sputum sample."

He began washing his hands. "You, on the other hand, are not good. You have strep throat, and it's not going away. I assume you have not been taking the penicillin pills I prescribed for you. And," he intoned severely, "I want to know why."

"I gave them to my granddaughter," Mrs. Wilcox said. "She had a sore throat, too, and her mama don't have any money for any medicine. So I gave the pills to the child."

"I see." Mickey Three wiped his hands on a paper towel. "In that case, I shall have to give you two prescriptions. One for you, and one for your granddaughter, who is how old?"

"Sixteen. She's sixteen years old."

"Sixteen." Mickey Three made his face resolutely cheerful as he scribbled on the prescription paid. "I don't suppose she would like to come in and have a chat with me? I could peek at her sore throat."

Mrs. Wilcox looked at Mickey Three. "Uh-uh, she won't come. I be telling her, come with me, see your granddaddy one more time 'fore he die, but she won't listen. She young, you know."

Mickey pursed his lips thoughtfully. "Young. And busy, I suppose. Lots of friends."

"Yes." Mrs. Wilcox and Mickey Three were silent, as together they contemplated the many possible time-consuming activities of a sixteen-year-old ghetto child with a persistent sore throat and a lot of friends.

"Well," he said at last, "you get the prescriptions filled, anyway, and you be sure to take yours, this time. And now," he asked, turning to Edwina when Mrs. Wilcox had gone out, clutching the prescription slips, "what can I do for you?"

Edwina raised her eyebrow. "Well, you can tell me if you really think the granddaughter has strep throat. Have inner-city health statistics for young adults' medical problems changed more than I realized, since I worked here?"

Mickey shrugged. "She could have strep throat. Or it could be pharyngeal gonorrhea. Either way, I've got her covered with the penicillin. If she takes it," he added sadly.

He squinted at the cubicle's window, clean on the inside, filthy on the outside, overlooking the city beyond the medical center: blocks of crumbling tenements, burned-out auto carcasses, and garbage-strewn vacant lots.

"You know, Edwina, sometimes I wonder if that swishing sound I hear is the sound of a whole generation, circling the drain."

She got up and took his arm, moving him from the window. "Come on. You need coffee, and I need information. Trust me," she added when he seemed not to want to leave the treatment room, "it'll be therapeutic."

The solarium was a hospital decorator's nightmare: old Naugahyde lounge chairs patched with friction tape; drab carpet, and faded paint. Patients were not supposed to be segregated by method of payment—private insurance patients to one ward, public assistance clients to another—but it tended to work out that way, because the public patients had so many more cases of tuberculosis, hepatitis, and AIDS, ailments that were grouped together for practical or epidemiological reasons. And of course when remodeling money was doled out, it headed in the direction of the insurance money, since money always liked the company of other money, in Edwina's experience.

"I don't know much about Bill Granger," Mickey Three said. "He's on the surgical side, and I know mostly medical people. But from what I've heard here and there, he's kind of a son of a bitch: brilliant, but not very well motivated. Charming when he wants something from you, and a little rat bastard if you cross him. Typical surgeon," Mickey joked, but he wasn't really joking; he obviously didn't like Granger's reputation.

"Anything else?"

"Not the kind of thing you're probably thinking about. I never heard serious bad talk; no big mistakes, outrageous neglect, or temper tantrums any worse than the usual around here. He told somebody who told somebody who told me, one time, that his wife was a dog, but she had a big trust fund and a pedigree so he kept her. Joked about obedience training. He's a wiseass. Short in the compassion department, from what I hear from my patients who've been on the surgical ward. But like I say, nothing major. Your usual wacko surgeon, but not extra-nuts."

As usual, Mickey had put the pieces together and come up with a correct diagnosis of her motives for asking the question in the first place. It was one of the reasons she liked him so well, another being his determination to take care of sick people come hell or high water, the bureaucracy and his own eminence be damned.

"Charming," she said. "He sounds like a real jerk. What about Sheila Klainberg? I'm seeing her in a little while."

Mickey was tall, blond, and blue-eyed; in addition to being filthy rich, courtesy of his father's wheelings and dealings, he had a crooked, confidential-looking grin the full force of which could make a sure-footed woman trip and fall down in the middle of a bare tile floor. The fact that he hadn't made a conquest of every unattached nurse in the hospital wasn't for lack of trying on their part, yet another reason she thought he was a prince.

"I know Sheila fairly well," he said in tones of approval. "Medical resident, here on the ward this year, going into OB/GYN next year. Smart and talented like Granger, and they graduated together. And there," he added, "the similarities end."

"I see. So Sheila's one of the good guys."

He nodded. "Never a show-off, not much of a gabber on rounds, but when she does open her mouth it's because she's got something to say. And I've never heard her say a bad word about anybody, unless it was both accurate and necessary to the task at hand. She's a good old-fashioned Southern girl, and I mean that in the nicest possible way."

"She was on the list of friends Granger gave to Ed Chernoff, people Granger said knew him well. If I ask her about Granger, do you think she'll tell me the truth?"

Mickey shrugged. "She told me once about a mistake she made with a patient, damned near killed the guy. It would have been easy for her to put it off on somebody else, or just deny that it ever happened."

He got up, draining his paper coffee cup and dropping it into the wastepaper basket. "I think she'll either give you the truth, or she won't give you anything. Young, still finding her way, but she's good people. Listen, I've got to get back, but before I go . . ."

Then he spent fifteen minutes telling Edwina which eminent cardiac surgeon had sewn an artificial heart valve backwards into which even more eminent city politician, then left the incision for his terrified assistants to close, whereupon the procedure had to be done over again before the patient could be taken off the heart pump.

"They should have just left him on the pump," said Mickey Three, whose proposal for a free children's vaccine clinic the politician had scuttled. "What the heck, he already acts like he's got a machine where his heart ought to be."

Which reminded him of the assistant clinical professor of endocrinology who had developed an obsessive crush on a pharmacy technician, sending him as many as twenty mash notes a day on her engraved letterhead via the hospital's antiquated but efficient interdepartmental mail-tube system. Unfortunately, one of the tubes got lost in the system one day and wound up on the desk of the overhead page operator, a well-meaning young fellow who read the missive over the hospital's general-address loudspeaker before realizing it was not a public announcement—except of course that by that time, it was.

"Glands," Mickey Three commented as they walked back

to the ward. "You'd think an endocrinology professor would know all the trouble glands can get you into, wouldn't you?"

Edwina laughed. Then, as an afterthought, "Do you know Frieda Schreiber? That is, well enough to have an opinion of her?"

Mickey made a face. "People's opinions on Frieda Schreiber tend to depend on where they stand on certain subjects. Some people think she's a grandstander; others think she's entitled to be as visible, as famous, as she can manage. But the main thing that divides people is this mind-body stuff she's so hot on."

"A little too far-out for the establishment?"

"Uh-huh." He paused at the nursing desk, selected several charts, and checked his pocket protector for a ballpoint. "Some of these older medical types, you know, they're about as flexible as a day-old corpse. But it's the way she goes about it that really gets to them. This place she's got up in Litchfield goes in big for aromatherapy, herb-oil massage, that kind of thing."

He turned toward the treatment room, where he would spend a few minutes making it look as if Mrs. Wilcox's strep throat, and her granddaughter's, had been suffered by legitimate hospital patients, so the insurance companies and the federal government could pay a little for treating them instead of a lot. For this, of course, Mickey Three could have gone to jail.

On the other hand, he was Mickey Two's son, and the kinds of lawyers Mickey Two employed ate insurance companies for lunch when they weren't too busy running the federal government.

"Bottom line, I think Frieda's kind of a fruitcake," Mickey Three said. "Which is nothing unusual, except she's a rich and famous fruitcake, and she wants to get richer and more famous so she can set up her own private operation, do what she thinks is right for her patients without a lot of people who haven't got a clue looking over her shoulder, giving instructions."

He gestured at the medical ward, with its decades-old paint and shabby furnishings and general air of clean but desperately pinch-penny impoverishment, in which he had to commit fraud in order to give penicillin to an old woman whose throat was sore.

"That answer your question?" Mickey inquired cheerfully, and strode off, whistling, to commit some more felony offenses.

◆ ◆ ◆

"Billy was okay. A little weird, but all medical students are weird. And by the way, don't get the wrong idea. I was his roommate, not his girlfriend. The apartment had two bedrooms."

Sheila Klainberg was a slim, strawberry blonde woman in her late twenties, with pale green eyes and a soft Carolina drawl. Wearing a lab coat over a pin-striped oxford-cloth shirt and navy slacks, she was all business as she met Edwina's gaze.

"What do you mean by weird?"

Klainberg had been sitting at the nursing desk, reading the *Physician's Desk Reference* and working out a dosage of something or other, when Edwina arrived. Around her, the ward was quiet, with the day staff gone and the afternoon people still lingering over coffee in the conference room. The air smelled of floor wax and rubbing alcohol; a television played quietly in the visitors' waiting area.

"Listen, I don't want to say anything that would get him in trouble," Klainberg said at last. "I mean, any more trouble. I haven't seen him in a while, but we were pretty good buddies."

"I understand. I'm just trying to get a sense of him. It's going to be difficult, you see, proving what his defense attorney needs to prove."

"That he wasn't responsible. That he was sane enough to get through med school and become a surgical resident, handle a lot of difficult, complicated cases, but he wasn't sane when he put a bullet through his wife." Klainberg's tone communicated just how easy she thought that would be to prove, which was just about how easy Edwina thought it would be, too: *not*.

From the conference room came the sounds of laughter and of chairs being pushed back. As if on signal, patients' call lights began blinking; a telephone rang, and a group of nursing students came onto the ward amidst much whispering and giggling, herded by a determined nursing instructor.

"I don't know," Klainberg said again, doubtfully.

"Whether what you say might help him or hurt him?"

"Not that. It's just that . . . well, Billy didn't like women very much. For all his lady-killing ways." She winced at her own choice of words.

"Are you trying to tell me he's gay?" Now, there was an idea nobody had mentioned, and one guaranteed to put Tom Whitelaw off his breakfast and onto the bourbon bottle; it was a fine reason for the old man to want to avoid a public trial.

But Klainberg shook her head again. "If he is, I never saw any evidence of it. Just the opposite." She got up, as the afternoon staff crowded out of the conference room. "No, it's just . . . you'd better come with me. We can't talk about it here."

"Dr. Klainberg," one of the nurses interrupted. Edwina recognized her brisk, beginning-of-the-shift expression; whatever didn't get whipped into shape right now probably wouldn't at all, and when the night shift came on, the evening shift would get the blame for it.

"Dr. Klainberg," the nurse said, "Mr. Upchurch says he wants dinner from McDonald's, his sister will bring it in for him, and he wants two beers with it. He says it's his basic human right."

"Oh." Klainberg sounded unimpressed. "His sister's going to bring the beer, too?"

"That's what he says. There he goes again," the nurse added as a call light blinked on at the desk.

"Please tell Mr. Upchurch," Sheila Klainberg said in her deceptively soft Southern drawl, "that if he asks me that again, I'm going to have him put on clear liquids, and if his sister brings in any beer I'll shut off his visiting hours. And if he gives you any trouble about it, tell him I said he should take his human rights to some other hospital, if he can find one that will admit him. Come on," she told Edwina over her shoulder.

"Upchurch," Klainberg explained as Edwina hurried to catch up, "weighs four hundred pounds, and if we can't get him down to safe surgical weight, his gall bladder's going to kill him. But he's sure that there's a pill that would fix him right up, and I'm withholding it from him because he's black and I'm white."

"One of your more difficult patients, I gather?"

Klainberg chuckled mirthlessly. "That's for sure. He's lucky there's not a pill that would make him vanish."

Edwina followed the medical resident into the on-call room, sparsely furnished with a bed, a desk, and a chair. Klainberg shut the door and sank onto the bed exhaustedly, one arm dangling over the side.

"I got into medicine to help people, but they don't want my help. They want to keep eating and drinking and smoking, only I'm supposed to give them a miracle pill so all that stuff won't make them stick."

"I'm familiar with the syndrome," Edwina said. "But that's not what I came to discuss. You told Ed Chernoff you'd talk with me about Bill Granger."

Klainberg sighed deeply. "I know I did. I'm just not sure that's the right thing to do. I'm really not sure what I think of the situation."

Join the club, Edwina thought. "Look, the situation is that if anything you know turns out to be of help to Bill Granger, it would be better if his attorney knew about it in advance. And if it doesn't, the same. Forewarned is forearmed, and all that."

"Right, but neither of the choices sounds very good. He's a nut, or he's a murderer. Isn't that about the size of it?"

"Dr. Klainberg," Edwina said, "I'm on his side, you know." Sort of, she added silently; actually, it was Chernoff's side she was on, a situation that was getting less comfortable by the day.

Klainberg sat up. "I know. To tell you the truth, I'm just trying to figure out whether or not I am. It's hard, you know, deciding whether to be a traitor to your sex or your species."

"I don't understand. Is there such a difference?"

Klainberg shrugged. "Billy was . . . is . . . my friend, but I felt embarrassed by our friendship sometimes. The thing is, when Billy saw a woman and decided he wanted her, that was it. He'd have her in bed before she knew what hit her, even after he was married. I felt so sorry for them, and for his wife. Almost as sorry," she finished, "as I feel for her now."

The sound of the overhead page operator's voice came through the closed door; Klainberg frowned and forced herself up. "I'd better get back out there before Upchurch starts a riot. Sorry about putting you to all this trouble, but I guess I also wanted to check you out before I decided whether to talk to you."

Coming from anyone else, this would have infuriated Edwina. From Klainberg, however, it didn't; the young doctor wasn't being difficult. She actually seemed to be wrestling with her conscience, a spectacle Edwina found so refreshingly unusual, she didn't even resent the inconvenience it cost her. "And are you? Going to, I mean?"

Klainberg nodded. "I'll be out of here around seven. You know the cafeteria behind the medical library?"

"I know it." Half a century old and looking every bit its age, the library cafeteria was famous for its glutinous macaroni, mystery meat casseroles, and salads that resembled forgotten science experiments. "That's where you want me to meet you?"

"That's where," Klainberg said.

• • •

Marion Bailey counted the money in her wallet, all that was left from the little fund she'd had in her bedside table. Fifty dollars would get her through a few days, and she had a paycheck coming; that would take care of next week.

After that, she had no idea. Chelsea Memorial's personnel department had given her two weeks' leave of absence, over the protests of the nursing administration people who believed that if a nurse couldn't work, she should quit or be fired. If there were a glue factory they could send broken-down nurses to, Marion thought bitterly, the nursing administration department would be lining her up for it.

In his bed, Gerry Junior shifted restlessly. The cloth cuffs he wore made chafe marks on his wrists; Marion had shifted the fabric and rubbed cream underneath it to no avail. Every so often one of the staff came to check his vital signs, change his IV bag and put medication in it. They tried putting feeding tubes in him, too, but he gagged them back out again.

So he lay there, and Marion sat beside him. They would be transferring him to Briar Hill as soon as there was a bed vacant, the chief psychiatrist on the ward had told her; he was sorry, but there was nothing he could do.

"If I could pay for it, there would be," she confronted him flatly. "I'll bet that would make a difference."

Her threat about a lawsuit had not been taken seriously, or if it had, the hospital had decided to brazen it out. As they should, she realized; giving in to her demand would only imply that they took responsibility. Besides, she could no more hire a lawyer than she could pay to keep Gerry at Chelsea Memorial.

"It won't change his outcome," the psychiatrist insisted. "Whatever's happening, it's going to take time for him to come out of it. If he comes out of it. We can keep him calm with drugs, of course, if he should need them, but beyond that . . ."

The psychiatrist was a skinny, stoop-shouldered man with

a long face and very dark brown eyes, wearing a wedding band. Marion liked him; whenever he drew blood from Gerry, or tested his reflexes, or did any of the other things that had to be done, she could see that he tried to be kind about it.

"Just a little stick," he would say as he plunged the needle in, "I'm sorry. I hope it doesn't hurt too much." And he always looked at Marion's tears, straight at her instead of averting his eyes when she wept; she appreciated not being found hideous, or at least that he pretended she wasn't.

"Look," he said to her now, "I have kids of my own; I can understand how you feel. But I have to be honest with you, Mrs. Bailey; time may be the only thing that can help your son. We don't know what's wrong, and we don't know how to fix it. We've done all the blood work, X rays, toxicology scans, ID workups . . ."

Infectious diseases, he meant; in case the infection in Gerry's ear had gone to his brain. But it hadn't; his ear was almost healed, and none of the other tests had shown anything, either.

"Something happened," Marion said for the hundredth time, or the thousandth. "Something happened that was so bad, he went away from it in his mind. He'll come back when he knows it's safe. I can feel it. I'm his mother," she insisted, "I know."

She looked up. "But how can I show him it's safe, if you put him in that place? Where children lie all day tied into their beds? Where six-year-old boys get bedsores, because nobody has time to clean them when they're wet or dirty?"

She took a deep breath, trying to control herself. "It's not their fault. I know they're doing the best they can. But you know the way a bed gets vacant at Briar Hill. You know the only way a bed will become vacant for Gerry is if some other little boy dies. And they do; they do it there all the time."

The psychiatrist looked uncomfortable. "Briar Hill has therapists. They have physical therapy and an excellent music therapy program. The people are dedicated."

Marion looked down at her two hands, the only two hands

she had. When she was not changing Gerry Junior's linens, turning him and washing and soothing him, she had been using them to turn the pages of the promotional materials the state put out about the "successes" of Briar Hill.

"Do you know how many children were discharged from Briar Hill last year?" she asked. "Alive, I mean? And in any kind of normal condition? So they could go to school, or be on a sports team, anything like that?"

The chief flinched; he knew the numbers as well as she did.

"None," she told him. "That's the grand total from Briar Hill. Now I ask you," she went on, "is that the track record you would accept for one of your children? Is it?"

The psychiatrist turned, looking out the window past Gerry Junior's bed at the buildings of the medical center, where space-age spires of steel and glass poked up through the red-brick remnants of a time when medicine was practiced with leeches. For all the good it was doing Gerry, it might as well still be.

"No," he said quietly, "I wouldn't. On the other hand, I have four patients down in the emergency room right now, and any one of them could use your kid's bed better than he can. One of them saw a drug dealer massacre her family; she only survived by playing dead, under the body of her little sister."

He sat down on Gerry Junior's bed. "One tried to hang herself last night; she's fourteen, pregnant, addicted, and HIV positive. The other two are your standard, garden-variety city disaster stories: a seventeen-year-old paranoid schizophrenic who does okay on meds, but his mom hasn't got the money to fill his prescriptions, and a retarded twelve-year-old whose father beat the shit out of him again last night. This time it was because the kid couldn't handle a paper route. The cops brought him here after he snapped and attacked the old man with an iron skillet."

The young psychiatrist gazed at the steel and glass spires. "It's no surprise the kid can't make change; he's got the mental capacity of a four-year-old. He doesn't belong here, and I'm looking for a long-term residential bed for him, prior to getting him fostered, but meanwhile if I don't bring him in, his father's going to kill him or he's going to kill his father."

"Why not send that boy to Briar Hill, and let Gerry Junior stay here?"

"Because that boy can feed and dress himself, and go to the toilet on his own, and your son can't."

It was true; Gerry Junior's state was perilously close to being vegetative. He focused his eyes, and she thought he understood what she said, but she couldn't be truly sure even of that much.

"Besides," the doctor went on, "Gerry's transfer paperwork is already done. I'm sorry; I'd rather your boy stayed, if only for your sake. But under the circumstances it's not possible."

He ruffled Gerry Junior's hair. The boy squinched his eyes closed and cringed away. "Ma-a-a," he whimpered, but it was only a sound, not a word.

"I'm sorry," the doctor repeated, and left the room.

When he was gone, Marion checked Gerry's IV again, to make sure it was running smoothly; he'd dislodged two already, and if he lost another one they'd have a hard time finding a decent vein to put in a third. She washed his face, straightened his bed, and fed him a spoonful of ice chips, which he spit out. Then she went back to the waiting area so he wouldn't see her cry.

Money, she thought; it all depended on money, and she didn't have any. Funny how when she was a nurse, she'd never thought of that. Some patients got transferred to one place, and others to anther; until they did, she treated them all the same, and then forgot about them. She'd never worried about what happened after they were discharged. It just wasn't her problem.

And now it is, she thought. This must be my punishment for never worrying about it before; about what happens to people who can't pay for the best. What happens is, they don't get it.

She could take care of Gerry at home, but she couldn't do it indefinitely, and that was what he needed. And if she did, what would happen to her job? Gerrald hadn't sent any money, and she doubted that he would. The last time she'd heard from him, he'd sounded drunk; he'd said he was having a crisis and needed time to find himself.

Good luck, buddy, she thought, wiping away her tears. Lousy husband, lousy father; why did he have to have his breakdown now? Wasn't Gerry Junior more important?

She took out a tissue and blew into it, trying to feel better. She had to go home and pay the bills that had come in the mail. She had never had to do it before; it had always been Gerrald's job. Still, the money in the joint account would cover things for a while; if she did take Gerry Junior home, they would at least have a roof over their heads. Gerrald had only taken his personal checkbook with him, thank God for small favors.

Then it hit her: there was enough in the account to pay for about ten days of hospital care. For a moment, she was elated; they wouldn't transfer him if she could pay. Gerrald, of course, would hit the roof when he found out, but when he did she hoped he got a fractured skull out of it. She was mulling the possibilities of this idea—put off the mortgage, pay taxes and insurance? pay the taxes but not the insurance?—when the door from the adult psychiatric unit opened.

Marion stared. It was the woman she had seen in the coffee shop a few days ago, when this whole horrible nightmare had just been starting. The woman recognized Marion, too.

"Hello," the woman said softly, taking in Marion's miserable condition. "At the shopping plaza, wasn't it? I was there with my mother, and you were alone." The woman approached tactfully.

Nurse, Marion thought. You didn't learn that way of getting next to people anywhere but on a hospital ward.

Watching, Marion felt the memory of it in her own body: walking into the hospital room of a complete stranger, someone sick and scared and probably in pain, and convincing the person that she was a friend.

"You're the boy's mother, aren't you?" the woman went on. "The boy who was in the emergency room, the other evening."

The woman was wearing a smart red wool suit and high heels, and a mink coat that looked like heaven. Close up, her face was bony and very severe, with a wide mouth and eyes that had seen plenty. The woman also wore a lot of good gold jewelry, and her haircut had cost a hundred dollars if it had cost a penny; each dark, glossy strand looked individually razored.

"Yes, I'm his mother," Marion said, feeling against all odds a little thrill of hope.

Money. If only she could get some.

◆ ◆ ◆

In Litchfield, the twins were treated like visiting royalty. After breakfast, the kitchen help took charge of them, playing with them and feeding them forbidden treats; as soon as Rita had finished washing their faces, which were laughing and smeared with jam, Mr. Watkins claimed them to show them, he said, what the menfolk did around the place. Mrs. Crusoe had dibs on them after that, hinting strongly that Rita should find something to do on her own so the old lady could have the boys to herself.

The trouble was that without them, there was nothing to do. Rita wandered around the big old house for a while, gazing at antique oil portraits of people whose features looked forbidding and smug; we don't have to look pleasant, they seemed to say, we can afford to look any way we like. Then she caught one of the maids watching her while pretending to be dusting, and realized that the staff must have been told to keep an eye on her.

Calmly, so as not to give the maid any satisfaction, Rita

went upstairs. The trinkets in the house were valuable, she knew, and she could have pocketed one of them easily: a crystal paperweight or silver stamp case from the desk, or one of the jewel-encrusted eggs that Mrs. Crusoe kept on a table in the library. Rita wouldn't take anything, of course, but the old lady's suspiciousness cut her deeply.

You couldn't just be nice to rich people in order for them to like you, she thought miserably; somehow you also had to pretend you didn't know they were rich. Otherwise, they were sure you wanted something, and that you would steal it from them the minute their backs were turned. In order for them to think you were sincere, in other words, you had to be two-faced.

Pulling on her gloves and hat, she stopped in the door to the sun room where Mrs. Crusoe and the boys were. "I'm going out for a while. Is there anything I can get you?" Daringly, she imitated the tone Mrs. Crusoe used whenever she was displeased: civil, but stony.

Mrs. Crusoe marked her place in the story she was reading. Her bright old eyes regarded Rita acutely; she had not missed the tone. "How kind of you to ask, but I think we have everything we need. Is something wrong, dear?"

Yes, Rita wanted to blurt out, there is. I'm not greedy for anything of yours. All I want is a chance to make my own life, and I just don't see how that's going to happen so of course I'm unhappy, and how dare you think I would steal your things.

"No, Mrs. Crusoe; I thought I'd get some fresh air, is all." *And you don't have to check my pockets,* Rita added bitterly to herself as she went out, past a Federal Express truck and a boy unloading a cardboard box marked "Perishable."

"Plants for Mrs. Crusoe?" he said, blinking at the house.

"In there." She pointed over her shoulder and kept going, her boots crunching angrily in the bright, white pea gravel which she figured must cost eighty dollars a yard and which looked as if it got refreshed twice a year. You could feed a whole family for what gets spent on this driveway, she thought as she slammed into the garage where Mr. Watkins's boy had put Edwina's Volvo; Miss Edwina, as the help all called her, had taken her own little Fiat sports car to town.

Miss Edwina; wasn't that a hoot? She was over forty years old, for God's sake, with a husband and two children; did these people think they were living on a plantation? Furiously, Rita twisted the key in the car's ignition.

"In a bit of a temper, are we?" It was Mr. Watkins, gazing shrewdly at her through the driver's side window.

Rita had had about enough of the old family retainer bit, too. "Yeah, we are. And I want to get out of here, all right? My knees are sore from genuflecting." She shoved the gear shift into reverse.

Mr. Watkins put his hand on the window well. "Got sniffy with you, I imagine. Got your dander up. She'll do that."

Rita sighed; just what she needed, a few rustic pearls of wisdom. As far as she was concerned, pearls of wisdom were what people who couldn't afford real pearls consoled themselves with whenever they felt sorry for themselves about being so damned poor.

Which in her case was getting to be most of the time, she realized suddenly, and let her breath out hard. "I'm sorry. I don't know how you put up with it, that's all."

Watkins nodded. "You could say I practice some selective remembering, in a manner of speaking. And then, I've been here a long time. But you, now, you're provoked 'cause she treats you suspicious-like. Makes you feel like a dirty-faced ragamuffin, 'eh? Little pickpocket, maybe you'll try to pinch the silver off the table."

It was such a relief to hear someone say what she'd been thinking. After all, she couldn't very well tell Edwina that her mother was a bitch. "That's right. And I'm not; I'm not what she thinks. I'm . . . what I am. But how did you know?"

Watkins's shoulders moved, under his heavy barn jacket. "She's that way with everyone at first. Cautious-like. And she's in a snit lately about something else, too; I dunno what. Anyway, it ain't forever, is it?" He stepped back from the car.

"Besides," he said, "if you're what you are, then she's what she is, ain't she? And she's been it for eighty years an' more. You got to try not to take it so personal, is all."

She looked at her hands on the steering wheel. Actually, she did feel better. "Thank you, Mr. Watkins," she said as she backed the Volvo out of the garage. "I'll try to remember."

The afternoon sun came slanting through the trees, making their bark silver; bittersweet clotted with bright orange berries netted the old stone fences along the drive. Passing through the gate, she reflected on what Watkins had said. It was true, she wouldn't be here forever; only a few more days or a week. After that, she would go back to New Haven with Edwina, to her life of taking care of the boys, and of trying and failing to save money.

Trying and failing; Watkins's advice was fine for the short term, she decided, but as she turned the Volvo onto the blacktop road leading to the town of Litchfield, it hit Rita again with a pang so intense it was almost nauseating that, as far as anything beyond bare survival was concerned, she had no idea where in the world she was going or, even more anxiety-provoking, how she was going to get there.

Nevertheless, once she got to town, she found her spirits lifting even as she resisted the charm of the place, with its row of stores on Main Street and its central green, complete with pretty white bandshell. There were white clapboard houses with gingerbread trim and neat gardens, a Congregational church with a spire covered in shingles shaped like the scales of fish, and a red brick Carnegie library with wooden shutters painted a fresh park-bench green.

Rita parked the car and got out, passing the hardware store offering shovels and snowblowers, the grocery whose butcher-paper signs proclaimed specials on pot roast and laundry soap, and a tiny store called the Women's Exchange, where homemade items were for sale: crocheted doilies, babies' sweaters, quince jam. Rita paused, then moved on as she caught sight of the price tags; she had money in her pocket, but not that much money. For all its rural charm, Litchfield was a rich little town.

The newsstand was a combination soda fountain, magazine store, and smoke shop; the smells of malted milk, newsprint, and cherry pipe tobacco mingled pleasantly inside the door, whose bell jingled cheerily as Rita entered. Red leather-covered stools lined the shiny counter; at the back stood a wooden phone booth with an old-fashioned folding glass door.

Rita scanned the magazine rack, looking for anything about design or fashion, or the city club scene, but the selections were tame: *Vogue* and *Rolling Stone*. There was a big assortment of country-living publications, crossword puzzle magazines, and periodicals devoted to money and investing. Maybe I ought to buy one of those, Rita thought, and find out what I'm doing wrong.

"Discouraging, isn't it?" said a voice at her side.

Rita turned; the woman was tall, blonde, and pretty, not much older than Rita; a little chunky, but on her it didn't look bad. She wore a yellow ski parka, houndstooth-checked stirrup pants, and a pair of shiny, pistachio green galoshes with lemon yellow fake fur around the tops.

"Yeah," Rita said. "I was looking at least for *Oasis d' Neon*. I figured *Retro Metro* would be too much to hope for around here. I mean, not to disrespect your town or anything, but . . ."

The woman laughed. "Don't worry about it, it's a burg. You stay here long enough, you'll be doing crossword puzzles, too."

She wore a good deal of makeup, carefully applied to look like none. Complementing her outfit were a pair of Day-Glo green earmuffs, multicolored wool mittens (from the Women's Exchange, Rita realized, and made a resolution to go back there) and red harlequin-style sunglasses on a green pop-bead suspension chain.

Rita was glad she had dressed in her corduroy knickers,

black silk socks, and leather wing tips, plus her buffalo-plaid wool shirt and man's black vest with the red silk lining. All in all, when you counted in the black-cat ceramic earrings and the glittery nail polish, she didn't look too shabby herself.

"What *do* you do around here, anyway?" she felt bold enough to ask. "For fun, I mean."

The woman gave Rita a disbelieving look. "Take the train to Manhattan, or stay here and eat ice-cream sundaes and get fatter, which was what I was about to do. Come on, you want one?"

Rita checked the clock over the soda fountain: four-forty-five. Outside, the bare-branched maples edging the town green had turned to sharp, black cutouts against a purpling sky. Mrs. Crusoe had dinner promptly at seven; Rita would be expected to take over with the boys.

"You want one or not?" repeated the woman, already perched on one of the red leather stools. The counterman opened the ice cream chest and got down one of the tall, cut-glass sundae dishes, turning to see if he should get down another.

In the mirror behind the counter, the woman's face was faintly challenging. Rita hesitated a moment longer. But what the heck, you only lived once, and it wouldn't kill anybody if she was five minutes late. "Sure," she said.

◆　◆　◆

Edwina Crusoe. Her name was Edwina Crusoe, and she said she was a consultant who helped people involved in health-care-related crimes. A snoop, she told Marion smilingly over coffee in the coffee shop on the hospital's first floor.

The next thing Marion knew, she was pouring her heart out to the woman, who had what Marion thought of as an exotic name and whose whole life seemed unimaginably glamorous and interesting, so much so that Marion felt she could easily have hated Edwina Crusoe.

But she didn't, because Edwina was so sympathetic.

Edwina listened while Marion told of Gerrald's departure and of Gerry Junior's injury, and she didn't just listen therapeutically, either, murmuring stock phrases about how difficult it all must have been. She listened with fascination, her lips parted and her eyes widening at all the right places.

"You're kidding," Edwina breathed when Marion got to the part about Gerrald needing to find himself.

Marion managed a giggle; just talking about it made her feel better. And it was pretty ridiculous, as if Gerrald had somehow fallen into a time machine and emerged back in the sixties.

"I know," she said. "I told him maybe he ought to buy some bell-bottoms and take up smoking pot."

"And what did he say?"

"Typical Gerrald, so articulate. He hung up on me."

This time they both laughed, but Marion stopped as it struck her: unloading her troubles on a stranger wasn't going to help, no matter how much better it made her feel for a little while.

"I haven't heard from him since," she added soberly, "and I don't know what I'm going to do. Not that he'd be much help. Meanwhile Tad Conway's mother is driving me crazy, calling every day to find out if Gerry's said anything. 'Did he say anything? Did he say anything?' " she mimicked in Janet's breathy, demanding voice.

"Tad's the boy who's missing? The one your son was camping with?"

Marion swallowed some coffee, to break up the fresh lump of tears in her throat. "Uh-huh. She thinks Gerry could tell the police what's happened to Tad."

But it was no use: a painful sob escaped her. "I remember when Gerry was a baby, and we kept waiting for him to say 'Mama.' And I had to keep telling myself he'd do it when he was ready."

Edwina put her hand on Marion's, and the kind touch was the last straw; she began to cry and couldn't stop.

"Oh, God, I'm so sorry," she wept. "But if he could only

say one word, just one word, then I would have some hope. I keep thinking that if I could just find out who hurt him, and show him that I would never let that person hurt him again, then maybe . . ."

"He could let himself get better," 'Edwina said quietly.

Marion was so surprised, her tears stopped all at once. It was a theory of hers, but a crackpot theory, according to all the professionals at Chelsea Memorial.

"Yes. Like shock therapy, sort of. If I could just *show* him. The doctors don't think so, but they don't know what they *do* think. They don't have a clue. And everything is piling up."

The bills, she'd meant to say, because this was her chance to let the obviously wealthy Edwina Crusoe know what she really needed: money. Gerry Junior's hospital bed, she'd meant to say, which he's going to lose because I can't pay for it except by ignoring other things that, sooner or later, I will have to pay for. But when push came to shove, she couldn't say these things, because this elegantly dressed stranger would only think Marion was giving her a sob story and hitting her up for cash. Worse, she would be right; so much for my great plan, Marion thought.

"I've heard that Dr. Granger may have said something to your son, just before he shot at him," Edwina remarked.

Marion looked up. The cafeteria, filling up with people and voices and the steamy, unappetizing smell of institutional food as the evening shift's dinner hour began, seemed suddenly still and bright. "No one told me anything about that."

Edwina's shoulders moved a fraction. She had thrown her mink coat casually over one of the molded plastic chairs; in her tailored red suit she looked slim as a knife.

"It's important?" Marion pressed. "What he might have said to Gerry?"

Edwina nodded. "It could show Granger's state of mind at the time of the incident. I'm working more on background stuff than on the incident itself, but I know Ed Chernoff would like to find out what it was he said. I'm surprised one of his other people hasn't gotten in touch with you. Do you have an attorney?"

"No," said Marion, bewildered by the change of subject. "I did call a few, but they all wanted a retainer. Besides, they all told me I would have to sue the hospital to get anywhere, and if I did that I'd lose my job. What would I do then, go on welfare? Nobody else would hire me while I'm in the middle of suing my old hospital, and I'm broke as it is." She stopped abruptly; this was part of what she'd decided not to say.

Edwina thought silently, her judicious expression causing Marion all at once to dislike her very much. It was as if Marion's misery, so intense that she sometimes felt she might actually die from it, had been turned into something lifelessly intellectual, like a mathematical equation.

Edwina must have caught Marion's injured look, for her own face softened. "Sorry," she said, opening her briefcase. "It's the old interesting-case syndrome, I'm afraid."

She dug around in the case, coming up with a plush squeaky toy, a packet of towelettes, and a small rubber locomotive with a Mickey Mouse figure sitting in the cab. "It always used to make me furious," she went on, "when I was a nurse. The surgeons would be on rounds, presenting the history of some poor patient with some miserable disease, taking a lot of painful treatments, he's in agony and the family is nuts with grief, a real train wreck of a situation. You've know the kind I mean, I'm sure."

She dug in the case some more. "Darn, I know I have a pack of business cards here somewhere, unless maybe my kids got at them. Aha, there they are."

She looked up, cards in hand. "And the surgeons would stand outside the room, and they'd say, 'This is a *very* interesting case.' As if the whole purpose of the poor guy's disease was to provide them with mental stimulation."

She laid the cards on the table. "Anyway, forgive me, but you are in a very interesting situation, along those same lines.

And the first thing you need is an attorney, only I can't refer you to the one I'm working for. I'm sure there's a conflict of interest there, real or perceived. See what I mean?"

Marion nodded, although she didn't. All of a sudden things seemed to be moving fast, only she didn't know in what direction.

"But what I can do," Edwina said, "Is refer you to another one. You see, legally speaking, our interests may be opposed. So if I get any more involved in advising you, the courts may say later that I was trying to influence you somehow."

Marion looked at the card. "I don't understand. Won't this other lawyer want money, too? And what do you mean, legally our interests are opposed?"

"If Dr. Granger is found not guilty by reason of insanity, he'll be committed to a hospital for psychiatric evaluation. If at the end of the evaluation or any time later he's found not to present a danger to himself or others, he'll be discharged."

Edwina finished her coffee and got up. "In other words, he'll go free. Which is what his attorney wants to have happen, but I wouldn't expect you to want it to happen."

"You mean you're trying to get him off?"

Edwina frowned. "Not exactly. I report everything I learn, not only the things that support his plea. Still, you can see how it would look. Your son's testimony could be crucial, and I work for Granger's side. I can't mess around with you."

She plucked both checks from the table, although Marion had had a sandwich and soup in addition to coffee. "And the reason the attorney I gave you isn't going to charge you a retainer is that she works on contingency; if you win, she gets a piece."

She peered at Marion. "Call her. She's a tough lady and you'll like her. And no, you can't have this check, I need to break a twenty for the parking garage guy. Okay?"

"Okay," Marion agreed, hoping she didn't look as grateful as she felt; the check would have taken most of the money she had allotted herself for the day, but she'd been so hungry.

"And thank you very much," she added, her mind whirling with all the things she had just heard.

Edwina paused at the coffee shop's exit, hiking her coat over her shoulders. Putting out her hand, she clasped Marion's and smiled warmly. "You're welcome. Good luck with your son."

Marion watched as Edwina walked away, her stride confident even in those glamorously high heels, the mink coat swinging around her ankles. Then she was gone, and Marion looked down at the small, white engraved card in her hand.

The call would cost a quarter.

◆ ◆ ◆

"That poor woman," Edwina said. "Her husband's flown the coop, her son's in awful condition, and from what I gather the hospital is jerking her around pretty good, too. She requires legal representation, Ed. She is a perfect example of the whole reason the legal system was invented in the first place."

Then she listened while Chernoff regretted aloud that she had referred Marion Bailey to anyone. Even a hint of influence, he reminded her, could queer his pitch, although being Ed he did not put it quite that way. Still, she got the idea.

"All right. I'm sorry. But I had to do it, Ed, and I knew it could foul things up if I didn't let you know immediately. Meanwhile, if any of your people are trying to get in touch with her, tell them to try the adolescent psych ward. From what I can see, she practically lives there, and although she won't say so, I get the idea her phone machine is filling up with bill collectors' messages, and I'll bet she's just erasing them all, along with any calls your people may have been making. She's pretty overwhelmed."

She listened some more. By this time of the evening, Ed liked to sort his thoughts aloud: progress made so far, progress planned for tomorrow. His voice, lazy and slow like that of the laid-back country lawyer he most emphatically was not, sounded more tired than usual.

"Another thing," she said when he had finished; "Emeralinda Whitelaw said something to my mother the other day about possibly giving some money to the boy's family, and I know his mom could use it. She practically fainted with gratitude when I picked up the coffee shop check; I had to give her a story about needing to make change, or she wouldn't even have let me do that much."

She took a deep breath. "Of course I put the kibosh on that idea of Emeralinda's right away, but I was wondering if. . . ."

Ed's voice lost its country-lawyer casualness completely.

"Yes," she managed to put in. "Yes, I know. No, I didn't say anything about any . . . no. No, I certainly won't. All right, I'll forget about it. Fine, Ed. I'll talk with you tomorrow."

Thoroughly disgruntled, she crossed the wide parquet floor of the dormitory entrance hall, between the tall plate-glass windows looking out onto the quadrangle. At this hour, the walks were full of students, hurrying in for a late dinner or out to the medical library for an evening of studying. They wore puffy down vests over bright turtlenecks and sweaters, corduroy pants or denim skirts with dark stockings, and boots or running shoes; almost all had backpacks slung over their shoulders.

Rita, Edwina thought suddenly, would say they looked MEGO, which was short for "My Eyes Glaze Over." The idea reminded her of how eager she was to meet with Sheila Klainberg and then get back to Litchfield and the twins. In a few minutes she would head to the cafeteria, and unless Dr. Klainberg had something fascinating to say, Edwina would deal very efficiently with her.

As she thought this, someone tapped her on the shoulder; turning, she regarded Sheila Klainberg's pale, unhappy face.

"I saw you from across the quad," Klainberg explained. "And I've been thinking about the question you asked me. Come on, there's something I think you need to see."

"What question?" Edwina followed Klainberg out into the

quad, up the lamp-lit walkway to the street. At the corner, the young doctor turned toward the high-rise apartment buildings a few blocks away.

"About whether I'm going to betray my species or my sex," Klainberg replied, "and whether there's a difference."

She turned up a sidewalk to the awninged entrance of one of the buildings, produced a key, and opened the outer door. In the lobby, a directory listed professional offices on the building's lower floors and apartments on the upper stories. Klainberg strode across the lobby without glancing at the directory.

"But I'm not really betraying either one," she went on as they entered the elevator, "because I've been thinking about Billy and the fact is, whichever one you're talking about, he's not a member. My sex *or* my species. And he never has been; it's just taken me a while to figure that out."

Gender, Edwina thought automatically; she doesn't mean sex, she means gender. Students headed for medical school seemed to end their humanities educations very early nowadays, the better to pursue hard sciences like anatomy and physiology; this, to Edwina, was like learning all about bricks and mortar without ever entering a building, but she doubled now was the time to lecture on the topic. "Mind telling me where we're going?"

The hall of the tenth floor smelled of dinners being cooked and roaches being exterminated. Behind the apartment doors, TVs played game shows, dishwashers rumbled, and a dog yapped once, then fell silent.

"Billy's apartment," Klainberg said, producing another key as she stopped before one of the doors.

Edwina stared. "This is Granger's apartment, and only his. I mean, his wife didn't ever live here, or even know about it?"

Klainberg swung the door wide and stepped in. "Yes. And no. Nobody knows about this place except me and Billy. And the girls he brought here sometimes. Nobody else knows."

Until now, Edwina thought. Prosecutors had ways of learn-

ing about hideaways like this: check stubs, utility bills, all
the telltale little bits of paper that scattered out behind
everybody like a trail of breadcrumbs.

Still, there was a chance it might have stayed secret until
now. Now, whatever was here might exonerate Granger, or it
might be time to stick a fork in him, because he was cooked.

"So you're not betraying your gender or species," Edwina
said. "Just your so-called good buddy, Billy Granger."

The pertinent question, of course, being why? But Sheila
Klainberg, gesturing Edwina into the apartment, was not
about to spill all her beans at once.

"I never claimed to like the idea," she said.

◆   ◆   ◆

Mrs. Crusoe was in a snit. Rita could tell by the way the old
lady was so polite and sweet, meanwhile setting her cup into
its saucer with a sharp little click like an icicle snapping. She
had insisted that Rita have dinner with her, and Rita could
not refuse, even though she would much rather have had her
meal in the kitchen with the cook.

So she sat in the dining room, at the enormous lace-
covered dining table with the candles and the silver, eating a
lamb chop that reminded her of the innocent creatures she
had seen frisking in the pasture of the Litchfield house. That
this particular lamb chop had come from the butcher shop
did not comfort her.

"I gather your outing was a success," Mrs. Crusoe said;
you were so late, she meant, you must have been having a
good time.

"Yes, it was very nice," Rita murmured.

If only she hadn't agreed to coffee and a browse through
the record shop. By the time she came out, the clock on the
spire of the Congregational church had already been striking
seven.

It might as well have been the stroke of midnight, to
judge by Mrs. Crusoe's look when Rita came through the

door, flustered and apologetic, only to find the boys bathed, fed, and in bed.

One of the maids had done it, Mrs. Crusoe reported. So if Rita wouldn't mind getting ready quickly (here Mrs. Crusoe had given Rita one of her up-and-down visual once-overs, about as pleasant as a dip in boiling oil), dinner would be in precisely fifteen minutes.

Rita forced herself to nibble the lamb chop, the potato which she did not even dare to butter, she was so afraid Mrs. Crusoe would think she was greedy and hold that against her, too, and the spear of broccoli that Rita wished intensely were a real spear, pointed and poison-tipped; if it were, she would grab it and put it through her own heart, she was so miserable.

"Rita, dear," Mrs. Crusoe began when the dinner things had been cleared and the coffee served.

Rita's heart sank. Why couldn't the old bat just let her go upstairs? She didn't belong here, everything she did was wrong, and no matter what Mr. Watkins said, she did take it personally; how could she help it? On top of that, Edwina was probably going to be angry, which she almost never was, when she heard what had happened; after all, she had left Rita in charge of the boys, not the maid.

"I'm sorry I spoke so sharply to you, earlier," Mrs. Crusoe said. "I know you think I'm hard on you, and for no good reason. But when you are my age, you depend more on certain things than you did. Order and routine. Having things the way you expect them to be."

"Yes, Mrs. Crusoe," Rita managed. Actually, she could see the old lady's point. At her age, anything could look like the beginning of the end; a wrinkle in the carpet could mean a fall, a broken hip, and bingo, time for the funeral.

"You, on the other hand, are young," Mrs. Crusoe went on. "Spontaneity, expressing yourself—'doing your own thing,' I believe it's called. These are important to you. I understand, and I know my daughter thinks the world of you. Which is why I doubt we need mention the unpleasantness of earlier this evening to her. As I mentioned, I'm sorry I scolded you so harshly."

"Thank you, Mrs. Crusoe," Rita said, thinking *If it hadn't been for you, there wouldn't have been so much unpleasantness.*

Still, Mrs. Crusoe had apologized, and she wasn't going to tell Edwina. Not that anything bad had happened to the boys, so it wasn't a real problem, just an embarrassment; Rita decided she would probably tell Edwina herself in a few days, when the sting had worn off a little.

Dessert was tapioca pudding, which to Rita always looked like creamed fish eyes. But she took a small spoon of it to be polite, and found that it was very good.

"That's right," Mrs. Crusoe said approvingly, "eat up your dessert like a good child. And while you do that, I'll fetch the surprise I had meant to show you before dinner."

"Surprise?" But Mrs. Crusoe had hurried off; she could move pretty fast for an old lady when she wanted to.

Rita relaxed and ate some more of her pudding; relief had given her back her appetite. The evening wasn't turning out so badly. Maybe if she tried harder to follow Watkins's advice, to understand Mrs. Crusoe and not take it so personally when she got upset, she wouldn't feel so much on the defensive all the time; she would feel more that she liked it here.

After all, what was not to like? A person could get used to china and crystal, paintings on the walls and having servants do everything all the time. A person would have to be crazy not to be able to get used to that. And now Mrs. Crusoe was going to give her a present. She put down her dessert spoon, which was silver instead of stainless steel, and folded her napkin, which was linen instead of paper.

"Here we are, dear," said Mrs. Crusoe, coming back with a garment on a wooden hanger. "I had meant to wrap it, but then I thought you might like to try it on right away. I hope it fits. I had to estimate your size, but we'll just see how this one is, shall we? And then, when I have a few more made for you, we'll do any altering that's necessary. What do you think?"

Rita stared at the garment. It was a dress of navy blue
polyester blend: a short-sleeved, self-belted shirtwaist dress
with a breast pocket, white collar and cuffs, and skirt pockets. It was, she realized, exactly what it looked like.

"A uniform," she managed, wondering if the tapioca pudding was going to come up right this minute, or later after
she had cried for an hour or two. "It looks . . . very well
made."

Mrs. Crusoe bridled. "Well, it certainly is. The woman
who makes the uniforms for all my girls made this, and she
charges a pretty penny. You see, dear," she went on confidentially, "I think the difficulties you have been having are due
to confusion. You don't know what's expected of you. At
dinner, for example, I could see that you were uncomfortable,
which proves my point."

You made me, Rita thought, you made me eat dinner
with you; I didn't even want to. But she said nothing.

"But when our costumes proclaim our roles," Mrs. Crusoe
continued grandly, "we understand those roles. We feel them
from within and can fulfill them to everyone's satisfaction,
including our own."

Rita thought that as far as feeling from within went, she
would rather feel a bleeding ulcer. The whole evening had
been designed for this, she realized: to put her in her place.
She only had one question, and if she got the wrong answer
she wasn't even going to stay the night; she would walk out,
and hitchhike back to the city.

"Does Edwina . . . I mean," she corrected at Mrs. Crusoe's
quick frown, "does your daughter know about this? That you
want me to wear a uniform?"

Mrs. Crusoe's smile returned. "Of course not. I thought it
would be a nice surprise for both of you. Now, wouldn't you
like to try it on?" She held the hanger out invitingly.

Slowly, Rita got up and walked around the table to take
the uniform from Mrs. Crusoe. The material felt slippery and
faintly clammy, and the white collar and cuffs would always

have to be washed by hand; a proper evening's activity for a servant girl, Rita bitterly supposed. "Thank you," she said.

Mrs. Crusoe tipped her head. "My dear, you don't look very pleased. There's nothing wrong with wearing a uniform, you know. It's the mark of a professional, wearing a uniform."

I've never heard of an artist who did, Rita thought, or a musician. Or a costume designer. "Yes, Mrs. Crusoe. I think I'll try it on in the morning, if it's all right. I'm a little tired, so I'll check on the boys and then go to bed."

"Fine, dear. Oh, and if either of them should wake, please don't let them sit up watching television as Edwina tells me you did last night. Both of them had circles under their eyes this morning, and although I know it is convenient for you to allow it, I do think their health comes first, don't you agree?"

"Yes, Mrs. Crusoe," Rita said for the hundredth, thousandth, time, and fled up the stairs.

Halfway up, she reflected that Edwina would put a stop to the idea of uniforms when she heard about it, but by the time Rita reached the first landing she knew that what Edwina thought wouldn't make any difference. Edwina let her mother do and say whatever she wanted, as long as it kept the peace.

Probably Edwina would ask Rita, apologetically, to wear the uniforms only when she came to Litchfield. Being Edwina, she would offer to pay Rita more for doing it; she would understand a little of how Rita felt.

A little, but not enough. Rita shut the door of her room very quietly instead of slamming it, so as not to wake the twins. She decided not to burst into tears, either; crying never helped anything. *If it did, I'd be the one to know.*

Instead she sat down to organize her purse; cleaning out the battered leather bag always made her feel better. Grimly, she sorted the items from the bag's voluminous interior: coins, eye pencils, a notebook containing the boys' health information, and a list of emergency numbers to call, arranged in order of the various disasters that might befall them. No

disasters ever had, of course, probably because she had prepared for them, but if any did, she was ready.

She reached into the bag again and came up with a scrap
of paper; on it were the name and phone number of the
woman she had met in Litchfield. The woman's image
popped into Rita's mind: blonde and pretty, confident in a
defiant sort of way, and rich—obviously rich. All the new, expensive stuff she was wearing, and the casual way she wore it;
the careless way she spent money in the record store, buying
anything she liked; even her car, a white Mercedes convert-
ible with a white canvas top, screamed cash and plenty of it.

"Hey, call sometime," the woman had said, pushing the
paper into Rita's hand. "We'll go out and have some laughs."
Then she had driven off, leaving Rita on the sidewalk.

Too rich for my blood, Rita had thought, but now she wasn't
so sure. She was stuck here until Edwina decided to go home,
and she could definitely use some laughs. She looked at the
scrap of paper again. Maybe she would give Lorelei Whitelaw
a call.

◆ ◆ ◆

Granger's apartment was large, nicely furnished, and clean.
There were handsome, expensively framed prints on the walls
and custom-made curtains on the windows; the furniture was
solid and tasteful. A wide-screen TV with remote control and
surround sound occupied one corner of the living room; in
one of the two bedrooms a state-of-the-art computer system
boasted the latest electronic accessories. But the furnishings
weren't the most interesting things in Granger's apartment.

Edwina sat on the carpet with her back to the television.
Niggling urgently at the back of her mind was the notion
that she ought to call Litchfield, to let Harriet know she
would be late and to check on the boys, but she couldn't: she
had no idea how Chernoff was going to want to handle this,
and until she did know, she didn't want phone calls to her
mother's number showing up on Granger's telephone bill.

She wished she weren't here at all, in fact; no way was

Chernoff going to be able to keep a lid on all this stuff. Heaped on the carpet were letters, photo albums, check registers, and appointment books, and a folder of photocopied newspaper clippings and certificates: birth certificates, mostly, of people who had died in childhood, and clippings about two different fatal accidents: one in Oregon, and one in southwestern Texas. Both victims were young women.

She looked up at Sheila Klainberg, who had brought all the items to the living room from their hiding places at the back of Granger's closet. "How long have you known?"

"Almost from the start, when we were rooming together. Not about everything. If I'd known about everything, I don't know what I would have done. Barricaded my door, maybe."

She laughed without humor. "Things he said didn't always fit together, but I thought if the school wasn't hassling him, why should I? Besides, it was a stressful time. We were all just trying to stay alive, fourth year of med school. Worried about clerkships, evaluations, getting a thesis done, where we'd be matched for internship. And scared to death about surviving internship. We all had our hands full, Billy included."

Edwina looked at the piles of paper and photographs. "Him more than anyone, it seems."

Klainberg cracked a sad smile. "Looks like it, doesn't it? I swear I didn't know it was this bad. But then when I heard he'd gotten arrested, I started thinking. And I thought I'd come over, have a look around. I guess it's true that if you don't want to find out any bad stuff, you shouldn't snoop on people. God, I wish I didn't know any of this."

You and me both, Edwina thought, wishing she had followed her own first instinct and stayed out of the apartment. All this was going to complicate Chernoff's life enormously, and that was nothing to what it might do to Granger's.

"Look, Sheila, what you're telling me doesn't wash. I'm going to ask you straight out what it was you were so desperate to find here. I mean, I'm going to ask you instead of letting it come up later when someone else is questioning you about all this."

Klainberg looked stricken. "Damn."

"Come on, it's obvious you didn't come here just to have a look around. You thought there was something of yours here; something you didn't want found except by you."

"All right," Klainberg gave in. "You're right. It's true what I said about not being his girlfriend. I haven't been for a long time. But for a couple of months right after we first met, we were pretty tight. I fell for him. God, did I ever."

"And then you had to go somewhere," Edwina guessed, knowing something about what a fourth-year medical student's schedule was like, and guessing about what Klainberg must have been looking for in the apartment.

Klainberg nodded. "I went on an exchange clerkship, to do pediatric oncology at a hospital in Oregon. Kids with cancer. It was awful, and I wrote a lot of letters to my friends, just trying to keep my head on straight. I couldn't afford to be on the phone all the time."

"And you wrote to Billy."

"Yeah. It's not that there's anything so terrible in the letters. But I was lonely and emotionally confused, and I just poured my heart out. It would be terribly embarrassing if anyone else found them and read them now, that's all. And maybe even bad for my career."

"So after Billy was arrested you came over here to look for them, and in the process, you found all this?"

"Yes, and I didn't know what to do about it all, especially with Billy telling people I would vouch for his character. I figured I would have to tell somebody, but I didn't know who, and then his attorney called me and you showed up."

Edwina got up and crossed to a pair of sliding glass doors leading out to a balcony. "You haven't said yet why you decided to tell me about it."

Klainberg shrugged. "Well, like I said, I thought I had to tell somebody. I mean, maybe somebody's noticed me going in and out of here, or in the lobby. And my fingerprints are all over the place, I'm sure. How would I explain why I hadn't told about it earlier?"

She made a helpless face. "So I just figured I might as well tell it all, instead of changing stories in midstream or adding things as I go along. Like you said, it won't be just one person asking me about things. If I start out telling the truth I've got a better chance of keeping my story straight, don't I?"

Edwina's respect for Klainberg went up another notch; she'd diagnosed the situation correctly. Before all this was over, she would be answering more questions than a game-show contestant.

"I don't think I did anything wrong," Klainberg went on. "They were my letters; I had a right to take them and burn them."

"Oh," Edwina said. "You burned them? That's too bad. Now you can't prove they were love letters, instead of—"

"Ones that incriminated me somehow?" Klainberg's voice took on a tinge of scorn. "And then I told you about them, when if I'd kept my mouth shut, no one would ever have known about them? I don't think anybody would believe that."

She looked down at the papers and photographs littering the carpet. "Anyway, I don't care. Maybe it was kind of dumb of me to burn the letters, but they were mine. And now I'm just going to tell the truth and let the chips fall where they may, whatever happens, even to Billy. I didn't notice him worrying about my reputation when he put me on his character-reference list."

Edwina thought Klainberg had caught the essential drift: she couldn't help Granger but she might still manage not to be harmed by him. Klainberg nudged a pile of Granger's documents with the toe of her shoe. "Is this all as bad as I think it is?"

"Well," said Edwina, who thought it could not be much worse unless a signed confession were found, "I believe we'd

better let the attorneys take care of forming an opinion on
that. Come on, we should get out of here."

Stepping out of the apartment ahead of Klainberg, she
waited while the other woman locked the door again. "Other
people's birth certificates, though," Klainberg said, "and clippings about those women who died. Isn't that how people
get fake IDs? With dead people's birth certificates? And the
last names of the two women who died are the same as the
ones on two certificates."

Bingo, thought Edwina bleakly.

"It's creepy," Klainberg went on. "I lived with him, even
slept with him for a while. Thought I was in love with him,
if you can imagine that. How could I have been so stupid?"

She didn't like thinking she'd been mistaken about a man.
Just how badly mistaken she had been, though, was still going to come as a shock to the young physician, if the documents in the apartment turned out to mean what Edwina
suspected they did.

"I did love him, actually," Klainberg admitted as they
reached the street corner. "No sense kidding myself about it."

"Consider yourself lucky, then," Edwina said. "Because
some other women loved him, too, and I've got a feeling that
at least three of them are dead on account of it."

◆ ◆ ◆

Gripping the stick of wood with the nail in it, Tad Conway
put his hand cautiously through the hole in the wallboard.

Nothing happened. Outside, everything was quiet, as
though nobody was there at all. Maybe no one was. Or
maybe somebody was sitting out there silently, just waiting
for Tad to emerge.

He could only remember bits of what had happened before
he got into the crawl space: running through the woods, falling, and a blow to his head that smacked him suddenly into
blackness. He had a headache now, an awful one that made
him dizzy and sick to his stomach. But that was nothing
compared to what might happen if somebody was out there,

waiting for him. He put his arm out a little farther and
waited again, poised to jab with the stick if anyone grabbed
him.

*Or if anything else happens. Handcuffs, what if the guy has
handcuffs?*

But the guy didn't, or if he did, he wasn't using them yet.
Maybe whoever it was knew what Tad was planning, and was
waiting for a better chance.

One way to find out. Tad put his face to the hole. After
so long in the darkness, the light sent bolts of pain through
his head. He squinted at a shabby kitchen with a bare bulb
dangling from the ceiling, a single window over the sink.

Staring at the window, he suddenly felt as if his whole
body had turned to ice water. There were bars on the window, inside the shade; no one on the outside could see them,
but they were there.

Now he remembered seeing those bars before. He remembered spotting the hole in the wallboard, scrambling through
it into the crawl space. But he couldn't remember *why* it had
happened, or *who* the other person was.

My head; I can't remember because I got hit on the head. His
throat felt sandy and swollen, and he was getting weaker.
Pain hammered his skull with heavy blows, as if something
were getting ready to explode up there.

Tad tried not to imagine what a relief it would be if that
pressure just let go: a hot, gushing splash of red behind his
eyes, then nothing. Instead, he thought about two facts.

First, nobody was going to get him out of here. If anyone
knew where he was, they'd have been here already. And second, unless he got out soon, he would die. This was it; his
head was screaming it to the beat of some nightmare music
video, drumming it from his bones: GET OUT OR DIE.

Holding his breath in terror, he eased himself from the
crawl space. Gasping, he crouched on the linoleum, gathering
his strength. Around him, the house seemed to expand and
contract in time with his labored breathing and his pounding
head.

No one jumped him.

Yet.

•   •   •

Marion Bailey sat on a bench in the park where the boys had been camping that terrible night, on a path between the duck pond and the children's playground equipment. A few yards away, a mallard pair moved on the water, the male's iridescent green head contrasting richly with the female's reddish brown one. The air on this freakishly springlike early December morning smelled of pine needles warming themselves in the wintry sun.

The incident that had put Gerry Junior in the hospital and made Tad Conway vanish belonged to some other park, Marion felt obscurely, one that was dark and full of secrets. She felt that this other park, the one in which awful things happened, must be where Tad Conway had gone; was in fact where Tad was right now.

After all, he had to be somewhere, didn't he?

The idea of Tad Conway's actual, independent existence was one that had occurred to her only a little earlier, as she emerged from the office of the attorney Edwina Crusoe had recommended. Until that moment, Tad had only been part of something that had happened to Gerry Junior, not an actual, separate, fully formed person about whom something could and should be done.

Like me, Marion thought with fresh surprise, recalling her visit to the attorney. Listening with great seriousness, the attorney had examined the bankbooks and tax documents Marion had thought to bring along, and had not sympathized with Marion's feeling that the whole awful predicament she was in was like an episode of bad soap opera. In the attorney's opinion, Marion's situation was clear; there was no question about what she should do, or at least about what she could do, because Gerrald was a tax cheat.

The documents showed what Marion had not known, or at any rate had not realized clearly: Gerrald had been moving money and property around and keeping things out of his own name so as to pay less. He had often asked Marion to sign forms and papers; sometimes she relinquished ownership of things or sums of money, but more often she took title to them. Gerrald had been vague about why, and she had not inquired.

Now she pondered the consequences of all those signatures, as the attorney had explained them to her. She owned the house, not in partnership with Gerrald, but alone. She owned the bank accounts except for his personal account; she owned the cars and a variety of financial instruments. In making his arrangements, Gerrald had severed himself from the sort of interest the IRS would find compromising, and that knife cut both ways; Marion could keep or sell the assets without asking his permission or even consulting him, and if he protested, he would trigger a tax audit.

Her first thought, as the implications of this sank in, had been that she could pay for Gerry Junior's hospital care. But the attorney had taken care of that, too, with a telephone call to Chelsea Memorial's chief counsel. Publicity surrounding the ER shootings had been copious, most of it negative; the hospital wanted no more of it. Gerry Junior would be staying right where he was for as long as Marion wanted him there. It was, the attorney remarked with a smile that Marion was already beginning to like very much, the least the hospital could do.

Meanwhile, Marion had things to do herself. There were the bills to be paid, her own leave of absence from the hospital to be demanded and, if necessary, her resignation submitted. She needed to visit a long list of bank managers, to explain that they would now be dealing with her and to revoke any powers of attorney she had granted. Her own attorney had cautioned her to bring along plenty of documentation to support her statements when she visited the bank managers.

Some of the documents had been out where Marion could find them, but others were in a locked section of one of

Gerrald's filing cabinets. Marion didn't know where he kept the key, but she knew that in the kitchen drawer underneath the Scotch tape and string there was a tiny screwdriver.

Marion had never jimmied a lock on anything and was not certain what the real-life procedure might entail. Still, she felt sure she could accomplish it in an afternoon, and if all else failed, there was always the hacksaw in Gerrald's workshop, among the heaps of expensive, neglected tools. Someone, she thought, might as well get some use out of those tools.

Finding Tad Conway was a more ambitious project; still, it too deserved a try. Tad's mother was frantic and the police had come to a dead end in their search for the boy, but since meeting Edwina Crusoe and the new attorney, Marion didn't feel frantic or dead-ended at all.

Quite the opposite, actually.

◆ ◆ ◆

"I thought you said his transcripts and recommendations looked okay," Ed Chernoff objected unhappily. "I thought you said you got them from the medical school, from the dean's own office."

Edwina sighed. He wasn't taking this well. "I did, and they did. But that was what the medical school had, not what he had."

She ticked off on her fingers. "He's got fake IDs. He's got blank letterhead from the college where he's supposed to have graduated, and what looks like access codes to the computer that generates transcripts. He's got letterhead from a private lab where he was supposed to be working a couple of years between college and medical school. And," she finished, "he's got a lot of clippings about two dead women with the same last names as are on his fake IDs. Women who died in separate accidents, in different states."

She let her hands drop. "I think he was married to them. He married them under assumed names, using those fake

IDs, and he kept clippings about their deaths. It's all there, sitting in his apartment."

"That doesn't mean he killed them."

"No, it doesn't. If I'm right, all it means is that he's been married three times and all three wives died violently, but as far as we know for sure, he only killed one of them. Ed, why are you resisting me on this? I thought it was what you wanted me to do: find out anything that could help *and* anything that could give you trouble."

Ed gazed miserably at her. "It is. I just wasn't expecting this much trouble."

It was trouble, all right; perhaps lethal for Granger. If he had been married to those women, and if the circumstances were as Edwina suspected, it would be nearly impossible to keep it out of the trial, and a jury's conclusions about it would not be pretty. But that still didn't account for the look on Ed's face.

"I don't get it," she said. "Whitelaw calls in a favor, big deal. Then you call me to find out whether Granger's naughty or nice. I say I think he's naughty and that I've got paperwork to support my opinion, whereupon you look like you might take the elevator to the roof, followed by the fast way down. Come on, Ed; sure the news is bad, but it's not your fault. Even Whitelaw can't ask you to walk on water, can he?"

He crossed to the window and peered out, looking beaten and old. From the street came the sounds of traffic. "Edwina, if I asked you to do something for me, would you do it?"

At his words, a series of memories flashed in her mind's eye: Ed as a young man in slacks and a blazer, eating cake at her seventh birthday party. Ed on his boat, tanned and handsome, tying up to the mooring at the Newport house. Ed, older and, as she had imagined, wiser, honorably not helping to mend her broken heart, when at the late age of twenty-one she discovered it could be broken.

She knew what he was asking. That he hadn't thought it through properly was more distressing than the request itself.

"I don't see how it could work. Even if I got back in and cleaned things up, it would come down to my word against Sheila Klainberg's, assuming she hasn't confided in anyone else, *and* assuming forensics doesn't pick up my trail in the apartment, which they probably will."

He nodded. "Of course. I'm not thinking very clearly. I'm sorry. I can have a check cut for you now, if you'd like. Get you off the case, and off the hook."

"And leave you on it? Sorry, pal, that's not the way it works. Besides," she relented, "maybe there is another, better explanation. Anyway, I could check it all out some more."

He looked so grateful, it nearly broke her heart. What in the world could he have gotten himself into for it to have come to this? To his contemplating even for an instant that she might tamper with the contents of Granger's apartment?

"Tell you what," she said, "I'll run down the story on those IDs, and on the time he was supposedly working in a lab between college and med school. Maybe I'll come up with something that puts another slant on things."

She hated bracing him this way. It felt as if the terms of their long friendship were changing permanently, and not for the better. "Also, I'll get the details on the woman. The nuts and bolts will be public record, and the newspaper stuff will all be on microfilm, any Granger hasn't collected himself."

Ed smiled, but his eyes were anxious. "I hadn't realized how good you'd gotten at ferreting things out."

It was not a pleasant image, but she forgave him for it. "Try not to worry," she told him, and left the office.

Half an hour later she was settling down to work in the only place she knew with instant access to research libraries, news wires, telephone directories, major crime bureaus, specialized reference books, credit bureaus, and motor vehicle departments, along with other information resources national and international: her own apartment, at her own personal computer.

Her system wasn't as new or fancy as Granger's; it took a few minutes to get the telephone hooked up to the computer.

Next she got the communications program loaded and running, the auto-dial function operating, and her ID and password logged on; after that it was all, as Ed Chernoff would say, smooth sailing. He wouldn't say it, though, about the information she compiled over the next few hours; for Ed and his client, the facts pouring from the computer terminal promised stormy weather, indeed.

"Hello," Martin McIntyre said, coming into the apartment just as she was about to go out again. "This is a good surprise. Are the boys with you? Hmm, I guess not."

Martin smelled pleasantly of soap, cold fresh air, and bay rum. The silence in the apartment was blessed. "I must leave," she murmured into his coat. He folded his arms around her.

"Just stay a minute," he said reasonably, which was how she still happened to be there an hour and a half later.

◆ ◆ ◆

"I hope you don't mind that I brought the kids," Rita said, glancing sideways for Lorelei Whitelaw's reaction as they sped along in the white Mercedes. "It just turned out to be a hassle, trying to get away without them."

Lorelei shrugged, downshifting skillfully through a tight S curve and accelerating again, up a long hill with spruce trees on either side. They had passed through the town of Litchfield and were heading now out into the countryside where Rita had not been before.

"More the merrier," the blonde woman said. "Glad you could get the car seats in the back. Be a drag if we'd had to take the Volvo."

"Yeah." Rita looked at Lorelei again, wondering if she really minded or not.

The boys hadn't been any trouble, at any rate; right now, both of them were asleep. Besides, if she hadn't brought them, Rita couldn't have come at all. Trust Mrs. Crusoe to have given the household help the day off, just when Rita wanted a free afternoon; trust the old lady, too, to be having her hair done, so she couldn't take the twins herself. Still, Lorelei seemed pretty mellow about it. She just wanted to drive.

"Where are we going?" Rita made room for her feet among the boys' extra sweaters, their spare hats and mittens and disposable diapers, and the bag of toys and snacks she had brought along to keep them from getting too fussy.

"Just around," Lorelei replied. "Cruising. Want to put some music in?" She nodded at the CDs in the console rack. "Put in Blondie, why don't you, or Talking Heads. I like the oldies."

Outside, fields and woodlots whizzed by, with here and there a mobile home or small house on an unkempt lot. Mailboxes stood in rows at the end of dirt roads. A dog ran out to chase the car for a while, barking, then dropped back out of sight.

Lorelei lit a cigarette. "Want one?"

"Um, no, thanks." God, the boys would go home smelling like ashtrays, and their grandmother would have a fit. Rita cracked a window and the cold breeze blew in, colder than it ought to be on such a bright day. It had been warmer this morning.

Lorelei smiled, glancing at her. "Good to get away, huh? I thought if I didn't get out of that house I was going to scream. You must feel the same way up at the Crusoe place. So boring."

"Sort of." Rita had left a note saying that she was going out and that she was taking the boys, but Mrs. Crusoe would be sure to find something wrong with that. Still, Rita didn't feel right complaining about Edwina's mother, so she kept her comments general. "It's pretty quiet there. But I'll only be staying for a little longer. Just another couple of days."

Lorelei slowed for a stop sign, then sailed on through it, flicking her cigarette butt out the window. Rita opened her mouth to say something, but didn't; they were coming into a town and Lorelei was slowing down anyway.

"What do you do?" Rita said. "To keep busy, I mean."

"Read, mostly. You don't have to look so surprised. I even go to New Haven for books. I buy them, and I have library cards all over. I'm very well read for a dumb blonde."

"I didn't look surprised," Rita said, knowing she had.

Lorelei chuckled. "And then I watch TV, listen to music, talk on the phone. I exercise a lot. Date the guys around here, for a laugh. You should see us at the country club, we look like Barbie and Ken dolls."

She sighed. "Someday I'm going to get out of here, though, and when I do, I'm never coming back."

Rita shook her head. "I don't get it. You've got money. Why don't you just leave now, if you don't like it here?"

Lorelei gave Rita a long-suffering look. "You're right, you don't get it. See, I've got money as long as Daddy says I've got money, and Daddy's little girls live at home until they go away to school or get married."

She shoved the car into gear nd peeled away from the stop sign in a spray of gravel. "And I'm too stupid to go to school, at least for anything he'd let me go to school for. So I have to wait for something else to happen, okay? Does that answer all your questions?"

"Sorry," Rita said, wanting to know what the thing was that Lorelei was waiting to have happen, but not daring to ask. The town they were passing through was not really a town at all, just a crossroads with a gas station and a run-down convenience store. A boy on a rusty bike stared as they went by, then flung a stone. "I didn't mean to be nosy."

Lorelei let her breath out, riffling her blond bangs. "Oh, forget it. I'm a bitch. Too much cabin fever. Come on, you put in some more tunes and we'll cruise. There's a place I want to see, up the road a little ways."

Jonathan whimpered; hearing him, Francis began to whine. Rita dug into the snack bag and got out a wheatmeal biscuit for each boy. "What place?" she asked.

"You'll see," Lorelei said. Her face was intent, gazing out over the steering wheel. Lorelei was pretty, except around the eyes; there, she looked like Jonathan always did whenever Francis pinched him: injured and faintly mystified.

"If I tell you where we're going you'll think I'm weird," Lorelei said.

I already know that about you, Rita thought, but now that Lorelei was driving more carefully, she didn't want to say so. Pulling an apple out of the bag, she munched on it, listening to the Talking Heads sing about being an artist and watching the scenery go by. To the right, sparkling blue between the pines, was a reservoir; the water looked clean and cold. To the left, on the far side of the valley, a line of clouds sat motionless on the horizon, dark gray and blurry as if one of the boys had scribbled them there with crayon.

Rita closed her eyes for a moment, content; when she opened them, the clouds were bigger and darker.

◆ ◆ ◆

Marion opened Gerry Junior's locker with the combination the school secretary had given her and pressed her hand to her lips. Taped inside the door as a magazine photograph of a girl in a bikini; someone had inked a mustache, fangs, and jagged stitches on her face, and a balloon saying "Hi!" coming out of her mouth, but her perfect, tanned body was unmarred, as if Gerry Junior hadn't quite dared to touch even a photograph of a girl's body.

Marion swept a pair of reeking sneakers, a canvas backpack, and Gerry's history and math textbooks into the satchel she had brought for the purpose. She took his comb and a jar of acne cream she hadn't known he had; his skin was breaking out terribly now that he was in the hospital, his face coated with a slick, oily sheen and his hair all sweaty and stringy. She took his sweater from its hook inside the locker and put it to her face, closing her eyes to inhale the sweet, normal smell of the healthy boy he used to be.

"Uh, Mrs. Bailey?" She whirled guiltily, nearly dropping the sweater.

The boy gazed at his shoes. "Uh, me an' the guys, we just

wanted to say we're sorry about what happened. We, uh, I mean, Gerry's a good guy. We think it's pretty rotten. Whatever it was."

Reddening, he glanced at three other boys standing a few feet away. Marion reached out and took a bit of lint off his jacket. It was such a normal, thoughtless action, and doing it nearly made her weep: normal lint, normal boy.

"Thank you," she said. "Tell your friends I said thanks, too. It was nice of you to come up to me and talk to me. I'll let Gerry know."

Then, before she could help herself, she burst out, "I just wish I knew what happened. I wouldn't get mad, or get anybody in trouble. Do you know? Did Gerry or Tad do or say anything that was weird? Was anything . . . *different* about either of them, that day?"

The boys looked at one another. "No. Our parents said if we knew, we'd better tell. But we don't."

One of the boys stood apart, a gangly redhead with pale blue eyes and a prominent Adam's apple. "Honest," he said, "all the kids are talking about it, but nobody knows anything."

Marion nodded. "Well, thanks anyway. I appreciate your telling me that much."

A bell rang, and more boys and girls came crowding from the classrooms, laughing and jostling and roughhousing. Behind them came a man Marion recognized as Gerry Junior's physical education teacher. He caught sight of her, too, and made his way through the tide of kids; glancing at one another, the boys moved away.

"Hi, Mrs. Bailey." The teacher stuck out his hand. "Fred Egloff, I don't know if you remember me."

The red-haired boy glanced back at Marion, his expression unreadable. "What?" she said, distracted. "Yes, I remember. You coached Gerry Junior in soccer last year."

The teacher was short and slender, with blond hair clipped close to his neat, small head, and wore a navy knitted vest over a tie and checkered shirt. "Hey, Waldrop," he called to one of the boys. "Get the lead out at practice. No more Mr. Nice Guy."

Then he turned back to Marion, smiling earnestly. "I'm very sorry about Gerry. He was good on the team, a pleasure coaching him. Hope to have him back at school real soon."

"As soon as possible," Marion replied, and watched him walk away, flashing the high-five sign to one boy, playfully punching the shoulder of another. Apparently the boys liked him well enough, although some of them did not seem to respect him. One made a face, capering like a monkey; another put two fingers up at the back of the coach's head.

And then she heard, really *heard*, what the teacher had said: he had lied to her. Gerry had not been good on the soccer team; Egloff had hardly let him play, and Gerry had bitterly resented it. He couldn't have been a pleasure to coach; probably he had been a pain in the neck.

Slowly, Marion zipped the duffel bag. Why had Egloff lied? If he'd wanted to be polite, he could have brought up something else. He'd looked, she realized, the way her husband had always looked, all the times *he* lied to her: bright and earnest, trying too hard. Nervous.

Slinging the duffel over her shoulder, she headed down the corridor past the classrooms and the principal's office. Girls' shouts and the tweets of a gym instructor's whistle echoed from the gymnasium; the steamy smell of dishwashing detergent drifted up from the cafeteria. The police had talked to Egloff, as they had to all the other teachers; Egloff had spent the evening at a sports bar the night Gerry was injured and Tad Conway vanished. Drinking Coca-Cola, he had assured them, and friends confirmed his story.

Still, he had lied just now. And the boys seemed odd around him; there wasn't the distance she recalled keeping with her own teachers, even ones she liked. And then there was the way the redheaded boy had looked at her, as if he'd wanted to say more.

Thoughtfully, Marion went down the front steps of the school building and put the duffel bag into her car trunk;

then she got into the car and sat looking at the ignition key. If she went to the hospital, Gerry Junior would be there, mute and restless. She had visited two banks and a savings and loan today, and had spoken to the managers of several more on the telephone; banking hours were over now, so there was nothing more to be done in that department. And if she went home, she would be alone.

Starting the car, she pulled it around to the side lot where the high school students parked their vehicles and turned the engine off again. She supposed a school guard might ask what she was doing here; if one did, she decided, she would say she was waiting for her son. It was true enough.

The school had several exits, and she couldn't watch them all, but from here she had a good view of one area she did want to watch, at least until a better idea came along: the junior high school teachers' parking lot.

◆   ◆   ◆

"The people whose IDs they really were died in childhood. Granger must have scouted cemeteries for little gravestones."

Propped up on pillows, Edwina sipped seltzer and watched her husband get dressed. "No one by any of those names, or Granger's own, graduated from the college he supposedly attended," she went on. "Assuming 'Granger' *is* his name. I'm beginning to wonder."

"You think he went in and fiddled the computer somehow, or got someone to do it for him? And then went back and unfiddled it, maybe, when he had what he needed: an official transcript."

She nodded. "Letterhead for the recommendation letters, a phone number and someone paid to answer it, or even in on the plan, in case anyone from the medical school called to chat about the applicant. Nothing impossible about any of that."

"What if someone from the medical school knew someone at the college?" McIntyre objected. "I mean, these people deal with one another year after year. So what if one of the admissions guys called somebody he'd talked with before, instead of the reference Granger gave, and found out Granger never went there?"

Edwina shrugged. "Chance Granger had to take. Besides, I'll bet he found out who knew whom before he picked the college. This boy does his homework, which is the part I don't get."

"Achieving type," he said, his glance meeting hers in the mirror over the bureau.

"In spades. Very smart, a genius in the fine-motor-skills department, and a glutton for punishment in the form of work, at least when he has to be. Mickey Three says he's kind of a bastard, personally, but otherwise you'd think he came out of a box marked 'Contents: One Perfect Surgeon.' "

"So how come he couldn't do it straight: attend a college instead of pretending he did, and go to medical school on the up and up?"

"Right." Edwina got out of bed and pulled on her dressing gown, an embroidered peach silk affair that always made her feel like a cross between Mata Hari and Madame Butterfly. "And why did he marry not one but two rich young women, both of whom later died in 'accidents,' under fake names? Which, by the way, I am now quite certain that he did; I scanned a photograph of him and e-mailed it to the authorities out there. They ID'd him positively as the husband in both cases."

"Really? How'd he make the fake identification fly? I mean, they must have been looking at him pretty hard."

She stepped into a pair of slippers. "Nobody ever looked at him very hard at all. Supposedly he was out of town both times, had a good story and witnesses. One girl fell down a flight of stairs; the other suffocated when a furnace flue malfunctioned. He wound up with a few hundred thousand dollars, free as air. But I still don't get it. As a surgeon he'd have earned that much in his first couple of years out of training, with a lot less risk."

"That's easy," McIntyre said, straightening his jacket. "He

used fake names so he could go back to his own eventually. He picked girls without a lot of family, so there wouldn't be a lot of questions, and either paid someone to kill them or did it himself and bought an out-of-town alibi. His wanting the money is understandable, too, assuming it's all part of the same plan: medical school is expensive."

Of course; it would have been Granger's hole card in getting into medical school at all: he could pay. No grants-in-aid, no scholarships or part-time jobs needed to be found for him; he had money in his pocket.

McIntyre glanced at his watch. "How are the boys?"

She kissed him. "Wonderful. Having their wits spoiled out. Rita's probably bored out of hers, though. Goes on tip-toe around Mother, too. I wish Mother could loosen up a little with her."

"Harriet's from the old school. Speak softly, and carry an electric cattle prod." He grinned, and ducked away from Edwina's playful swing at him. "Going back tonight?"

"After one more chore here. It turns out that during the time Granger was out west, marrying and becoming a widower twice, he says he was working in a private research lab about ten blocks from here. And he had a recommendation letter to prove it, because of course he had to account for that time when he applied to the medical school."

McIntyre's smile was the one on the face of the tiger, only ten times handsomer. "Going to pay a social visit, are we?"

"My dear," Edwina replied, "I'm the original social animal."

When he had gone she took a brisk shower, resisting the impulse to steal the rubber duckies from the twins' bathroom and line them up on the edge of her own tub. She had left Litchfield that morning before they were awake and would return after they were asleep. Pulling her robe on, she felt a pang of longing for them and went into their room to gaze at their ceiling of stars. McIntyre had painted it azure and stenciled it with silver; standing in the middle of the room with their quilts in her arms, she allowed herself to miss

them intolerably for a moment before hurrying to finish
dressing.

The discomfort she felt was merely guilt at leaving them,
she told herself as she gathered up her coat and bag, and that
was silly. They were fine with Rita and Harriet; it was good
for them to get along without her for a few hours, and besides, she would see them again tonight. Thus lecturing herself, she went out of the apartment.

The walk from York Street to Prospect Street was one of
the few decent walks of any distance remaining in downtown
New Haven, much of which seemed lately to have been
soaked in a peculiarly destructive sort of social-contract-
dissolving acid. Still, a few routes remained where a person
could go unmolested; turning right onto Chapel Street past
the Repertory Theater and the university art and architecture
building, Edwina smelled coffee roasting, hotdogs steaming,
and souvlaki, egg rolls, and pizza being prepared in eateries
along the way. Crossing the Green, she passed the courthouse,
Clark's Dairy, and one of her favorite New Haven bookstores,
Black Cat Mysteries.

On my way back, she promised herself, coveting equally
the newest by George V. Higgins, a new paperback of Sayers's
Gaudy Night, and as a gift for Harriet, a volume entitled *Forensic Pathology*; Harriet adored reference books, the better
to make her romance novels as accurate and authentic as
possible, and she particularly liked gruesome ones.

Cheered by the promise of these treats, and by the prospect of a chat with the Black Cat's witty and charming pro-
prietress, Carmela (not to mention the store itself, which was
a mystery lover's dream of a bookstore: brick fireplace, Gorey
prints, and acres of lovely books to be lingered over), Edwina
turned left onto Trumbull Street and had a brisk stride up
Hillhouse Avenue, whose still-graceful mansions behind
wide, flat front lawns one could almost forget were no longer
private residences; at least most of them weren't. Edwina
smiled sadly for the mahogany wainscoting hidden behind

wallboard panels, Italian moldings under acoustic ceiling tiles, and fluorescent fixtures in place of Tiffany glass.

Probably it was a sign of age to long in such politically incorrect fashion for the good old days; the Italian artisans, after all, had been paid a pittance and had gone home to sleep in ghettos. And I'm wearing mink, even if it is second-hand, she scolded herself, but was not able to summon up much sorrow over this delinquency; at four o'clock on an early December afternoon the sun had begun going down, and it was getting very cold.

She turned onto Prospect Street and, shivering a little, consulted the card upon which she had noted the address of the research lab. Surely that white Victorian house could not be it? Equipped with what must be the original gingerbread porch trim, rotted and crumbling in places, a side veranda whose floorboards appeared positively treacherous, and a front walk whose crazy paving looked as if Hansel and Gretel ought to be wandering along it, the house loomed tipsily over the sidewalk.

She looked uncertainly at the card again, and at the house again. All the windows were covered by lowered shades, and there was no sign or door placard to indicate that any but domestic activity went on here; in fact, there was no sign of any activity at all, and there was no doorbell. Edwina wondered if she had gotten the address wrong, or if the research outfit had moved, sensibly, to more appropriate facilities. The only research she could imagine being done here was research into the possibility of life after death, conducted in the form of seances.

As she thought this, one of the window shades twitched. The finger doing the twitching, she felt quite sure, was not made of ghostly ectoplasm but of good old-fashioned proto-plasm. That meant there was a live human being in the house.

Pleased, for she was a fan of weird window-shade twitch-ings as well as of unusual old houses, and she wanted to talk

to the human being, Edwina went up the curving front walk
and knocked on the door. In a moment, it opened.

* * *

After Egloff had visited five different houses, Marion figured
it out: today was the first of the month, and he owned property. He was collecting the rents. Gerald had done that for a
while when he first got into real estate: driving around to
each address, checking on the place, picking up checks and
noting any repair work or other jobs that needed to be done.

Of course, Gerrald had been working on a larger scale: at
his peak, he had managed dozens of properties, some of them
palatial. Marion had asked once why his own family lived in
a small frame house in a lower-middle-class neighborhood
when his tenants, some of them, lived in mansions. His reply
had been scathing: houses were not to put money into, he
said; they were to take money out of. Marion had never asked
again.

Now she drove slowly through the streets in the gathering
dusk, stopping when Egloff stopped, waiting while he went
into his houses and came out again. Sometimes the tenants
joined him on porches or in doorways; mostly they didn't.
The houses were small, with postage-stamp yards, neatly
kept at first; gradually the neighborhoods began deteriorating, until abandoned buildings and junk-strewn vacant lots
appeared between desperate-looking little dwellings.

Finally he parked in front of the smallest, shabbiest house
of all, a one-story stucco bungalow with drawn shades, a
single lamp burning behind one of them. A padlock glinted
on the side door; Egloff opened it and went in while Marion
watched from her car.

Ten minutes passed; twenty. The house must be unoccupied; otherwise, why would it be locked from the outside?
The lamp was meant to discourage break-ins, Marion supposed. Just as she was beginning to think he might not come
out again at all, Egloff did come out. He resecured the padlock, got into his car, and left.

Marion sat thinking. So Egloff had a vacant property; he'd spent the time checking it, perhaps with a flashlight, or maybe he'd been doing some small repair job. That was why he'd stayed so long in the house; it was all perfectly innocent. Still, she could not quite bring herself to leave.

Around her, the neighborhood sulked under a single working streetlight: trash-littered, packed-earth front yards, junk cars hunkering at the curbs, and some boys loitering ominously on the corner, casting hard-eyed glances.

Once she would have been afraid, but everything was changed now. She felt as if, between one step and the next, she might sail up off the earth, higher and higher until she vanished into the sky. The hard-eyed boys were barely even a distraction as she pulled her car into the driveway of Egloff's house, got out, and climbed the porch steps.

She tried peering in the window, but no space showed between the shade and sill. She walked around back and was barked at by a neighbor's angry pit bull that slammed its muzzle between the slats of a wooden fence. The cellar doors of the house were locked with a shiny padlock like the one on the side door.

A FOR RENT sign tacked to a discarded fence slat leaned against the house, crumbs of earth still clinging to the slat's sharpened end, as if it had been pulled up recently. The phone number on the sign was familiar, Marion realized; very familiar.

On her way here, she had passed a run-down convenience store with a pay phone only a few blocks away. Backing her car out of the shabby driveway, she hoped the pay phone worked.

◆ ◆ ◆

Inside the Victorian house on Prospect Street, Edwina listened as the man who had answered her knock introduced himself and briefly explained his work. In his laboratory, supported by a group of financially well-set visionaries and entrepreneurs whom he refused to name, Byron Chulovitz was attempting to bring dead mice back to life, and in a separate but related project to keep them from dying in the first place, as initial steps toward making people immortal.

He had not done it yet, Dr. Chulovitz confided, rubbing his hands together with kooky enthusiasm, but he would do it soon: next year, or next week, possibly even tomorrow.

"How interesting," Edwina murmured. Never having met a mad scientist before, she was unsure how to proceed, but it turned out there was no trouble on that score.

"Go ahead, look around," Chulovitz said. He was a small, balding man in a white shirt, corduroy trousers, and a long white lab coat. "No secrets here. None casually observable, at any rate. And even if there were, no one would believe you if you told them. Bringing dead mice back to life; that's ridiculous." He emitted a yelp of laughter.

The inside of the house had been gutted, leaving only the supporting beams, so that the whole first floor was one large, well-lit work area. There were lab benches with microscopes and dissecting pans and smaller work stations with computer screens glowing atop them; in these areas, young men and women in jeans, sweaters, and short white lab coats labored intently.

The room smelled of Bunsen burners, preserving solution, and glassware sterilizing solution, overlaid with a pleasant minty aroma; Edwina noticed small bottles with wicks protruding from their necks placed at intervals around the workroom. There was no reek of animals, which she found surprising considering that the rear wall was covered with a huge, wire-enclosed mouse cage.

Rather, it was a mouse metropolis: white mice running on exercise wheels, scampering across bridges painstakingly woven of string, up and down ladders, and through complicated obstacle courses; mice eating mouse chow, drinking water from dispensers, and smuggling into nests made of something that looked very much like cashmere.

As Edwina watched, a timer buzzed sharply somewhere and a pretty girl began cleaning the cage, inserting her rubber-gloved hands through sliding gates set at intervals in its mesh. The animals went on pursuing their activities, unconcerned at the intrusion.

"How often do you do that?" Edwina asked; the cage looked cleaner than her apartment.

"Every half hour," the girl replied with a smile, as if this were the most natural thing in the world. "We don't think it's very nice to make them live in dirt."

Chulovitz beamed proudly. "It's only right to arrange their lives pleasantly. After all, they make the ultimate sacrifice for us."

Edwina squelched a mental picture of a white mouse wearing a little blindfold, bravely smoking a tiny, final cigarette. "And then," she managed, "what happens to them?"

The scientist shook his head. "That's an exception to the no-secrets policy. Proprietary information for now, I'm afraid; I wouldn't want my competitors to get the jump on me."

Edwina looked at him, trying to decide if he really thought science was racing with him in a competition to make white mice immortal. She decided that he did.

"I can tell you, though," he went on, "that it has to do with preventing the cell damage that occurs during the course of aging or disease. For example, some of these animals are eight years old."

"Eight *years*?" The standard mouse life was measured in months, Edwina recalled.

"The revivification portion of the project," Chulovitz said as he led her away, "is carried on at another location, and it, too, is confidential at present. How old do you think I am, Ms. Crusoe?"

She blinked at the sudden change of subject, then realized it wasn't one. His eyes, knowing and amused, told her that he was older than he appeared; perhaps much older.

"But that's not what you came to ask me about, is it?" he went on smoothly. "My scientific endeavors are to you merely an obstacle, something to be gotten past. You want to talk about my erstwhile friend."

He pressed his pawlike hands together. "Let us go upstairs to my parlor, then, and I will tell you about William Granger, the man among men whom I should most not like to make immortal."

Chulovitz's parlor resembled the display room of an interior decorator specializing in Victorian re-creations, only Edwina had a feeling no decorator had ever seen any of this stuff; it looked as if it had been here a hundred years. Moroccan poufs, lacquer tables, wicker stands, and tasseled upholstery pieces crowded together on a threadbare Turkish rug whose remaining pattern was more in the breach than in the observance. On one of the low tables, a candy box encircled in a ruffle of gold foil like an expensive bouquet smelled invitingly of chocolate mints.

"Have one?" Chulovitz offered, then stuffed a pipe and waved Edwina to a chair. Firmly, she ignored the candy, determined that although she might be a middle-aged mother of two, she was not going to look like one, or at least not around the waistline.

"It all happened quite by chance," he said, puffing fragrant smoke. "Granger lived in the apartment building next door, a very charming young man, or so I thought at the time. May I ask how you learned of our acquaintance?"

Edwina described the letter of recommendation Granger had submitted to the medical school, a letter written, apparently, by Chulovitz.

"I see. How foolish of me to have thought the arrangement would never come to light."

"So he didn't work for you? Why did you write him a letter saying he did, then?"

"Blackmail, essentially. He had me where he wanted me, so I did what he asked me to do."

Chulovitz frowned at his pipe. "He did work for me for a brief time, soon after we met. Like many other youngsters, high school or college students wanting laboratory experience: animal care, equipment maintenance, basic record keeping." He waved at the floor to indicate the workers below.

"But Granger was different."

"Yes. Older. More personable, or so it seemed at first. I confided in him; most unwise of me. A financial irregularity, all settled now. But had it become known when he threatened to reveal it . . . well. Immortality may make me a rich man someday, Ms. Crusoe, but at present there's not much cash flow in it. Rather, cash flows, but all in an outward direction. He could have ruined me in an instant."

"This was after he'd been away for a while? Do you know where he was?" Do you know, Edwina meant, that he'd been in Oregon and Texas, marrying and possibly murdering two women?

"He was away," Chulovitz agreed, "for nearly two years. And no, I didn't know where he was. In fact I'd almost forgotten him. But when he returned, he demanded a letter saying he'd been with me all that time, and I'm ashamed to say I gave it to him."

"And you recommended him by telephone, too, I suppose, to the medical school admissions committee?"

Chulovitz nodded. "One of the deans over there followed up on him, some poor gray-faced functionary whose name I blessedly disremember. I was able to improvise something, I've forgotten now just what. It was very distasteful and I suppose I did know that eventually it would return to haunt me, but I didn't feel I had much choice."

He puffed on his pipe. "And now here you are. Rather a relief, actually. Telling you about all this feels like going to confession, only I'm worried about what the penance will be."

"No penance. Not from me, anyway. But there is one other thing." She fingered the antimacassar on the velvet settee. "I don't know quite how to ask you this, but . . ."

"Why should a recommendation from a deluded old crackpot like me carry any weight at all with a prestigious medical school admissions committee?"

She felt herself reddening. "Well, yes, actually I did mean that. Forgive me, but you see how it seems. Mouse immortality."

"No apology required," Dr. Chulovitz replied. "When we want the truth, we can't always be worrying about whether our questions are polite, can we?"

He tipped his head at her. "But Ms. Crusoe, I believe you will find I'm more than just a crackpot, if you check into my academic reputation. I am currently a lecturer in microbiology at the university medical school, and I speak regularly to learned groups around the country. I am massively published, voluminously lettered, and so loaded down with degrees both honorary and earned, I can barely move under the weight of them all."

He preened delicately. "I am, in short, a fine reference giver despite my somewhat unorthodox current interests, a fact that Mr. Granger, with his nose for the news that might benefit him, spied out at once."

"Have you heard from him lately?"

"No, nor do I wish to. I suppose, though, that now I will have to testify at some hearing or other, or at a trial."

She went out onto a landing that overlooked the laboratory. "Possibly. It's not yet clear what will be done. Thank you for seeing me, Dr. Chulovitz, and for being so frank with me. It has cleared up a puzzle."

"Has it." His wise old eyes were undeceived. "How pleasant to be able to do that."

She started down the stairs, her hand sliding easily on the silky wood of the old banister. Outside it was fully dark; she thought she would catch the university shuttle bus across town to her car, even though it meant skipping the book store this trip. As she reached the bottom step, Chulovitz's voice came again from the gloom above.

"Ms. Crusoe. Aren't you even a little curious? About what might make you live forever, I mean?"

"Of course." She turned, smiling. "But I thought that part of your work was a secret."

"I can give you a hint."

He stood in the doorway, his back to the lighted room behind him, his face in shadow. "Broccoli," he said. "Eat plenty of broccoli."

She let herself out. Broccoli, of course. Why couldn't the key to immortality be cream cheese, or pie? She was getting very hungry, she realized, as her pocket pager beeped.

"Listen," McIntyre said when she called him from the pay phone in Clark's Dairy, "I got to thinking about those women Granger was married to, because it still struck me as odd that he never came under much suspicion."

The smell of grilling hamburgers made Edwina feel faint; she wished Chulovitz hadn't mentioned food at all.

"I mean," McIntyre said, "it's always the husband. A woman can fall out of an airplane and you know it's the husband unless he's a thousand miles away. So I made a couple of phone calls."

"And?" Harriet would have planned a perfectly lovely dinner with wine and little baby vegetables, maybe a baked salmon or a pork roast. Firmly, Edwina put the idea of an enormous bacon cheeseburger out of her mind.

"And he was a thousand miles away, just like you said. Once on a ski trip, and once driving a trailer for some friends who were moving out of state. Plenty of witnesses. That's why no one rattled his cage, even though he did inherit a fair amount of money; he really couldn't have killed those women."

"I see. How annoyingly coincidental their deaths are, then."

"Right, and there's more. Cops out West faxed me a couple of photographs of Granger. They could ID him okay from the one you sent them, but back then he was forty pounds heavier, flabby and sloppy-looking, had longish hair and a big mustache. You knew him then, you wouldn't recognize him now."

Edwina remembered the trim, well-exercised man she had met the day before. "That is interesting. Easy enough to cut off your hair and mustache," she mused. "But going from flabby to fit takes some long-term commitment."

"Right. And maybe a long-term plan. Like, for instance, if you think you might be getting some national press, and you don't want your old acquaintances making connections."

Edwina sighed. The prosecution was going to have a field day with all this. Never mind that he hadn't come under any suspicion when the first two women died; the fact that Granger was now a widower times three was almost as prejudicial as if he'd actually been charged with their deaths, and a lot easier to get into trial testimony. The fake IDs and fraud to get into medical school just made it all worse.

"But wait, there's more," McIntyre said. "He didn't get a couple hundred thousand; that was just what he got right away. Total, it was more like a million."

"Good heavens. Talk about your basic motive."

"Right. So if he's spent a couple hundred thousand since then, which is generous considering he's been too busy to spend much money, where's the rest?"

"I gather that's being looked into," she said resignedly.

"You bet. Feeling is, when that money gets found, it'll be somewhere fishy. Like maybe with whoever killed those women."

"The consensus around your office being that he's sane and guilty, then?"

McIntyre's voice hardened. "What makes you think that? He's just a victim of circumstance. Walks around with a little black cloud over his head, every once in a while it causes one of his wives to die. And so far, it's batting three for three."

"I have to admit I'm having difficulty rooting for him myself," Edwina admitted. "He's got at least one shrink getting ready to say he's a multiple personality, but I don't like any of his personalities. The stunt he pulled yesterday was creepy in the extreme, and he got one of his fake recommendation letters by blackmailing an old employer who was supposedly also a friend."

A waitress walked by, carrying a tray loaded with sandwiches and plates of onion rings. Edwina shook her head, to clear it of a sudden, nearly overwhelming craving for saturated fat.

"Which is another thing that bothers me," she went on. "I mean, could he have been working on all this for *years*? Because it's sure starting to look to me as if he was."

"First he knocks off a couple of moderately wealthy women," McIntyre agreed, "to get the money for medical school. Fakes his way into medical school, then marries a really rich one, the kind who makes a million look like pocket change. And then she dies. Sounds like a plan to me."

"Even if he gets away with it, he'll never practice medicine again," Edwina said, remembering Frieda Schreiber's objection.

"Why would he need to?" McIntyre asked reasonably. "By the way, have you checked his library activities?"

She frowned. "I don't follow you."

"Well, if he's not really nuts, he's got to seem nuts. He's got to fool the experts. He's going to be tried for this crime, remember, not those. And I don't think he'd want to ad lib it, do you? I think he'd look it up. In, say, the medical library?"

"Oh, my gosh . . . prosecution's already doing that, I'll bet. Checking on his library card. And if Granger didn't take out any psych material, at least Ed Chernoff will be able to say Granger didn't. I have to go, now, Martin; thank you very much. You're wonderful and I love you."

"Of course I am, and of course you do," he said. "Kiss the boys for me." He hung up.

She punched Chelsea Memorial's main number and got the page operator to page Mickey Hasbrouck.

"Mickey? I need a favor. I need you to go to the medical library and get a list of every journal and monograph our friend Dr. Granger has requested or checked out in the past two years. Also, all his MEDLINE searches, any journal articles he got the computer to locate for him. You'll have to get the librarian to pull his library card bar-code number for you and key it in by hand, but once she does, I'm pretty sure the system will pull up the whole record and list it for you. Get a printout."

True to form, Mickey neither hemmed nor hawed at this rather unusual request. He did, however, raise a practical objection. "I don't think they'll give me his bar-code ID number without his permission."

"Right. I'll call Ed Chernoff, get him to call the library in advance; he can give the permission for Granger. And listen, I appreciate this; I'd do it myself but it's starting to snow and I haven't seen my kids today. I'm getting the Mommy Guilts."

Mickey laughed understandingly. "Yeah, it's awful, isn't it? I was an intern and a resident when my kids were little. The older one thought the telephone was named Daddy. I'll call you later, let you know if I find out anything."

"Thanks, Mickey. I owe you."

"Not really," he said pleasantly. "All you ever did was restore my faith in the human race by keeping my confidences, once upon a time. Or some of my faith, anyway." He hung up.

Good old Mickey. Probably he was happy to have something to do when he left the hospital besides go home to an empty house. Edwina stepped out of the restaurant and stopped. Fat white flakes were floating out of the sky in the unhurried way that in her experience generally signalled a huge snowstorm.

Nothing significant had been forecast, and besides, it was too early in the year for serious weather. Still, dervishes of flakes whirled along the sidewalk, collecting in miniature drifts against the buildings. University students hurried by, wearing hats and winter parkas and boots, and the cars in the street all had their windshield wipers on.

"Excuse me," she said to one of the passing students, noticing with sudden suspicion how jocular they all looked, how gleeful with holidaylike anticipation. "Excuse me, but do you know if it's supposed to snow much tonight?"

The student stopped, grinning. "Haven't you heard? We

are going to have a *major* blizzard. Up in Litchfield they've already got a foot. Hey, see you on the slopes!"

"See you," she murmured, watching him hurry to catch up with his friends. She might still make it back to Litchfield if she got on the road soon; the Fiat was surprisingly good in snow, and the plows would be out in force. Turning, she gathered her coat, raised her collar, and prepared for a fast march straight across town. But before she could take the first step, her pocket pager went off again.

"Edwina," said the scratchy, static-distorted voice coming out of the device. "This is your mother. Rita's gone with the boys, and they haven't come back. It's snowing like blazes here and I'm dreadfully worried. Please call at once."

◆ ◆ ◆

"I really appreciate this," Marion said as the rental agent unlocked the door to Egloff's little house. "I happened to be passing by and saw the sign."

She didn't mention that she had also moved the sign, so that it would be plausible for her to have seen it from the street.

"A friend of mine will be moving into town soon, and she's desperate for a small, inexpensive place. She'll be working with me at the hospital," Marion went on. "Isn't it funny that my husband's old company should be managing the property?"

It was what she'd counted on: that mentioning Gerrald's name could still get a favor done for her. And it had.

"Good little house," the agent said, working the padlock. "Good landlord, too, does all the work around the place, collects rents himself. We just show it for him, he's got a schedule and can't always be available."

"Mr. Egloff; yes, I know him. He teaches my son."

The door swung open. "That so? Well, here it is. Small place, but everything works. Oil furnace. Needs paint. And furniture, of course, and the rent doesn't include utilities."

The agent, a big, ruddy man with graying hair and

bloodshot blue eyes, waved at the refrigerator, an old, slope-shouldered Frigidaire. Beside it stood a newer freezer; scuff marks on the floor showed where this appliance had been pushed into position against the wallboard rather recently.

The freezer was running. Marion stared at it, and at the bars on the windows. They were the sort of cast-iron welded bar units one might expect to see on the outside of a house, bolted to the window frames. The rental agent cleared his throat.

"Uh, I guess the last tenant was pretty security-conscious. Those could come off if your friend didn't like them."

"Yes, I'll tell her." Marion's gaze kept returning to the freezer. Casually she tried the water at the sink and pulled the cord hanging from the light over the counter, getting nearer to the big white box. She didn't want to look, but she had to.

"Sizable bedrooms, bathroom's in good shape, plenty of hot water." The agent's voice echoed hollowly from the living room. "When did you say your friend is coming?"

"A few weeks." The freezer hummed smugly, gleaming in the light from the naked bulb over the sink. Holding her breath, Marion reached out and lifted the freezer's lid. It was empty.

"Want to take a look at the other rooms?"

"No!" Startled, she dropped the lid; it fell closed with a thud. "I mean . . . no, thank you." She managed a shaky smile.

The agent was looking oddly at her. "I . . . didn't realize the house was so small," she said. "My friend has four children and a . . . a big dog. There wouldn't be room for them all."

The agent let her out, snapped the padlock shut, and handed her a card. "Send her along when she gets into town," he said, clearly not believing there was a friend at all. He backed out in a roar of exhaust without waiting to see if she got off all right; she had wasted his time.

And her own, apparently. The pit bull began howling;

Marion felt like joining in. She took a step, tripped on one of her own shoelaces, and went down hard. *Damn, what else could happen?*

Wincing against the pain, she reached to tie the lace and stopped as a small, shiny object caught her eye. A tiny brown bead, or . . . no. A small, round seed.

A marijuana seed, stuck between porch floorboards. There had been a lecture at Gerry Junior's school, so parents would recognize drugs and drug paraphernalia if they came upon them. Slides had shown marijuana growing and seeds of the plants.

Gazing at the seed, Marion remembered again the way Gerry Junior's friends had looked at Egloff: as if they knew something about him that they didn't want to let on to her. As if he was something more than just a teacher.

Leaving the seed, she drove home and took a shower, then fixed herself a grilled cheese sandwich and a cup of coffee; after supper, she called the hospital to check on Gerry Junior's condition and was told that there had been no change.

She had not been expecting any. Gerry would remain the same for as long as she let him; it was up to her now to change the situation. Somehow, she would have to show him that it was safe to get better.

Somehow. Thinking this, she looked up the Egloffs' number in the telephone book and tried it. Mr. Egloff was not at home, but his wife was there, her voice sounding gruff and manly. Marion explained who she was, and asked if she could come over; she hoped it wasn't terribly inconvenient, but what she had to say was important.

After a brief hesitation, Mrs. Egloff agreed.

◆ ◆ ◆

I'm disappointed in you, Tad. Very disappointed. But I'll get you out somehow. You can count on it.

The crawl space was completely dark, the hole covered over. Tad had crept out through it and found himself imprisoned in the house. He had gulped water from the faucet, located the bathroom and managed to relieve himself without falling down, scoured the kitchen for food and gobbled some Hostess Cupcakes he found in a cabinet. Then he had tried every way he could think of to get out.

Unsuccessfully: the house had locked doors, barred windows, and no phone. He shouted, but no one heard him, and the bars kept him from breaking the glass. When he heard the car pull into the driveway, he had scrambled back into the crawl space. Moments later he had begun feeling much sicker than before; the cupcakes, he realized.

Then came the scraping sound, as the freezer was shoved up against the hole. Later came new voices: a man's voice and a woman's. They had been out there, and he had tried to shout, to hammer with his fists, so they would find him and save him. But when he opened his mouth, only a faint croak emerged, and when he raised his fist it fell limply, without a sound.

His stomach had rejected the cupcakes and whatever was in them, but he still felt very sick, poisoned even, and his head hurt so much that he almost couldn't breathe. He felt hot and cold, drenched in sweat, his teeth chattering like a jackhammer.

Things happen, Tad. You see them on TV all the time: gas leaks. Fires, explosions.

A feeling of doom poured through him as he realized: this voice wasn't real. It was in his head; he was hearing things that weren't there. And this *wasn't* TV, where no matter how bad a situation looked, the kid always got out of it.

The kid got saved, because everybody knew you couldn't let the kid get killed. Kids lived forever, didn't they?

Didn't they?

◆   ◆   ◆

The wipers batted clots of snow from the windshield as the Fiat fought gamely for every inch along the storm-swept highway. Route 8 up through the Connecticut River valley hadn't been too treacherous, but in the Berkshire foothills the driving had gone from miserable to sheer murder.

Or suicide, Edwina thought, peering through the wedge-shaped opening the wiper created. The only other vehicles on the road were snowplows, hurling white gouts from their slanted blades as they bulled through the storm.

The Fiat's rear end slid out warningly. Edwina let her foot off the accelerator, her hands resting lightly on the wheel. Any aggressive move could send her into one of those snowbanks the plows had heaped along the side of the road, and on a night like this one she wouldn't get out again.

At last she glimpsed the dirt road and Mr. Watkins at the end of it, waving a flashlight. Obediently, she took the turn, downshifting to muscle the Fiat as far as possible off the paved roadway, feeling the tires spin.

When she switched off the engine, the only sound was of the snow brushing the car's canvas top. She rolled down the window and gasped in the frigid air, trying to loosen the band of fright that had tightened around her heart.

"Throw 'er in neutral," Mr. Watkins called, "and leave the brake off. When I tell you, just keep the wheel straight. We'll 'ave you up in a bit."

From the darkness came faint snufflings and jinglings; then, looming like apparitions, the huge, pale shapes of four horses hitched into a team materialized, vapor chuffing from their flared nostrils. Watkins bent to the Fiat, hooking up a chain.

"Is there any word?" Edwina called to him. "Does anybody know what's happened to Rita and the boys?"

His face pinched with worry and cold. "No, Miss. Let's get on, now, she's up waitin' for you at the house, and she's in a bad state. Put the 'eadlights on, can you? The 'orses know the way, but in this weather I'm not sure I know mine."

The chain tightened clankingly and the car began to move as Watkins shouted to the animals, urging them on. In a few minutes the windows of the big house appeared, floating like the lights of some enormous, ghostly ship set sail on an ocean of white.

Harriet started up from the kitchen table as Edwina came in. "I should never have left her alone with them, I knew she wasn't to be trusted, especially not after the night before. Oh, it's all my fault, how could I have let her take them?" Harriet cried.

"Mother, it's not your fault. I would have let Rita take the boys if I had been here; she does it all the time."

Edwina looked around at the kitchen; there was no sign of any washing up, which meant Harriet had not eaten anything. On the sink sat a teapot and a box of tea, abandoned when Harriet had become too distraught even to make herself a cup.

Harriet herself looked pale and haggard, speaking in rushed, disjointed fragments. ". . . In this *weather*, what could she have been thinking of, and Martin, has anybody told Martin? Oh, dear, I've forgotten to take my medicine. Do you see it? Where is my medicine?" She peered around wildly.

"Mother, sit down. Martin is in the city, coordinating the search from there, and Watkins says the local police have been in touch with Martin. And nobody knew we were going to get snow; it was only supposed to be a few flurries, everyone thought."

She picked up Harriet's pill dispenser to examine it. "And you've taken your medicine already. Now, I'm going to make some tea and toast, and we're both going to have some."

"I'd have gone looking for them myself, if I were younger," Harriet fretted. "Oh, if only I'd been more firm with her; I saw the look in her eye. If only I hadn't let them go or I'd stayed home myself, none of this would ever have—"

Edwina put her hands flat on the counter. "Mother, stop."

Harriet's eyes were puffy, her perfect makeup smeared and her hairdo falling. Her left hand plucked at a loose thread on her cardigan.

"Rita got caught in the storm," Edwina said, "and pulled

in somewhere, and she's waiting until the roads get clear. Maybe the phone's out where she is. None of it is your fault, but if you make yourself sick with a lot of fussing and I have to take care of you on top of everything, that will be your fault."

Harriet nodded solemnly. "But she was angry with me. You must know that. I didn't mean to offend her, but . . ." Her voice trailed off.

"Never mind," Edwina said. "You can tell me about it later, after you've calmed down and eaten something."

Outside, billows of snow swirled in the light from the kitchen windows. From the barn came a pale, intermittent gleam as Watkins rubbed down the horses, settling them for the night. Wind whistled in the clapboards and rattled the wooden shingles of the big old house.

Edwina filled the teapot and sliced some bread. Wind made the lights flicker, but they came on again. She put the bread into the toaster, gripping the sink's edge as another wave of fright slammed through her; the absence of the boys was like an endless black hole she was falling down, falling and falling.

"Rita could call, I suppose," Harriet said dubiously after a sip of tea and a bite of toast; she was beginning to get her wind back. "If she got to a working phone."

"Yes, she certainly could," Edwina agreed.

But the hours went by, and the storm raged on. Midnight came, and one o'clock, and two-thirty, and there was still no word.

"Mother, you should go to bed," Edwina said.

"I wouldn't sleep a wink. Pull that afghan over you; it's getting cold in here."

Harriet got up and put another log into the woodstove in the sitting room. She usually spent her mornings writing in this room, but now Edwina thought Harriet's desk looked unusually neat: no spiral-bound notebooks, scattered index cards, or piles of the reference books Harriet used to check everything from the number of deaths due to toothache in

1775 to the proper method of transporting a lady's wardrobe along the Oregon Trail, and of transporting the lady, too.

"Aren't you working on anything?" Edwina asked idly. If she thought about the boys for another minute, she would go mad.

Harriet looked uncomfortable. "No. I'm taking a rest."

Taking a rest came about as naturally to Harriet as taking poison. "Really? What's the occasion?"

Harriet's lips tightened; she looked down at her hands. "If you must know, I've had a setback. I suppose it's why I've been in such an awful temper lately. Properly researched, decently written historical romances seem not quite the thing nowadays, at least not according to my new editor. She was hired by the liquor distributors who bought my publisher, and she's well over twenty-two years old, so I suppose she should know," Harriet added scathingly. "She wanted me to think about ghosting a book in someone else's series, a fellow called Claudio or some such ghastly personage. She says he is very hot."

"Oh, dear." Edwina was familiar with the image of the gentleman in question; his public relations organization was as big as the Pentagon. His face and the musculature of his upper torso had appeared on the cover of dozens of romance novels over the past five years; now someone had decided that his name might as well appear on the covers of some of them, too.

"I'm meeting with him on Tuesday," Harriet said. "My agent and the promotion and advertising people all insist that I at least talk with this creature. Assuming he can talk," she added.

"Oh, Mother. No wonder you've been in such a bad mood."

"Yes, well, I could refuse, of course, but they're making me feel that if I do, it's only because I'm a narrow-minded old lady who is too senile even to consider new ideas."

"Maybe he'll run off with a movie actress, and you'll be off the hook," Edwina suggested.

"Or," Harriet said wickedly, "an actor. You haven't been very cheerful yourself lately, I've noticed. What's wrong with this business you're working on for Ed Chernoff?"

Edwina felt a pang of guilt; the last thing she wanted was for Harriet to get wind of any deep, dark secrets Ed might be trying to keep. Harriet treated secrets the way cats treated mice: she played with them for a while, then laid them open.

"I don't think it's going to go well for him," Edwina said. "Nothing I've come up with has been very helpful to him. To the contrary, actually; Granger is shaping up to be quite a monster, and Tom Whitelaw's pushing Ed hard to show otherwise."

Harriet switched off the lamp. The stove's red flames flickered, making weird shapes of the furniture; outside, the storm hammered and howled. Edwina remembered this room from her childhood, late at night with the grown-ups talking over her head as she drowsed on the sofa where Harriet sat now.

"Tom Whitelaw," Harriet said, "is a monster himself. He likes to think everyone has forgotten, and most people have. But old ladies have long memories."

"What do you mean?" A gust rattled the windowpanes. Edwina closed her eyes, trying not to think of how cold it was outside, how frightened Francis and Jonathan must be.

"Remember the story I began telling you," Harriet asked, "about Tom and Emeralinda? Well, as it happens there's more to it. I was her best friend after her parents died; I was married, older, only a little wiser. But I think she felt safe with me."

The old lady sighed, remembering. "She used to come here in the afternoons. To get away from the lawyers, she said, but then she learned that one of them was stealing from her. Tom Whitelaw discovered the discrepancies and told her about them."

Edwina's eyes had been drifting shut; now she opened them. "Which one was stealing?"

"Emeralinda wouldn't say. I wondered why she was

protecting whoever it was. Soon, though, that difficulty paled beside a new one; she was pregnant, and Tom Whitelaw was pressing her to marry him. He knew she didn't care for him in that way, but he wanted what he wanted: a beautiful, wealthy wife. And he wasn't above threatening to put her at the center of a scandal if she didn't go along with him."

"He knew she was carrying another man's child?"

"Of course. It was part of what he would use to blacken her reputation if she didn't marry him. The wedding was just a month after she told me of her trouble, and they left at once on a year's tour of Europe; when they returned, the baby was three months old. Or six, depending on whom you believe. Lorelei didn't come along until years later."

"And was the lawyer who stole money from Emeralinda also the father of the baby?" They were talking, Edwina realized, about Charity Anne, whose conception had forced Emeralinda's marriage to Whitelaw, and who was not his child. No wonder the poor thing had never been sure of her welcome.

Harriet glanced at her daughter. "How interesting that you should ask; it's what I wondered myself. It would explain her failure to accuse the thief, wouldn't it? But I don't know for sure. It's not the sort of thing that comes up in ordinary conversation. Or extraordinary conversation, either; Emeralinda stopped confiding in me after she was married."

Harriet poked the fire. "Ed Chernoff was married once himself. Did you know that?"

Edwina blinked at the information and at the seeming change of subject. "He never told me."

Harriet stood by the stove. "It was quite tragic. He was a struggling young lawyer, and she was a poor girl. Some town family, I don't remember which one. They were happy at first, but then she became ill with tuberculosis. So many things to die of, in those days. She died just about the time Emeralinda married Tom Whitelaw."

"And then Emeralinda went to Europe and had a baby, and came back. And by that time, Ed Chernoff was gone."

"Yes. He'd started up his practice in New Haven. On what, I have no idea, and it's all ancient history now. I thought I'd tell it to you, to take your mind off things."

She opened the curtains. Outside, it was getting light; the storm had passed, and it was going to be a brilliant day.

"To take my mind off things," Edwina repeated. But Harriet never told stories merely to take people's minds off things.

The telephone rang.

◆   ◆   ◆

At seven in the morning, the smells of coffee, breakfasts, and hot, soapy water wafted through the hospital corridors. TVs were tuned to chirpy morning shows, carts bearing fruit baskets and flowers were arriving, and the sky outside the big plate-glass windows was a pale, promising blue.

In Gerry Junior's room, Marion Bailey spread out the towels, fresh bed linen, and clean hospital gown she had fetched from the cart in the linen room. Tuning Gerry's radio to the station he liked, all screeching guitars and frantic shouting, she filled a basin with water and unwrapped a fresh cake of soap.

Looking down at him, she considered opening a disposable razor; a few dark hairs sprouted on his sweat-beaded upper lip. As she debated the idea, he rolled his eyes and made flopping motions with his puffy hands.

But no; a young man's first shave should not be administered by his mother. He would shave himself, someday. Calmly, she began giving him his sponge bath; it was an important morning and she knew that he would want to look good.

"Now, Gerry, if I'm wrong, or you can't do it, that's okay," she said, sluicing warm water from a pitcher over the back of his head. "I promise I won't be mad at you."

Gerry arched his back. His mouth was like a fish's mouth, opening and closing.

"You're going to have company in a little while," she went on, untying his wrist restraints.

His gaze zigged to the right, his fingers fastening onto her sleeve. "Wa," he whispered, blinking.

"*Very* good. Okay, now, over you go." A long red mark ran diagonally across his back, the result of a wrinkle in the sheet he had been lying on.

She finished washing and drying him, changed his bed linens, rubbed him down with lotion. As she was combing his hair, she caught a glimpse of movement and looked up, but it was only the reflection of an aide in the mirror over the doorway, outside the room. It was a psychiatric ward, after all, and the security was subtle but thorough; the mirror was to prevent anyone leaving the room from being surprised by someone waiting, mischievously or otherwise, outside the room.

"They like it that your mom's a nurse," Marion told Gerry. "So I can help them out." Adjusting his bed to a sitting position, she refastened his restraints, then bundled the soiled sheets and towels into the linen hamper.

"There," she said. "You look much better. Feel better, too, I'll bet. Now remember; if you can't do what I said, or if I've made a mistake, it's all right. No one will hurt you or punish you, and I will always take care of you."

Gerry turned his head away. Being sick had thickened his skin and enlarged his pores, so that he seemed older than he had only a few days ago; the hairs on his upper lip were almost a real mustache, but in profile he was still only a little boy.

Outside the room, aides pushed carts of dishes back to the dietary department; wheelchairs and stretchers bore patients away for tests or X rays; doctors in white coats moved from doorway to doorway on their morning rounds. Over it all the page operator's voice droned steadily.

"Everything will be all right," Marion said.

Gerry's eyes focused; she thought he might be listening to her. But when she followed his gaze she saw that he was watching the people and vehicles in the corridor, their shapes and faces distorted but perfectly recognizable in the large, round mirror.

♦   ♦   ♦

The breakfast room at the Whitelaws' was done up in painted white wicker and green cushions with touches of sunny yellow. At the center of the table was a Meissen fruit bowl heaped with grapes and apples, but the only fruit either of the Whitelaws consumed regularly, Edwina realized at the sight of them gazing blearily at one another, was the kind that came impaled on little plastic daggers in double old-fashioned glasses.

"I don't understand," she said, frustrated in her attempts to get anything sensible out of them. "Why didn't you call yesterday, or last night?"

Thomas Whitelaw looked up from his coffee. "We didn't know your car was here until this morning, when the plow came to open the driveway. The driver wanted someone to move it. You can't see it from the house, and we didn't go out." He turned a page of his *Wall Street Journal*.

"Didn't you notice that Lorelei hadn't come home?"

Emeralinda turned languidly, her extravagant silk kimono wrapped sloppily around her and hooded eyes dim with what Edwina suspected was a ferocious hangover. "She stays out sometimes. We've asked her not to, but what can you do with young people, these days? Would you like a cup of tea, dear, or a piece of toast? We have some wonderful English marmalade."

Edwina considered grasping the Whitelaws by their necks and banging their foolish foreheads together. "My children," she said, "have been missing since yesterday, along with their nanny and your daughter. I assume they're together. Aren't you the least bit worried?"

Whitelaw frowned at a headline, apparently trying to focus on it. "I'm sure they'll turn up. Lorelei's a big girl. She's learned to take care of herself."

I'll just bet she has, Edwina thought. She's gotten about as much parenting from the two of you as a glob of frog spawn. "You won't mind if I have a look at her room. Maybe she's left some hint of where they were heading."

Whitelaw bridled faintly, but Emeralinda waved his objection away. "Of course not, dear," she told Edwina. "Lorelei has such a pretty room. Do stop and say good-bye before you leave, and give your mother our love."

Edwina stared for a moment longer in disbelief. It was as if the two of them lived under a glass bell, or packed in moth balls. Nothing outside their little world touched them, or even reached them. The charitable explanation was that they were paralyzed with grief over Charity Anne, but Edwina wasn't feeling very charitable; besides, she didn't believe it.

Whitelaw turned another page of his paper. Could he really be blackmailing Ed Chernoff, as Harriet had all but come right out and suggested? Emeralinda sipped her tea, looked aggrieved, and rang the little silver bell beside her plate impatiently.

At the stairs, Edwina met a uniformed maid hurrying toward the breakfast room. "Somebody rang?" the maid asked anxiously.

"Yes. Mrs. Whitelaw saw something nasty in her tea leaves. Which way is Lorelei's room?"

The maid directed her, and Edwina went down the long hall past door after closed door until she came to the last one. It opened onto a bright, sunny chamber decorated in pink and white, with gauzy priscilla curtains and a white lace bedspread, pink lampshades, and pink striped silk on the upholstered chairs.

At first Edwina thought she must have mistaken the maid's words; the room was so neat and clean, so entirely without any personal items in evidence, that it seemed as if no one could ever have lived in it. The only thing that would not have seemed out of place in a hotel room was a row of what looked like big photograph albums or clipping books filling one whole shelf of the white-painted wooden bookcase along the far wall.

Harriet had books like those; she kept all the reviews of her novels and news articles and publicity pieces about herself in them. Edwina took one of the books down and opened it; then she took down the next one and the next, spreading them open on the white lace bed.

Fifteen minutes later she was back in the Fiat, heading toward Route 7. The secondary road was plowed but still covered with packed-down snow; she drove as fast as she dared. Route 7 would be bare pavement, or nearly so, and if her theory was correct, that was the way Lorelei Whitelaw had gone with Rita and the twins.

Fourth gear was dicey, even on the Fiat's Michelins, and fifth was a distant dream; once she reached cruising speed, Edwina drove with one hand and operated the car-phone buttons with the other, punching out her home number and then the code for the remote playback mode on the answering machine there. McIntyre would have left a message for her by now.

"Hi, it's me, I'm on my way." His voice was crisp and businesslike, betraying no trace of what he was feeling. "The word's out, local, state, and federal. I have to check a few things up in Litchfield, and if they're not back I'm going to drive around a while. I love you, Edwina. We'll find them."

No good-bye, just a click and the next message: "Hey, Edwina, it's Mickey Hasbrouck. Don't know if this is good news or bad news, but I checked those library records."

Edwina blinked; her interest in Billy Granger and whether or not he had researched symptoms of multiple personality disorder seemed now to have been part of another life, one in which little boys were safe at their grandmother's house where they belonged, not lost somewhere out in the snow.

Billy Granger was someone's little boy once, too, a voice in her head reminded her; she silenced it viciously. Even the memory of his ghastly self-mutilation act, if it had been an act, failed to move her now. If the twins could vanish then anything was possible, and Billy Granger was of no interest; he could take his eyes out with a teaspoon, for all she cared.

". . . nothing on him," Hasbrouck's voice went on. "He didn't use the library much, and what he did get was surgical stuff."

A burst of static from the answering machine tape broke up his voice. ". . . sorry there wasn't more," Mickey finished. The message ended.

So Granger hadn't researched his symptoms, or if he had, he'd done it the old-fashioned way: finding references in the printed *Index Medicus* volumes and sitting in the library to read them. And if he had done that, there was no computer record of it, so it was as if he hadn't done it at all.

At the intersection with Route 7 she turned right onto the wider pavement, which a nightlong barrage of salt from the road crews and the morning sun had almost completely cleared; between the high banks of plow-thrown snow at either side of the highway, the road was black as licorice.

She flicked the Fiat's wipers, peering through the sandy spray thrown up by the car ahead of her, and tried to remember the last time she had filled the car's washer-fluid reservoir, then punched out the number of McIntyre's car phone, but it was busy.

Hang up, she thought impatiently at him, but she knew he wouldn't. He would be in touch with the local and state police, with the staffers on the national missing-children emergency hotline, and with people he knew all over the Northeast, trying to find Francis and Jonathan. He would not rest, he would have to be forced to eat or sleep, and he would not let anyone else rest either, until he had the boys back.

Which meant she wouldn't be able to reach him. She could call up the local police and ask for their help, but what she had to say wouldn't sound very sensible: that she believed she knew, from the contents of Lorelei's scrapbooks, where Lorelei had been headed when she, another young woman, and a pair of toddlers had vanished in the snowy darkness: to her sister's fresh grave.

The side road angling uphill off Route 7 led into what Harriet called the boondocks; tiny four-corners settlements and clusters of run-down trailer homes that might as well have been in the back hills of Kentucky for all they shared with the richer parts of Litchfield County. Edwina passed a battered pickup loaded with logs, its snow tires jingling merrily in defiance of the scowl on the driver's face; the fresh, cold air smelled of pine sap from branches broken under the weight of the blizzard, and chain saws buzzed in the distance. People here heated with wood, roofed their houses with tin, and as often as not met unknown visitors with their shotguns near to hand.

But Edwina wasn't planning on visiting anyone who would object to company. The inside front covers of the clipping books in Lorelei's bedroom were inscribed with the words "Property of Lorelei Whitelaw," but the items in them commemorated nothing in Lorelei's life except the activities of her sister. There was a baptism certificate and all Charity Anne's school report cards. Later came diplomas, honor roll citations, a piece from the *Litchfield Times* noting Charity Anne's graduation from nursing school, and her wedding announcement.

And there was more, much more: everything admirable that Charity Anne ever did, all catalogued by Lorelei, who in spite of her good looks and popularity, her girl-next-door freshness and healthy glow, was not the golden girl. Charity Anne was that, to Lorelei, at least: Charity Anne who got away and made herself a life, who did things that mattered, even got married. Awkward, homely, uncertain: still, she was the successful one. Last in the scrapbook had come Charity Anne's obituary, with its notice of her burial.

We were never close, Lorelei had said, but they had been, only Charity Anne never knew it, hadn't wanted to know it. All the things she hadn't been able to be, she had decided to scorn, and the sum of them was her younger sister, Lorelei, so pretty and charming, so much what Charity Anne could not be.

And yesterday, forgotten by everyone but Lorelei, had been Charity Anne's birthday: not according to the Whitelaw family legend, which put the girl within the bounds of legitimacy and made her Tom Whitelaw's daughter, but according to Charity Anne's birth certificate, the first of Lorelei's scrapbook mementos and one that told the truth.

Edwina pulled the car as far as she could off the traveled part of the narrow lane; a covered barrel with a shovel leaning alongside it held sand, or perhaps stove ashes. A cast-iron arch beyond was worked with the words "High Hill Cemetery," and led to a pristine snow-covered slope studded here and there with snow-laden cypresses, hunched like trolls.

But yesterday, the lane under the archway would have been open; Lorelei could easily have driven up it, over the hilltop to the edge of the graveyard. Edwina got out of the car and pulled her coat around her. The frigid wind cut across her face, bringing tears that froze in her eyelashes. She trudged up the hill with no idea of what she might find on the other side; still, she was certain that Lorelei had come here. Perhaps she had left some sign of what had happened next.

The wind shoved like a bully on the unprotected slope. Snow filled the tops of Edwina's boots and puddled around her ankles. But when she reached the top, there was no sign of where Charity Anne's new grave might be. Tall granite obelisks poked through snow so brightly white that it hurt to look at it, their polished sides glinting and their shapes casting blue shadows; the rest of the stones were white, indistinct humps, row upon silent row of them, as if the legions of the dead were pushing to the surface but had not yet quite emerged.

◆　◆　◆

The light hurt Rita's eyes. Her feet felt like solid frozen blocks at the ends of her legs. The air smelled of wood smoke and burned like fire going down. Beyond the sand-streaked heaps the plows had piled up at the sides of the road, the snow spread endlessly.

She wanted to eat some of the snow. She wanted to fall into it and sleep. Ahead, the road curved into a grove of pines.

A car appeared; slowing, it pulled alongside her and stopped. Mr. McIntyre got out. Rita wondered if he was real.

"Where are they?" He gripped her shoulders. "Where did you leave them?"

She looked around. There was the road, but she had only been on it a little while. Before that she had been in the dark, in the snow, walking and falling and getting up again.

She looked at her hands. They were bloody. "I don't know."

"Rita, think, now. Which way did you come?"

Her head fell back. A hawk drifted overhead, in the silent sky. It was getting harder to breathe.

"Footprints," she said, fighting to get her head up, but it wouldn't stay up. "My footprints. In the snow."

◆   ◆   ◆

Edwina drove mechanically, hardly caring which way she went. Turning back onto Route 7, she got stuck behind a slow-moving plow spewing slushy snow to the shoulder of the road. The piles of snow rose higher than the Fiat's roof at either side of the highway. I don't know what to do next, she thought clearly.

Her car phone ringer trilled; she fumbled at the speaker button. McIntyre's voice came through, but raggedly. He was trying to give directions, but the reception fuzzed in and out.

". . . Lime Kiln Road . . . Crooked Brook . . ."

Crooked Brook, she realized, and Lime Kiln Road was just off that; to him, they were unfamiliar locations, but not to her. If she had gone on uphill instead of turning around at the cemetery, she would have come down on the other side, straight past the old quarry that, until she was well into her teens, she had thought was devoted to the production of rhinestones, not limestone.

Flipping on her headlights, she leaned on the horn and swung aggressively out around the snowplow, whose startled driver shot her a one-fingered salute as she left him in her spray. By the time she reached the quarry and Crooked Brook, she could already hear the sirens on the emergency vehicles coming up fast.

Young men in bright yellow jackets were digging with shovels into the snow heap at the side of the road. McIntyre waved a rescue squad in the direction of his car, then rushed to Edwina. As he reached her, one of the shovel crew shouted.

"Where are they?" she demanded, following McIntyre's look of grim hope to where the crew had begun shoveling faster. A corner of something white appeared, glinting in the snow.

Then she understood. "My God. They're under there?"

"They went off the road sometime last night, and the plows came along and covered them. Rita got out, but she couldn't get the others out. Her tracks led here."

"Easy, easy," one of the men shouted roughly, "there's a lot of weight. And watch it with those shovels, that's a rag top on that car. Kids' heads in there, and a woman."

Edwina turned away. The rescue crew were getting Rita out of McIntyre's car, lowering her onto a backboard. Rita's head fell sideways; she caught sight of Edwina and called out weakly.

"Rita." The girl was barely recognizable, her face bruised and windburned, her lips blistered and split. Her mottled hands were swollen masses of bloody scrapes.

"I'm sorry," she whispered. "We were . . . going back. But we spun into the ditch, and the plows . . . covered us."

Edwina looked at Rita's nails, all broken and torn, and at the height of the snow heap the men with shovels had excavated. "You dug out with your hands?"

Rita's shoulders moved under the ambulance blanket. "There wasn't . . . anything else. Are they . . . all right?"

"Not yet," the shovel crew leader shouted as McIntyre hovered beside him. "Watch that side, you got a cave-in started there. A little more, a little more . . ."

The rescue squad crew lifted Rita's stretcher. "I'm sorry," she wept. "I shouldn't . . . have gone. But I was so angry . . . it was all about . . . money."

"Ma'am, we have to go," said the ambulance volunteer at the head of Rita's stretcher.

A hoarse cheer went up from where the men were digging. One of them handed something up out of the hole. A weak, angry wail filled the air. Rita began crying hard; then her sobs turned to coughing, and the skin around her lips went briefly blue.

"No," Edwina said, getting hurriedly up, "not Litchfield." It was a perfectly good hospital, only not good enough.

"Clear it with whoever you have to," she called back over her shoulder, "but go straight to Chelsea Memorial. We'll meet you there."

She hurried to where the men were still digging. McIntyre had one of the boys in his arms and was looking down into the hole, his face unreadable. The rescue squad roared off, sirens blaring; the men by the hole shouted something Edwina couldn't hear. Fearfully, she took a step nearer, and then another.

◆　◆　◆

Three hours into the workday, and the nurses' aides on Chelsea's adolescent psychiatric ward had had enough back talk out of their teenaged patients, many of whom were sullen, sarcastic, or smart-alecky in the extreme. When Marion Bailey went to greet Fred and Barbara Egloff at the nurses' station, a screaming battle had just erupted between a skinny redheaded girl with braces and thick glasses and an aide who thought ten days was long enough for the girl to be wearing the same smelly, unwashed flannel shirt.

Fred Egloff looked anxious. "Guess she's kind of upset," he commented in a near whisper, glancing nervously around as if he expected some pyscho kid with a butcher knife to fly down the corridor at him.

Egloff's wife showed no such discomfort, looking bored and contemptuous as the aide led the girl away. A big woman with iron gray hair and strong, capable-looking hands, Barbara Egloff wore a plaid shirt, denim skirt, and flat leather walking shoes; her size and the impression of physical power she conveyed made her husband look even smaller and more ineffectual.

"Thank you for coming," Marion said, wondering why Mrs. Egloff had come at all; it was the teacher Marion wanted. "Gerry's room is this way."

Fred Egloff blinked nervously several times. "Be good to see the boy," he said, obviously not meaning it. From one of the rooms came the crash of a washbasin being hurled against a wall.

Egloff jumped. "Never did like hospitals," he squeaked, taking one unwilling step and then another.

"Many people don't, but you get used to it after a while," Marion replied coldly. She had told Gerry's doctor as much as she dared early this morning. If Gerry had a sudden emotional shock, she had asked, like the one that got him into this mess; if he saw the person who hurt him, close up, could that possibly snap him out of it? Could it help, or might it make him worse?

The doctor had looked at Marion for a long moment. When he did speak, he hadn't seemed to be answering her question at all, or at least not at first.

"We're going to put a gastrostomy tube in him," he said. "I don't like doing it, but there isn't any choice. We've got to feed him, and he won't eat normally. I don't have to tell you about the risks of infection, but it's the lesser of two evils. As for his mental status, we're taking it day by day."

"In other words, he's starving. If you feed him he could get septic and die. If you don't feed him, he'll die anyway. And he's not showing any improvement, mentally or emotionally."

The doctor had nodded, which meant Marion had her answer. Nothing she did or didn't do could hurt Gerry Junior. Now she paused at the door to Gerry's room.

"He doesn't look well," she confided to the teacher and his wife. "He doesn't speak, or even give any sign he knows you're there. His eyes are open, but he doesn't seem really conscious."

Was it her imagination, or did Egloff look relieved? Barbara Egloff stood a few paces behind him, looking ready, if necessary, to give her husband a shove.

"But I thought if he could see a familiar face," Marion went on, "someone he likes and admires the way he does you, then maybe he'd know at least that people were thinking about him."

Egloff took an unwilling step into the room, while his wife waited out in the corridor. In the mirror over the door, Barbara's face resembled a bad-tempered bulldog's, her jowls sagging dourly and her eyes narrowed in chronic irritation.

"Hey, guy," Egloff said from the foot of Gerry's bed. "We, uh, miss you at school. Hope you get better soon."

Gerry moaned, his arms flopping limply in their restraints. Egloff looked as if he wanted to run from the room.

"Here," Marion said, "why don't you sit down?" She took a grim pleasure in herding Egloff to the chair on the window side of Gerry's bed, where the light was brightest.

Gerry, look, Marion thought at her son. *I'm here, no one can hurt you. Look at him, honey. Please, look.*

Gerry's head rolled restlessly. Egloff's gaze skittered around the room, taking in all the indelicate items of equipment needed for the care of a patient like this one. "Hey, guy," he said again weakly.

Marion stood beside Egloff's chair, hoping to draw Gerry's attention. Gerry stared straight at Egloff for a moment, then went into one of his blinking fits and wrenched his gaze away. Out in the corridor, a boy in a wheelchair zoomed by, and another one right after him; they were having a forbidden race.

Barbara Egloff glared after the boys. If she were running the asylum, her look seemed to say, she would start by instituting some discipline among the inmates.

Gerry muttered something incomprehensible.

"Well," Egloff said, getting up, "I guess that's all I . . ."

Gerry muttered something else.

"Wait," Marion said sharply.

Gerry moaned, grimaced, and muttered again.

"Honey?" Marion bent over him. "Honey, did you say words? Talk to Mommy, honey. Look, there's someone here to visit you."

Gerry blinked. His gaze was distant but focused, a faint frown creasing his sweaty forehead. He was looking at something in the corridor.

"Sorry, kid," he said. "Sorry, sorry."

Egloff looked confused. "Does he always say that?"

"No. This is the first time he's spoken. Gerry, I want you to obey me, now. Are you listening to me? Look at Mr. Egloff. You look at him, Gerry, and you *tell me what he did to you*!"

Egloff took a step back. "What I did to him? Are you out of your mind? I didn't do anything."

"Sorry, kid, but I gotta make this look good," Gerry Junior pronounced thickly.

He was staring out into the corridor, fascinated by what he saw there. "Gerry, he's *here*," Marion pleaded, bending over him.

Then, turning, she saw what he was staring at. His body stiffened, his wrists straining against the straps holding him. His face flushed as he shouted at Barbara Egloff, who stood as if trapped in the corridor-revealing mirror, her mouth dropping open in shock.

"You!" Gerry shouted hoarsely. "You! You!"

♦ ♦ ♦

The pediatric intensive care waiting area's two big windows looked out over the east side of the city to the harbor. At the docks, a little red tugboat backed away from a container vessel, jaunty as one of the twins' bathtub toys.

"They're here because I left them," Edwina said.

"Nonsense," McIntyre replied. "The car hit a patch of ice. It could have been you driving; it still would have happened."

"But it wasn't. Why did I do that, Martin? Why did I leave them, when I love them so much?" She clenched her fists on the windowsill, wanting to beat them against the glass.

"Edwina. I leave them too, you know." He turned from the view. "You can't have the responsibility all to yourself. It's not yours."

He put his arm lightly around her. "We're in this together, remember?"

She gave in and leaned against him. "I know. It's selfish of me to take some special kind of blame, as if they're more mine than yours. But if I had been there, they would be all right. If I'd been home baking cookies for them, or something."

"Considering your record in the cookie-baking department, I'm not so sure of that." He smiled at her; she managed a faint smile back. Whoever had coined the phrase "It's the thought that counts" hadn't sampled any of her baking efforts.

"How's Rita doing?" she asked after a while.

"Okay. No major frostbite. Cuts and scrapes, mostly, and the emotional shock. She's a tough little character. I don't know about Lorelei. They were still working on her when I went down to check. She didn't look too bad when they got her out of the car, though."

He looked at his watch and at the intercom speaker with its button for alerting the intensive care unit secretary. "Do you suppose we should call in again and ask them how long it will be before someone can talk to us?"

"No. They know we're here. They'll be out when they have something to say."

As if on cue, a young man in khaki green scrub clothes

came into the waiting area. He looked well over fourteen years old, but the expression on his face was cheerful; once Edwina realized that, she didn't care about his age.

"Mr. and Mrs. McIntyre?" The young doctor stuck out his hand. "I have good news for you. It looks as if your children are going to be all right."

Edwina felt as if all the blood had been let out of her and replaced with champagne. McIntyre, normally the most reserved of men, flung his arms around the young pediatrician and bear-hugged him, nearly lifting him off the floor.

"Now, the nurses are still getting them settled, and I need to caution you that we're not out of the woods yet," the young doctor said. "They got very cold. We need to warm them slowly, and watch them while we do. But whoever bundled them up did a good job, got some calories and fluids into them, too, so they're in better shape than we expected them to be."

Rita, Edwina thought; when she couldn't get them out, she packed their extra clothes around them, wrapped them up together. Fed them, and made them drink. Got them ready to wait for help.

"So what I think you two should do," the doctor went on, "is go downstairs, get a cup of coffee or something, and come back in an hour. By then, they'll be ready for you to come in and visit with them."

Edwina bit her lip. She wanted to see them now; she wanted to hold them. "Are they . . . are they crying?"

The young doctor smiled kindly. "No. They're being real troupers. Francis grabbed the end of my stethoscope and wanted to keep it, and Jonathan's staring around, looking interested in everything. You've got two real confident, secure little cowboys there. Congratulations on them."

"See?" Martin said when the pediatrician had gone. "I told you that you'd done everything right."

"We. We've done everything right." Edwina felt stunned and a little shaky, as if the world had jolted back into motion after a jerky halt, like a reel of defective film. They walked toward the elevators. "Do you want coffee?"

"No. But I don't want to sit here for an hour, either. I've got about a ton of nervous energy I need to burn off." He veered toward the stairwell. "Let's take the stairs down to the lobby level and just walk around."

So they did, which was how they happened to run into Marion Bailey, pushing Gerry Junior in a hospital wheelchair. It was one of the old-fashioned wooden wheelchairs, less maneuverable but much handsomer than the shiny metal variety, and Gerry looked every bit the recovering invalid in it: pale and dazed but aware, dressed in brand-new pajamas, a red flannel robe, and green Ninja Turtle slippers.

Edwina reintroduced herself and introduced Martin. "Your son seems to have made some remarkable progress," she said.

"Yes," Marion began doubtfully, a frown creasing her face. "He has, but . . ."

Gerry turned his dark, tousled head. "Sorry," he said. "Sorry, kid, but I gotta make this look good."

"It's all he'll say now," Marion said helplessly, "after he screamed at Mrs. Egloff, and she just denied everything, and I've told the police, but they won't help, and I'm so scared for that other poor boy, but the police won't *do* anything. I don't see *why* they won't do anything, and Gerry won't say anything else."

"Sorry," Gerry repeated amiably again.

McIntyre listened puzzledly, his attention caught by the word "police," while Edwina wondered why the boy's jabbering troubled her so. "Let's sit down somewhere," she suggested.

Ten minutes later in the cafeteria, Marion had spilled out the whole story: how she'd been sure that if she could only show Gerry that he was safe, show him the face of his attacker while she was there to protect him, it would jolt him from where he was stuck, in his mind and in his feelings.

It was a remarkably unscientific idea, Edwina thought.

She also thought that it made perfect sense, and that it had worked.

But it hadn't worked completely. "The Egloffs left? They just denied doing anything wrong and took off? And the police said thanks, but no thanks, of course."

She looked at Marion. "An accusation by an emotionally traumatized and possibly mentally ill teenaged boy not being," she added gently, "their favorite form of communication, and his mother's unsubstantiated 'bad feelings' being even less so."

Marion nodded resignedly. Beside her, Gerry sat smiling at people as they passed with their trays of pastry and coffee, their sodas and afternoon snacks. His lips moved soundlessly.

"Let me make sure I understand what's happening," McIntyre put in. "You got the feeling there was something wrong about this Egloff, so you followed him. One of his rental properties is unoccupied, and you got into it thinking the missing boy might be there, but you found nothing except a marijuana seed on the porch. Then Gerry, here, got a look at the wife, got upset, and started talking."

"Yes, but he'll only say . . ."

"What *was* in the house? How thoroughly did you search it?"

Marion looked perplexed. "There wasn't much to search. Not a stick of furniture except in the kitchen, a refrigerator and freezer. I looked but the freezer was empty."

McIntyre frowned. "Freezer? Part of the refrigerator?"

"No, a big chest freezer, a fairly new one. Running, even; plugged in. I hated looking in there. I was afraid I'd find Tad Conway in it."

Edwina looked at McIntyre. McIntyre looked back. "Why," Edwina wondered aloud, "would there be a freezer running in an unoccupied rental house?"

"My question precisely," he replied, getting up. "Excuse me, ladies, but I think I'll make a couple of phone calls. Just," he added, "to satisfy a curiosity of mine. I'll be right back."

"You know, you've been quite something through all of this," Edwina told Marion. "Hanging in there, I mean. And following your hunches about Egloff and about what might help Gerry. That was brave."

Marion flushed, although the new, steely look in her eyes did not fade. "It was because of meeting you," she confessed. "The way you seemed to approach things head on. I'd never done anything that way, but it started me thinking. Then the lawyer you sent me to found out I wasn't broke, and that Gerry wouldn't be transferred to Briar Hill, so I had time to figure things out, to try to do things. And I felt I wanted to. Had to, really." She shook her head. "But I don't know what to do next. I thought if I could just show him. But I guess I didn't show him enough."

"Sorry, kid," Gerry Junior whispered. "Sorry."

It was an odd phrase for a teenager to be repeating, like something out of an old gangster movie. "Where do you suppose he got that?" Edwina asked, and then it hit her, as if it had been hanging in the air all along.

"You don't suppose it's what Granger said to him?" she asked Marion.

Their eyes met. It was so obvious, neither of them felt the need to debate the idea any further. Gerry Junior was repeating his attacker's words.

"What can we do?" Marion asked. "They won't let me take him into the adult psychiatric ward. They don't allow children under fourteen."

Edwina got up. There was still half an hour until she could see the twins. "I might be able to get around that, but maybe we won't have to. Stay here, and tell my husband I'll be back in a minute."

A picture, she thought as she hurried toward the elevators. There was one back at the apartment, but she believed she knew where to get one here that might finish the job Marion Bailey had begun. It might finish Ed Chernoff, too, but she couldn't think about that now; Ed wouldn't want her to.

Whatever he'd done in the past, he would not sacrifice an innocent boy to preserve his reputation.

Or so she hoped. The elevator opened on the surgical ward, with its sharp smells of disinfectant and benzoin. It was just past change of shift, and the nursing station was deserted except for the secretary, putting together new charts. Edwina spotted what she wanted pinned to the corkboard on the wall behind the counter.

If she asked for it, she would have to explain; instead she took advantage of a little-known fact about hospitals: a person who is decently dressed and who looks as if she knows what she's doing and where she's going can go almost anywhere and do almost anything in a hospital.

Stepping behind the counter of the nursing station, she took down the glossy sheet. The ward secretary snapped the metal rings of another chart shut, not even looking up. Moments later, Edwina laid the sheet with its head shots of smiling young men and women on the cafeteria table in front of Marion.

"These are the residents and chief residents on the surgical staff at Chelsea this year," Edwina said. "The first-year residents' photographs aren't very big, but the second-year ones are quite recognizable. There's William Granger, third from the right."

She turned to Marion, who was regarding the photograph thoughtfully. "Do you want to give Gerry Junior a look at it?" But the boy had already glimpsed the sheet, leaning forward to see what his mother and Edwina were examining.

Suddenly his expression of cheerful idiocy faded. The color drained from his cheeks, and into his dark brown eyes came a look of mystification, as if he were trying to solve a puzzle.

"Sorry," he said hesitantly, reaching out to touch the photo with his index finger.

"Gerry," Edwina asked gently, "did this man do something to you? Did he say something to you?"

"Gerry," said Marion in firmer tones, "answer the lady's question. No one is going to hurt you, because if they try, I am going to stop them. And I can do it, too," she added in tones that Edwina thought boded well for mother and son.

Something had happened to Marion in the past few days, and whatever it was, the result was clear: anyone who laid a finger on Gerry Junior would be lucky to escape with his kneecaps intact, because Marion was perfectly capable of removing them, and of enjoying the process, too.

The click, when it came, was nearly audible: the last piece of the puzzle snapping into place. Maybe there wasn't such a thing as being paralyzed with fright, or at least it wasn't in the medical books, but that was what had happened to Gerry Junior, and now it wasn't happening. He was back.

"Mom," he said thickly, his mouth unaccustomed to normal speech, "that guy shot at me. He said, 'Sorry, kid, but I gotta make this look good.' And he shot at me."

Gerry began to cry, sobbing like the brokenhearted child he was. Marion let him do it, only pressing a tissue into his hand.

McIntyre returned. "I reached out to some guys I used to work with," he told Edwina, "down at the station. They're going to take a look inside that house, as a favor for an old buddy."

"Martin, they'll need a warrant. There's nothing to get one on, is there? And even if they do get it, it could take time, and if that other boy is in there . . ."

McIntyre pursed his lips. "I did my best, Edwina."

There was something more he wasn't saying, but it was no use trying to get it out of him now; McIntyre always said just what he wanted to say, and when he was finished, he stopped.

She glanced at the clock. "We should go back upstairs; the hour's nearly up."

"What should I do about this?" Marion asked, indicating the photograph of Granger.

"Nothing," Edwina said. "Nothing now, anyway. You two take care of yourselves, and I'll be in touch."

"Kid remembered something?" McIntyre asked on their way to the elevators.

"Enough to put a serious wrench in Granger's monkeyworks," she replied. "I don't know how I'm going to tell Ed about this, but it sounds as if Granger said something purposeful and sane while he was in the midst of the act."

"Not good for the defense," McIntyre agreed as the elevator rose. "Kinda leaves poor old Billy just swingin' in the breeze, doesn't it, now?"

She nodded. "Trouble is, from what Mother as good as told me last night, Ed might end up swinging right alongside him. I still wish I could figure out one thing, though."

"What's that?"

The elevator stopped; two nurses, some visitors, a pair of orderlies, and an X-ray technician got on, accompanied by an X-ray machine whose wheels stuck in the elevator's entrance. Cursing them all mentally, Edwina stepped forward and gave the machine a practiced lift-and-shove, whereupon it rolled smoothly in.

"Like riding a bicycle," she commented acidly to McIntyre as the elevator began moving again. "Assuming you ever learned. Anyway, there's one thing everyone agrees on, about Granger: he's acting like what we used to call EFN, back in my student nursing days when we laughed about things just to keep from crying about them."

"EFN?" The doors opened and they stepped out. There was no one in the waiting area; Edwina couldn't decide if that was a good sign or a bad sign.

"Mr. and Mrs. McIntyre," she announced into the intercom, and stared at the automatic doors of the intensive care unit, willing them to open.

"What," McIntyre persisted, "is EFN?"

"A staff diagnosis. It stands for Extremely Freaking Nuts. And what I want to know is, if he isn't, how did he learn how to behave that way?"

She was about to go on, to explain to McIntyre that Granger hadn't requested or checked out via computer any references that would have enabled him to research the topic, and that as a resident he couldn't have had time to identify and locate the materials by hand; the task would have been daunting even to someone who wasn't working a resident's harsh on-call schedule.

But she didn't, because at that moment the automatic doors of the pediatric intensive care unit swung open, and to Edwina, they looked just like the gates of heaven.

♦ ♦ ♦

The unit was a long, dim-lit room with cubicles divided by curtains. Along one side of the room was a nursing desk with banks of monitors, rows of chart racks, and a shelf of reference books. At the far end, two metal cribs stood side by side, each with a twin in it.

Sound asleep, they resembled little angels. Jonathan's forehead bore a small, blue bruise, and Francis had suffered a bloody nose, but otherwise they seemed uninjured. They had IVs and heart monitors and warming lights over their cribs, but that was all. Holding McIntyre's hand, Edwina bent and kissed each boy's soft cheek; neither stirred.

"They're exhausted," said the nurse. "You can sit with them for a while, but I think they'll sleep for a few hours, at least." She checked each IV drip and made a note on each twin's clipboard. "If everything goes as we expect, they'll go to the ward tomorrow morning," she added. "They're doing just fine."

McIntyre sighed, releasing pent-up tension. "I guess we're getting through this in reasonable shape, then," he said.

"I guess so. I'd better call Harriet." Edwina felt suddenly as if she could crawl into one of the child-sized beds and sleep for a week.

"I called her. There's something unnatural about an eighty-year-old woman with more energy than two forty-year-olds," he added with a tired smile.

"It's true. Harriet thinks natural human frailties are for common folk, like paper plates and public beaches. How are the police going to get into Egloff's house without a warrant?"

"Gas leak," he replied in tones that suggested he'd rather not say much more. "Wouldn't want a place to explode."

"I see." She dropped the subject, having known McIntyre and his cronies long enough to figure out how it would go. An officer patrolling his sector, alerted by a passing citizen to the smell of gas, might investigate a dwelling. If he suspected the presence of a victim inside, even if it were only an animal (thus accounting for the door being locked on the outside, as Marion had described), he might break a door open. Then he might check the place thoroughly before concluding that the citizen has been mistaken, said citizen having gone about his business.

Out in the waiting area, McIntyre sank onto a sofa while Edwina fell into a chair, exhausted.

"One of us should go see Rita," he said. "And check on Lorelei. Has anyone spoken to the Whitelaws?"

"Ambulance guys called them," she replied with a rekindling of dislike for the old couple.

She looked at McIntyre. "I wish I didn't have to tell Ed Chernoff what I have to tell him. That kid's testimony is going to nail Granger's feet to the floor."

McIntyre raised a tired eyebrow. "But since you do have to tell him . . ."

"Right. If it's going to go against him, I could at least save him the battle. If I could show that before Granger did the deed, he'd prepared himself to fake the symptoms of a specific, medically recognized mental illness . . ."

"And not in a haphazard way. He's faking it well enough to fool experts."

She rubbed her forehead; now that the twins were safe, it was letting itself begin to ache. "For a while, I thought Lorelei might be the answer: with Charity Anne gone, Granger would inherit whatever she'd left him and Lorelei would wind up with the rest. Together, they'd have what even

Harriet would call a fortune. She might even have done the research, if he showed her how; Harriet insists that Lorelei is no fool, just doing the dumb-blonde act. But then I found out that Lorelei worshiped the ground Charity Anne walked on."

"How about that Chulovitz guy, the mad scientist? Or maybe that woman doctor Granger had roomed with, Sheila Klainberg? She'd have library access, and she could have taken you to the apartment, shown you those clippings about Granger, just so the defense would get them first. Knowing they'd come up anyway."

Outside the big plate-glass windows, light drained from the sky. A pigeon perched on the window ledge, peering at a shred of leaf frozen into a crust of snow.

"Possible, but not likely. Chulovitz says he hasn't been in touch with Granger since Granger as good as blackmailed him for a fake recommendation. And I don't see what his motive could be; he's an eccentric scientist who only cares about mice, as far as I was able to tell."

She thought a moment. "As for Sheila Klainberg, she didn't have to show me the apartment. She could have gotten rid of those clippings and documents before anyone found out about them. It doesn't make sense for her to help destroy the plan if she'd been part of putting it together."

She turned on a lamp. "I do think Granger messed up on a few things, though. For one thing, he overestimated his own importance in other people's lives: he didn't expect Klainberg to give him away or he'd never have named her as a friend of his, for example. And he overestimated his ability to control events: a more realistic person would have gotten rid of that clipping file altogether."

She looked at McIntyre. "Most damaging of all is that he generalized a principle he learned as a surgeon, assuming that it applied not only in the operating room."

McIntyre's eyebrows rose quizzically.

"He overestimated," she said, "his ability to control life

and death. In the operating room, it's all in his hands. He is literally in control of whether a person lives or dies."

"But not everywhere," McIntyre said comprehendingly.

"Right. It explains why he couldn't resist saying something self-incriminating to a kid he was about to kill: he forgot that in the real world surgeons are not all-powerful. Other variables can apply. He forgot that Gerry Bailey might live."

Outside, the lights of the city were flickering on. "If you can stand another acronym," she said, "he's got what we nurses used to call an FGC, back when we used to make fun of doctors so we could keep from murdering them. It stands," she added, "for Freaking God Complex."

"A necessary bit of psychological equipment for a surgeon, I should think," he said.

"Uh-huh. But now I've got it, too; I think that if I can't find out how Granger prepared himself to do all this without leaving any record of it, nobody can, and I think that without such a link he might still get an NGRI. And I don't want that to happen. I want that bastard convicted."

McIntyre leaned forward. "You can square it with yourself? I thought you and Ed Chernoff were old buddies."

"I can't square it completely. Ed's going to get hurt, one way or another, and if he'd left me out of it in the first place, maybe he wouldn't have. But he didn't leave me out."

The lights of the harbor twinkled, ringing an expanse of deepening blue. She squared her shoulders, trying to work the kinks out of them. "I can't sit here; I'm going back downstairs. Feel like coming along?"

"No. I might catch a nap. Take your time; I'll be here."

He stretched out on the sofa in the glow of the floor lamp, its pale shade reflected in the big plate-glass windows; beyond them, it was full dark.

◆   ◆   ◆

In the gift shop, Edwina bought a magazine for McIntyre and a newspaper for herself, noticing that the Granger story had migrated to the sensation spot, top right-hand corner above the fold. It made hay on the possible upcoming insanity defense, with the help of the psychiatrist Frieda Schreiber, who managed to imply that in her professional opinion, Granger was several clams short of a casino, laying the groundwork for the trial testimony she would give.

It was a smart performance and Edwina admired it, even as she noticed how chatty the doctor became the minute it looked as if she might get some publicity for herself out of the situation; maybe I should have told her I work for the *National Enquirer*, Edwina thought sourly.

But prosecutor Ginny Fowler had spoken to the media, too, and the gist of her remarks was that if Granger didn't have something incredibly interesting to say for himself at the very next opportunity he was given, he was going to find out just how thorough an investigatory department the DA's office possessed. Furthermore, at that point Granger's window of opportunity would be closed, and no more plea-bargaining chances would be offered.

In other words, Ginny Fowler was thinking the same thing Edwina was: that Granger was faking, somebody'd helped him, and the helper had covered it up; thus the hinted offer of a deal, if Granger would name his co-conspirator.

Chernoff had been going through the right motions, according to the report, including one for another psychiatric exam (granted), one for a hearing on the matter of Granger's mental status (also granted), and one delaying a hearing on the DA's request to move Granger to a state forensic institution immediately (denied). The judge set to preside over this latter hearing, Vonda Keller, was a hard-nosed, hot-tempered gavel banger with a mean streak, popularly known as "Killer" Keller; history suggested that Judge Keller was about as likely to let Granger keep lying around in his cushy private hospital bed as she was to send him to Disney World, pending sanity hearing or no pending sanity hearing.

The upshot was that by tomorrow afternoon, Granger

would be sent to the equivalent of a prison; there would be no bail set, partly because the prosecution wouldn't stand for it given the well-known wealth of the Whitelaw clan, and partly because Judge Keller was the type who would rather choke on her own spit. And that, Edwina thought, changed things dramatically; Granger was going away, and he was going tomorrow, unless he got in the game by saying something the prosecutors wanted to hear.

Such as, for instance, the name of someone else they could prosecute. Edwina took the papers into the cafeteria and got some saltines and minestrone. Crumbling a few of the crackers into the soup, she wondered whether Granger was considering shaving some weight off his load by trading in his helper. Ed Chernoff must have tried already to convince Granger to do it; she wondered if he would.

She finished her soup and crackers and decided to walk the length of the lobby three times quickly before going upstairs; her body felt heavy and sluggish, and exercise might help. At this hour of the evening, the lobby was busy with visitors and staff: In the gift shop, a woman was buying a Mylar balloon and some comic books. A man stood at the pay phones feeding change into a coin slot. An older man helped his wife out of the elevator, and a couple of nurse's aides went into the stairwell, their footsteps echoing hollowly in the enclosure before the heavy metal door thunked shut.

As Edwina passed the long half-oval of the admitting desk, a man was struggling through the big glass lobby doors, pushing a dolly loaded with cardboard boxes. Two more men came in behind him, each with another dolly; the third man set down his burden as the first went out for more. By the time she returned, they had begun opening the cartons, taking out electronic components and lining them up on the counter, tossing the packing materials back into the boxes.

The uniformed lobby guard smiled and nodded at Edwina. "New computers," he said approvingly.

"So I see," she replied. "Lots of them."

"Whole new system," the guard pronounced, happy to chat. "So they can get all kinds of information, credit and insurance and so on, over the phone lines. Type in a number, social security, credit card number or your insurance number, get all the rest."

"That sounds very efficient." Guards were always lonesome, surrounded by people but with nobody they could talk to.

He shook his head. "Kinda makes me feel like a little bug under a microscope, all those things they can find out. But it is modern. Cheaper, too. Ec-o-nomical."

"Really. How do you happen to know so much about it?"

The lobby guard was a tall, distinguished-looking black man with salt-and-pepper hair, amused brown eyes behind gold-rimmed bifocals, and a thoughtful way of speaking.

"I stand right here all evening, and hear them all talking about it. Whether this one is better, or that one. They all finally decided on this one. Call it from anywhere, give it your password, and it hooks you right up."

"Isn't that remarkable," Edwina commented, feeling like an idiot but deciding that the vanishing of one's children entitled one to a brief lapse in concentration. And perhaps it was not too late to repair that lapse. "You know," she told the lobby guard, "you've just solved a big problem for me."

The guard peered quizzically through his bifocals, then broke into a smile. "Well, isn't that nice?" he said. "Always glad to help solve problems."

At the pay phone, she punched in Chernoff's number. "Ed," she said when he answered, "has Granger given himself any help?"

"No." Chernoff sounded tired and old. "And he's not going to. Somehow he still thinks it's going to work; he's got Frieda Schreiber on his side, and he thinks that together she and I can pull a rabbit out of a hat. Tom Whitelaw does, too, and I can't get any of them to listen to reason. You've seen the papers?"

She indicated that she had, and that she thought the timer on Granger's goose was just about to pop out. He agreed.

"By the way," he said, "the Whitelaws have also decided that girl of yours, Rita, put their daughter's car into a ditch somehow. That's how rational they're all being."

His tone was so morose, she barely had the heart to drop the Gerry Bailey testimony bombshell on him; when she was finished, he only sighed.

"Look," she said, "what if you gave up the conspirator? I mean, we all know there was one; maybe if you explain things again to Granger, he'd tell you who it is. You could strike a deal with the prosecutor on that, and I could get Harriet to bring her influence to bear with Whitelaw. So he'll keep quiet about Charity Anne, I mean, and the money."

There was a silence. "So you know."

"Harriet told me enough so that I figured it out. You were stealing from Emeralinda, weren't you? And sleeping with her at the same time. The latter to distract her from the former, I suppose, or maybe not; it doesn't matter. And you couldn't marry her, even if you wanted to, because you were married already to a dying woman. And Whitelaw found out about all that and he's held it over you ever since."

She took a deep breath. "But what he wants can't be done, Ed, any more than he could turn Granger into the perfect son-in-law just by willing it. It can't be done."

Ed sighed. "Oh, Edwina. You were the one I hoped most would never find out. I'm so ashamed and sorry."

I'm sorry, too, she thought clearly. You're not the man I thought you were.

And then, suddenly, she felt as if she were back upstairs in the pediatric waiting area, staring into the darkness. She was not the mother she had meant to be to the twins: neither perfect nor infinitely patient, nor involved in their lives to the exclusion of everything in her own. She couldn't even bake good cookies. But she was the mother they had.

The parallel was not perfect either, but then, nothing was. And Ed was the friend she had. "Ed, do you remember the day you first tried teaching me to sail?"

She shifted the receiver to her other ear. "I got the lines tangled, lost a sail, and dropped a custom-machined clip over the side. We were aimed straight for Death's Head, in Narragansett Bay, about to go aground. I started crying and telling you how sorry I was, and do you know what you said to me?"

There was a brief silence, and then a dry chuckle. " 'Sorry, hell,' " Ed Chernoff quoted himself. " 'Get the freakin' sailboat straightened out.' "

"Aye, aye, sir," she replied crisply, ignoring the fact that the order had been given thirty-five years earlier, and hung up before he could try arguing with her.

◆ ◆ ◆

It was not, after all, such a terrible job being a secretary on a psychiatric ward. Most of the patients ate dinner in their rooms, or if they felt like being sociable, in the common room. Sometimes they played cards, did jigsaw puzzles, or read. Some, less able to pursue purposeful activities, walked up and down the long, fluorescent-lit corridor, looking like the homeless people Jennifer sometimes saw downtown, shambling and mumbling; that was what they would be if they weren't in here.

The walkers, as Jennifer was coming to think of them while she sat at the nursing desk, weren't organized enough to live in houses, have jobs, or keep families or friends together. They could put one foot in front of the other, but not one thought in front of the other, which was sad but not scary, or at least not as scary when you got used to it. Even the girl who made faces and stuck her tongue out was just . . . sad.

Jennifer finished filing lab slips in the charts and began picking out the consult requests, the orders for new medications, and the orders for tomorrow's tests and procedures. The doctors were supposed to flag any charts that had these, but sometimes they didn't, and if things didn't get done it was Jennifer who got the blame, not the doctors. That was the same whichever ward you worked on: bad stuff ran downhill, and nobody was lower than the ward secretary.

Someone at the unit door buzzed for entry; leaving the chart she was paging through, she checked the closed-circuit TV screen that showed the waiting area, then pushed the electronic release. An anxious-looking delivery guy came in carrying a package.

"Geez," he said, "a psycho ward. I delivered a lotta things a lotta places, but never to a psycho ward. Sign here."

He shoved the package and a clipboard across the counter at Jennifer, glancing over his shoulder. "I told 'em downstairs, I said, I'll leave it, you bring it up. But no, they don't wanna come up here either. Can't say I blame 'em."

He leaned forward confidentially. "Say, you got that crazy doctor here. One murdered all them people, I read in the paper. This's for him, that's how I knew it was the loony bin. How you stand this job, anyway? Ain't you scared somebody's gonna jump out at you with a butcher knife or something?"

Jennifer eyed the delivery guy levelly. "No, I'm not," she said. "Here's your sheet back. I'll buzz you out."

"Well, ain't we hoity-toity." He looked affronted. "So long, then. Don't let the wackos bite."

Jennifer waited until she heard the interlock click; then she examined the package. It was about eight inches wide, twelve inches long, and maybe three inches thick; she guessed it was a box of candy. It had been sent from one of the mailing services downtown, addressed to Dr. William Granger in care of the hospital.

Jennifer took it down the corridor to the office where the charge nurse for this evening was frowning over the staffing schedule. Harmless-looking or not, all mail for the patients had to be checked.

"Okay," the nurse said when she had removed the wrapping, examined the accompanying card, and poked at the candies in their crinkly pastel papers to make sure nothing was hidden beneath them. "Smells like chocolate mints. Okay, you can take them down to him."

"Me?" Suddenly, Jennifer's confidence evaporated. Sitting behind a desk was one thing; actually entering a patient's room was quite another, even if the patient did have a cop stationed outside his door. Especially if he did, actually.

"Yes, you," the charge nurse replied with heavy patience. The schedule she was working on was filled with X marks and angry crossings-out; the Christmas and New Year's holidays were coming, and everyone wanted them off. "Unless maybe you want to do this damned thing and I'll play delivery girl."

Reluctantly, Jennifer took the candy box. The card was a simple flowered one with a brief printed message: Best Wishes for a Speedy Recovery, it said, signed by someone named Jim. Reminding herself of all the intelligent, broadminded things she had been thinking about psychiatric patients only a little while ago, Jennifer brought the candy down to Granger's room. It did smell good, very minty and chocolatey, only more minty.

"Candy for Dr. Granger. The charge nurse checked it," she told the cop in the chair by Granger's door.

Barely looking up from the sports page of the *New York Post*, the uniformed cop waved her in where she most emphatically did not want to go. In the room, the TV's sound was turned down, and the light from the screen flickered weirdly on the face of the man sitting motionless in the bed.

Jennifer hesitated, but she had to do it. How awful would it be to have to admit she was too scared even to deliver a box of candy?

"Dr. Granger?" she said, and was horrified when it came out a quavering whisper.

"Come in," the man in the bed replied, snapping on a light; she entered nervously. But one clear look at him made her feel better: he was handsome, or at least not horrible-looking, with dark, curly hair, a nice smile, and intelligent, pale green eyes. Except for the bandages on his wrists he didn't look crazy, and he certainly didn't look dangerous. He didn't look anything at all, in fact, except lonely.

"Come in," he repeated, "I don't bite. I used to scratch, but they've clipped my nails." He laughed a little, raising his bandaged wrists, but stopped when he saw her face.

"I'm sorry," he said. "That wasn't nice of me. What have you got there?"

She held the box out; seeing it, he brightened. "I'll be darned. Somebody remembers I'm here; I thought everybody had abandoned me."

He looked at the signature on the card. "Jim. Which Jim? Jim from surgery? Jim from the intensive care unit? Jim from the gym?" He laughed again.

Despite her nervousness, Jennifer smiled; he was so delighted at his gift. She would have to remember how a simple thing like a box of candy could cheer somebody up. Or a card; anything, really.

He opened the box. "Oh, chocolate mints, my favorite. Boy, these look fantastic, don't they?"

He held the box out. The sweet, minty smell of the candies wafted deliciously into the hospital room.

"Have one," he invited.

◆ ◆ ◆

The computer search service's office was a small cubicle off the medical library's main foyer, with a window looking out onto the street. Under a streetlight, students crowded onto an idling shuttle bus, its exhaust billowing whitely in the chilly evening.

"But you would still have to see the books," said the young woman behind the desk in the cubicle. "Or journals, or whatever. You generally can't get whole-text articles sent to you via computer."

Drat, Edwina thought; seeing the new computers in Chelsea's lobby had given her a brainstorm.

Granger had a computer in his apartment. From it, he could do library searches by linking his terminal to the library's database via the telephone. He might even cover the electronic tracks he would generate, possibly by using a stolen or borrowed password. Doing so would ensure that no one ever knew he had performed the reference search at all.

But he would still have to read the materials, and as it turned out he could only do that the old-fashioned way.

"He could come in here and read or copy the stuff," the librarian said, "or get the reference service to copy and deliver it to him. Those are the only two ways to actually get text."

"A delivery service?" Edwina said, surprised; now there was an interesting idea. "Could you check that list? Or better, I could give you a list, and you tell me if any of the people on it have used the text delivery service, or done any data searches for psychiatric references, or both?"

"Sure, no problem," the librarian said, turning to her own computer terminal, but twenty minutes later, she handed Edwina's list back. "A couple of these people have used the delivery service, but not for psych material, and none of them have ever had any database searches done on any psychiatric topics."

"Rats." The librarian had asked the computer to check on Sheila Klainberg, Byron Chulovitz, and as a long shot on Lorelei Whitelaw and Charity Anne herself. Then she had gone down the list of friends and acquaintances Granger had given as personal references. She'd even tried Frieda Schreiber, and as a last resort, Emeralinda and Thomas Whitelaw: no dice.

Finally, she'd checked in the other direction: had *anyone* searched for the pertinent references, whether or not they'd had them copied and delivered?

"Nope. Dead end," the librarian said. "Either no one has looked this stuff up, or they looked it up by hand."

"Or in some other medical library," Edwina added.

"Possible, but I doubt it; a lot of the material is obscure. Such small, specialized journals, not many places subscribe."

The librarian peered at her screen. "Here's one that's only available here, in Tokyo, and in Sydney, Australia. The rest of the issues go to private practitioners, I suppose."

Clearing the terminal, she got up. "What you're telling me is that somebody got this stuff, and what the computer is telling me is that if they did, they did it in a way that's untraceable. But the only way to be untraceable," she went on, "is to do it by hand, and come to think of it, I was wrong: you couldn't do that, either. Not with this material."

"Why not?" Outside, the shuttle bus roared away in a rumble of exhaust; glancing at her watch, the librarian began clearing her desk.

"The library remodeling caused some damage in the periodical stacks," she said, "mostly to older bound volumes. Dust and so on; nothing that bothered anyone except the antique enthusiasts. But there was one exception."

She let Edwina out of the research office ahead of her, shut off the lights, and closed the door, locking it with a key from a ring of them. "The plumbers used acetylene torches. There was a fire and some volumes were destroyed. We ordered replacements, of course, but the dean of the library at the time was a big fan of miniaturization. You know, minimizing storage needs."

She crossed the foyer, past the antique medical instruments glittering in their glass case. They were, Edwina realized, the only items in the building that looked as if they might be more than twenty-five years old, the exception of course being the students, most of whom looked as if they would never be more than twenty-five years old.

"Remodeling was his idea, too," the librarian went on. "Glitzing the whole place up with wall-to-wall carpet and Danish modern furniture. Heaven forbid anyone's surroundings should suggest that anything important happened before they were born."

Edwina followed, pleased to hear her own opinions being spoken by someone else. "What about the fire?"

"Well, the thing is, the replacement issues of the journals that got destroyed weren't ordered as actual paper copies. They were ordered on microfilm. And because of where your references were located when the fire happened . . ."

"They're only available on film now. So even if somebody located them with a personal computer and an on-line electronic database search, or by hand in the printed *Index Medicus* . . ."

The librarian nodded. "You can't just walk in and read, or copy, most of the things you've got on your list. They have to be requested at the reference desk and checked out from the microfilm department, which means you can't get at them without leaving a record. Let's go look at those."

But when they did, even Edwina could see that the boxes in which the pertinent microfilm resided were still covered in the original shrink wrap; neither Granger nor anyone else had ever opened them, much less read the text inside. And that was that: nice try, no cigar.

"There is one other thing," the librarian said as they went out through the foyer. "I don't want to tell you your business, but I'm always on the hunt for things in the databases. And when I look for something that ought to be there, only it isn't, I don't decide that it doesn't exist. I decide my assumptions about it are wrong, and I alter my search strategy. Widen it, for instance."

"I'm not following you." Somehow, Edwina was not feeling up to a romp through the theory and practice of database searching, fascinating as that topic undoubtedly was to a person who had not just recently had her missing children rescued out of a ten-foot snowbank and whose good friend was about to be ruined by a rich old jerk and his murdering bastard son-in-law.

"There are other places to get journals and monographs," the librarian said, as if explaining something to someone not quite bright, "besides in libraries. For example, a person could buy them. Find out their addresses and order copies. Order them by mail."

Oh, good, Edwina thought sourly, quick-stepping back across the street to the hospital. Anyone could do that, which meant anyone could have acquired Granger's MPD research materials for him. The list of possible co-conspirators had just enlarged to include the entire population of the world, and she had until tomorrow, when Granger's transfer hearing would be held, to narrow it down—possibly to nothing.

After all, Granger could have ordered the journals himself. All he needed to cover that were some money orders and a post office box under a fake name, the latter being something he had plenty of practice at getting, and even if the journals reported mailing any issues to a post office box, it couldn't necessarily be proved that the box was Granger's. Irritably, she punched the elevator button; so much for providing Chernoff with a bargaining chip.

As if to prove the point she was mulling, the elevator doors opened to reveal a group that had just come from completing evening rounds: four medical students, two interns, a couple of residents, and a chief resident, along with their attending physician, who was still lecturing to them as they all filed off the elevator. All the students were carrying medical books and journals: the rest carried clipboards with journal tear sheets among the papers clipped to them. Even the attending physician had an issue of *Annals of Internal Medicine* sticking out of his briefcase.

Then the overhead page operator began reciting, over and over again: "Code Five, Adult Psychiatric Ward."

A scrub-suited anesthesiologist ran out of the cafeteria, straight-armed the stairwell door, and hit the stairs at a gallop; code team members were not allowed to use elevators, because an elevator on its way to an emergency inevitably stopped at every floor. Two nurses and a respiratory therapist followed, their beepers still whistling from their uniform pockets.

Wrong again, Edwina realized as she stepped alone into the elevator and it began to rise: she didn't have until tomorrow, after all.

◆   ◆   ◆

"He ate some candies," the ward secretary said shakily. "He ate three or four of them while I was in the room with him, and I don't know how many after I left. He offered me one, but I didn't take it."

Down the corridor, the resuscitation attempt continued, but it was not going well. The blood-gas technician hurried out with a glass syringe filled with arterial blood; it was almost black, which meant that Granger wasn't getting enough oxygen despite the anesthesiologist's efforts. The charge nurse rushed down the hall with a gastric lavage kit and a big bottle of liquid charcoal, but from what the secretary was saying, it was also too late to do much good by pumping Granger's stomach; whatever he'd eaten in the candies had already had plenty of time to be absorbed.

"This is the wrapping that the candy box came in?" Edwina asked. "And this is the card?"

They wouldn't be much help either. You could walk into a mailing service, hand over whatever you wanted mailed and ask to have a card included, and pay cash, giving any fake name you liked. If you did it in the middle of a business day, the mailing place would be so busy and crowded that no one would remember you, especially if you made sure they didn't by wearing a disguise.

She sniffed the mailer: mint. "Did he say anything else to you?" she asked the secretary, whose name was Jennifer.

The girl shook her head. "Only that he was glad everybody hadn't forgotten him, and that he didn't know which Jim had sent him the candy. And . . . that he didn't bite."

The mingled aromas of mint and chocolate reminded Edwina of Byron Chulovitz's Victorian-style parlor, with its ornate candy box full of confections. And the work area in his house had smelled of mint, only not the edible kind; a suspicion struck Edwina as she recalled the bottles standing among the laboratory furnishings, their wicks wafting the minty scent into the air. The scent, actually, had not been ordinary mint, but wintergreen, a substance which from the culinary point of view bore about the same relationship to mint as amanita did to a truffle.

The trouble was, Byron Chulovitz hadn't looked up any

MPD references either, and Edwina doubted that facts about obscure mental disorders were the sort of knowledge the mouse researcher would come to casually; he was a physical scientist, not a—

The interlock buzzed, interrupting Edwina's thought. Jennifer pressed the door-release button and a half dozen people hurried onto the ward: patient-transport aides pushing a gurney in case Granger survived to go to the medical intensive care unit, the hospital chaplain with his last rites kit in case Granger didn't, a pharmacy runner carrying some vials of whatever last-ditch drug the medical people hoped would prop up Granger's collapsing circulatory and respiratory systems, and a trench coat clad—police detective whom the cop outside Granger's door had summoned.

Behind them all came the psychiatrist Frieda Schreiber, wearing her usual bright makeup and trademark black cape, her auburn curls flying. "What happened to him?" she demanded. "I got a message that something's happened to William, that they think he's been poisoned. What's going on?"

From her briefcase protruded the mail she had apparently grabbed up in a hurry, on her way here: envelopes, circulars, and several professional journals. Edwina gazed at them, feeling illuminated. Down the hall, the uniformed officer conferred with the detective outside Granger's room. "Why don't you come with me," Edwina said, "and I'll fill you in on everything. How did you know anything had happened to him, by the way?"

"I asked to be notified at once if his condition changed. But I didn't mean anything like this. What in the world is wrong with security around here? I insist on getting an explanation."

And you shall have one, Edwina thought, stopping within earshot of the detective. "I believe what happened," she told Schreiber, "is that you and William Granger conspired to murder Charity Anne Whitelaw. The idea was that he would kill her, and you would get him off by building a fake insanity case for him."

The police detective looked up interestedly. Edwina favored him with one of her sweetest smiles; she was very happy.

"He might have to spend time in a hospital being treated for his 'mental disorder,' " she said. "But eventually you would get him released, by teaching him how to get well, plausibly, and the two of you would be very rich. You could build a private clinic; he could do what he liked. As I say, it would take time. But then, getting rich almost always does take time."

Under her makeup, Schreiber's face had gone white. "That's crazy."

"Maybe. Or perhaps just very wicked. I suppose it depends on whether or not you accept the 'evil as illness' theory of human nature. Which in your case, I'm afraid I don't."

In Granger's room, intense activity continued; on a young guy like him, the code team would go far beyond the call of duty. But from the way the EKG technician was shaking her head over the heart monitor's readout, Edwina knew the effort was futile.

"This is ridiculous," Schreiber said. "I don't know why I'm even listening to you."

"So you can find out how much I know," Edwina replied; this was almost too easy, like impaling a bug on a pin.

"You met him," she said, "at the Whitelaws', and because you are perceptive about people—you are, after all, a psychiatrist—you knew he was unsatisfied, unprincipled, and willing to take advantage of other people. He was already planning to kill his wife; it was part of a plan he'd been pursuing for years, and you thought you could be part of it. And that you could use him."

In Granger's room, the burly technician who'd been doing cardiac compressions shook the stiffness out of his arms. The respiratory therapy technician unhooked the resuscitator bag from Granger's endotracheal tube and popped the flowmeter from the wall outlet. The EKG tech turned off the cardiograph; paper stopped spewing from the machine.

"But he never told you about his earlier two wives," said Edwina. "I suspect when their cases are reopened, we'll find he hired someone to kill them. He didn't tell you he got into medical school on fake records and with letters that he got by blackmail. And after he shot Charity Anne, he didn't tell you about a remark he made to one of his other intended victims in the emergency room."

One of the aides pulled the curtain around Granger's bed; it was over. The police detective took a step toward Edwina and Frieda Schreiber.

"And this morning," Edwina finished, "a newspaper article appeared. The insanity act wasn't working, and the prosecution as good as said that Granger had better roll over on whoever taught him how to act mentally ill, or he was going to prison."

"That's ridiculous," Frieda Schreiber spat. "You can't say things like that about me. I'm a professional."

"You knew," Edwina said, "he'd be likely to save himself by naming you."

The code team members filed out of Granger's room, their silence hanging in the air like a wisp of smoke after the candle has been snuffed.

"Isn't it interesting," Edwina said, "that they were mint candies? And that oil of wintergreen has such a minty aroma? It's deadly poison, you know: methyl salicylate. And used as an aromatic lubricant, I believe, in massage therapy."

She turned to Schreiber. "Which is among the kinds of therapy you practice when you are not providing expert commentary on the topic of multiple personality disorder."

The detective moved up closer to Schreiber on one side, and the cop on the other. "This is outrageous," she repeated. "I'm a respected psychiatrist, an *expert* on multiple personality."

"Which is why you have most of the facts on it already in your head. Even more interestingly to me, you also subscribe to the relevant journals and own the relevant texts. You're the one person Granger knows who wouldn't need to do any research on MPD, Dr. Schreiber. You coached him, and when you thought he was about to betray you, you killed him."

The detective stepped forward. "Look here, I don't know who you are, but you're making some very serious accusations. You'd better have something more to back them up. Anyone can get hold of a medical journal, you know."

Frieda Schreiber tossed her auburn curls, trying to appear confident. "You see? He doesn't believe you either. You've just got some ridiculous notion in your head."

"Do I? Or if the police searched your office now, might they find a needle and syringe bearing oil of wintergreen traces? If not, then they are in the briefcase you're carrying; it's how you got the poison into the candies, by injecting it. But psychiatrists' offices don't often have facilities for disposing of needles or syringes, and you couldn't risk their being found in your trash, or your being seen tossing them out a car window. To be perfectly safe, you'd have had to carry them away."

She thought a moment. "To carry them here to the hospital, for instance, where needle-disposal boxes are so common that no one would even notice your using one. All you'd have to do is act as if you know what you're doing, which of course you do, and presto, you'd be rid of the evidence."

Schrieber's fingers clenched the grips of her briefcase; she took a step back. The detective came to his decision.

"I wonder," he asked the psychiatrist, "if I might have a word with you?" Then with immense professional tact and civility he led Frieda Schreiber away.

The young ward secretary stood watching as the aides rolled Granger's covered gurney away. The patients watched, too, from their doorways, many of them appearing confused or upset, thrown off by the disruption in their routine.

The girl who made faces and stuck her tongue out at people made a face and stuck her tongue out. As if by reflex, the ward secretary made a face and stuck her tongue out

right back. Then her look turned to horror as she realized
what she had done.

But the girl who made faces was laughing, and after a moment the secretary began laughing, too.

◆   ◆   ◆

The smell in the crawl space was worrisome. That was how
the young cop had learned to think of things he found in the
houses that he entered: worrisome, or not worrisome. In this
house, he was supposed to be checking for a gas leak, but gas
definitely wasn't what it smelled like in here. It was like an
animal had crawled in and died, or was trying to; he hoped,
anyway, that it was an animal.

Behind him, outside the ragged opening in the wallboard,
the freezer he and his partner had shoved aside hummed
gently. Ahead loomed a pile of junk building material: ends
of two-by-fours and the raggedy remains of a roll of tar paper, broken cinder blocks, a lot of other stuff that somebody
had been too lazy to haul away and had just shoved in here
instead.

"Hey," his partner called; the young cop grunted in reply,
inching forward to aim his flashlight into the corners of the
crawl space. "You wanna tell me how come somebody's got
an empty freezer running in an empty house?" his partner
asked.

"That," the young cop muttered, "is worrisome, too."

He crept forward a little more. Maybe whatever had
crawled in here had also crawled out, and had gone off to die
somewhere else. One more pass with the flash and he was
leaving, too, the young cop decided firmly, and the hell with
whoever the goddamned desk officer wanted a favor for, goddamned goose chase.

He swung the flash into the far corner, cringing as a
swarm of beetles skittered out of the light. Then he swung it
back again, not believing his eyes. "Hey! There's a kid in
here!"

His partner shouted something, but he couldn't hear it; he

was making too much noise shoving and wiggling himself forward on his belly. The kid wasn't moving.

"Hey, kid!" Hell, it was a goddamned dead kid. The young cop reached forward to pull the dead kid by the leg.

The dead kid moaned.

"Holy shit," the young cop whispered to the kid, who was obviously not dead, but not far from it, either.

"Hey, radio an ambulance, he's alive! And tell 'em send a unit to see the people who own this joint, the ones we were s'posed to do a drive-by on after we got done with this place."

Let's just see what they have to say, the young cop thought as the kid struggled to breathe. Every time the kid's chest went up and down, it made a sound like a sodden sponge being squeezed and released.

"Yeah," the young cop said, "you keep on breathing. The bad part's over now, buddy. All the bad stuff is over now for you."

The kid's eyelids fluttered. No question but he was the kid everyone had been looking for, vanished out of the park the other night like he'd vanished off the face of the earth. And now here he was in the crawl space of a vacant house, stuck behind a great big freezer that he sure as hell couldn't have shoved up against the wall himself. And if somebody hadn't found him here pretty quick, the outcome could have been . . . worrisome.

"Hang on, cowboy. Help's on the way. Things were bad, but they're getting a lot better. We've got," the young cop told the unconscious kid, "a whole new goddamn situation here."

◆ ◆ ◆

"No uniforms," Edwina said sternly. "And no giving of any orders, instructions, guidelines, advice, commentary, or critiques whatsoever to anyone in my employ, unless first approved by me. Is that clear, Mother?"

"Yes, dear," Harriet replied, looking meekly up from a pile

of knitting, itself enough to make Edwina suspicious. Ordinarily Harriet was about as interested in creating hand-made items as hornets were in making honey, and she was about as accomplished at the process, too.

"Drat," the old lady muttered, "another dropped stitch. But I must finish this scarf; winter is here, and dear Claudio's neck will be getting cold."

From behind McIntyre's newspaper came a snort that he tried too late to disguise as a cough.

"Laugh all you like," said Harriet, unperturbed. "Claudio usually spends his winters in the south of France, only this year he's staying here with me. To carn," she elaborated, "his share of the substantial advance we have been offered to write our new book. So far, his ideas have been very interesting."

From what Edwina had been able to gather, Claudio's ideas were not the only interesting thing about him. At the moment he was sitting on the floor, ignoring the talk going on over his head, contentedly playing with Jonathan and Francis.

"Zoom," he said, running a toy car across the floor. "Zoom, vroom."

Francis goggled at the enormous man with the craggy, tanned face and yellow, shoulder-length hair. Claudio's torso was as wide as the boy was tall, a fact that had helped elevate Claudio to romantic hero—superstar status, first on the covers of romance novels and now, putatively at least, as the co-author of one.

Giggling, Jonathan tried to climb Claudio's shoulders, as if he were a tree. The young man's ability to speak only about fourteen words of English did not seem to trouble the twins, and when Harriet talked about a substantial advance she usually meant plenty of zeroes in groups of three, so she was not about to let any little deficiency in the language department bother her either. She looked, in fact, inordinately pleased with herself, and this went on making Edwina feel uneasy.

"I don't understand," Rita said from the wicker chaise

where she was lying, "what that other boy was doing in that house. Why did the teacher put him there?"

In the days since she and the twins had been released from the hospital, the three of them along with Edwina and Martin McIntyre had been recovering nicely at Harriet's house. Only Rita's energy level did not seem what it had been, and something else was bothering her, too, but Edwina didn't know what.

"Not the teacher," said Lorelei Whitelaw, who since her own recovery from a concussion had taken to waiting hand and foot on Rita, making her take walks and swim laps in Harriet's pool and urging her to eat healthy foods. To Edwina's surprise, Lorelei was very good at her self-appointed practical nurse role; with the elder Whitelaws off to Florida for the season, Lorelei had moved into the big house in Litchfield, too.

She had not bounced back quite as well from the loss of her sister, but she was working on it. She needed, Edwina realized, something to do, something that needed doing; it was all Lorelei had ever needed. And she adored the twins.

"The teacher's wife," Lorelei told Rita. "Her husband was selling marijuana to the students at the high school, and Tad Conway—the one the police got out of the house—he found out and was going to tell the principal. He *told* the teacher he was going to."

She took a deep breath. "So the teacher got scared and told his wife, and she cleaned the dope out of the freezer where he kept it. Then she decided to scare the kid, so he would keep his mouth shut."

"To scare him," McIntyre put in darkly, "with a loaded gun."

McIntyre thought Mrs. Egloff's story of what had happened in the park that night, and afterwards, left much to be desired, and he was looking forward to prosecuting her wits out.

"Which she fired," he went on, "accidentally or with intent, wounding Gerry Bailey, whom she thought she had killed, whereupon she proceeded to assault, kidnap, and imprison the sole witness to her crime, Tad Conway, who got away into the crawl space of the vacant house. So she did what any right-thinking lady would do in the same situation: after a couple of halfhearted efforts to get him out, she trapped him in there, and left him."

He rattled his newspaper for emphasis. "She's going away," he said, "and so is that twerp husband of hers who says he didn't put her up to it. He says he didn't tell her the boys would be in the park, then hang out all evening in a bar just so he'd have witnesses to where he was."

McIntyre scowled. "But I say he overheard the boys talking about their camping trip, and I say he's as dirty as she is."

"What," Harriet inquired, "about the handgun? The one the Conway boy supposedly had. The papers say Mrs. Egloff claims *he* shot the Bailey boy."

McIntyre's scowl turned to a grin of mirthless, merciless ferocity. "She doesn't know it yet, but that gun was found in the bushes, in the park. Unloaded, and it hadn't been fired. The Conway kid must have dropped it when she hit him on the head. With," he added, his voice dripping disgust, "her fist."

It was almost six in the evening, and Ed Chernoff would be arriving soon for dinner; Edwina got up to begin getting ready. She wasn't quite sure what Harriet had told Emeralinda Whitelaw to persuade her to provide the document that Ed would receive later tonight, in private. But the document said that many years ago, Emeralinda had given Ed substantial gifts of money, and that statements alleging otherwise, no matter who made them, were to be considered utterly false, malicious, and fully actionable.

Trust Emeralinda, Edwina thought, not only to establish the facts to suit her purposes, but to try to legislate how everyone felt and what they did, too. Still, Edwina suspected that tonight Ed Chernoff would get not only one of Harriet's excellent dinners, but also his first good night's sleep in quite some time.

"Dear," said Harriet, "I have a confession to make."

Oh, good, Edwina thought sourly, another confession. Frieda Schreiber's had been remarkably complete, and so repulsive that it had quite put Edwina off hearing any personal revelations, confessional or otherwise, for the forseeable future.

Still, she supposed she had better make an exception for Harriet; who knew what the old lady might have been up to in her constant quest to keep all physical, mental, and emotional pots at a perpetual boil?

"Yes, Mother," Edwina said cautiously, wondering what bombshell Harriet was about to drop.

"I have made a few arrangements without consulting you," the old lady replied. "And without consulting Rita or Lorelei."

The girls turned, and McIntyre lowered his newspaper; this sounded serious.

"I have enrolled Rita in the Rhode Island School of Design," Harriet pronounced. "She will begin the spring semester, by which time I trust she will have regained her health."

She peered at Rita, whose mouth formed an O of happiness mingled with disbelief, and who looked healthier already. So that, Edwina realized, was what was troubling the girl; escaping death did tend to bring sharply to the forefront the question of what to do with one's life.

"It's true," Harriet assured her. "Talented young women should not spend their lives as babysitters, merely because they haven't the money to do otherwise. I persuaded friends in the admissions department, and the money will be supplied by me."

"Oh, Mrs. Crusoe," Rita breathed. "How can I thank you?" She looked as if she might start by crying.

"Work hard and do well," Harriet said. "And throw out that uniform."

"Mother," Edwina asked Harriet later in the pantry, "what

about the boys? What you're doing is wonderful, but where am I going to find anyone else like Rita to take care of them?"

Harriet finished counting the butter knives and started on the spoons; having devoured their dinners, the men were in the television room watching a soccer game. Claudio, it turned out, knew plenty of English words, most of them sports terms; if he and Harriet could come up with a romance plot that happened to take place in a hockey arena, the two of them would collaborate quite nicely.

"I think I've taken care of that, too," said Harriet, "and Lorelei's reaction to Rita's good news only confirms my opinion. Lorelei forgot that I had mentioned her at all, in her happiness for her friend. Most encouraging, wouldn't you say?"

Harriet closed the silver chest. "I think Lorelei ought to come and work for you, taking care of the twins. It would get her out of her parents' house and give her something useful and pleasant to do, and it would provide you with a replacement for Rita. You've seen how devoted and responsible she is, caring for Rita, and she loves the boys. Perhaps you'd give her a try?"

Edwina blinked. She had been ready to argue, but it was a good idea, and she was sure Lorelei would jump at it. "But what about her parents? They've kept her on a pretty short leash."

"Her parents won't be back for months," Harriet observed. "And if when they return they object to an arrangement I've made for the benefit of all concerned, they can take it up with me. I've gotten," she added wickedly, "rather handy at persuading the Whitelaws of things."

"So you have." Edwina put her arm around her mother, who smelled as sweetly as always of Pear's soap, scented face powder, and Joy perfume. "You've taken care of everything so thoroughly and well, in fact, that I'm afraid we have nothing to do tomorrow."

"Good," said Harriet, pleased. "Then let's go shopping."

* * *

Marion Bailey sat in the living room of the small wooden house she had moved into on the day she got married. Upstairs, Gerry Junior slept like the dead, tired out from helping to pack suitcases and boxes with his clothes and personal possessions.

She wasn't sending him back to school this year, even though he was almost well enough to go. She wasn't going back to work at the hospital, either; her lawyer said she would have more than enough income not to have to, even before the house was sold.

Gerrald's lawyer wasn't arguing anything, since in order to do so, Gerrald would have to admit to enough tax misdeeds to put him in prison for years. It was, Marion's own lawyer said, a monkey trap: in order to get free, Gerrald had to let go, and it seemed that he had. Marion, at least, had not heard from him.

She finished her coffee and took her cup to the kitchen. Tomorrow morning they would be leaving early, driving first to Arizona for the winter and in spring to Canada, maybe as far as Alaska. She was excited, and Gerry Junior seemed even more so, marking out their route on a map, choosing towns for them to stop in at night, and picking attractions for them to see along the way.

Setting her cup on the drainboard under the kitchen window, Marion felt overcome with emotion; she recognized the feeling as happiness.

Beware; it is an illusion. It can be destroyed. It can be swept away in an instant.

But for now it was enough.

ABOUT THE AUTHOR

MARY KITTREDGE, a former respiratory therapist for a major city hospital, is the author of five previous novels featuring Edwina Crusoe, including *Fatal Diagnosis* and *Desperate Remedy*. A native of Milwaukee, she lives in North Branford, Connecticut.

If you enjoyed Mary Kittredge's KILL OR
CURE, you'll want to read FATAL
DIAGNOSIS, featuring Edwina Crusoe.

coming soon in Bantam paperback!

Turn the page for a special advance look at
FATAL DIAGNOSIS.

"This won't hurt a bit," Helene Motavalli told the little girl as she swabbed the small outstretched arm with an alcohol wipe.

"I know," the child replied. "It's OK, I'm not scared."

Turning, Helene readied the plastic syringe and the small glass collection tubes, shielding the child from the sight of them until the final moment. "My, you're a brave one, aren't you?"

The little girl was nine, with big brown eyes behind thick tortoiseshell glasses. She wore a denim jumper, dark green sweater and green cable-stitched knee socks. Her long dark braids were tied with green ribbons, and on her feet were a pair of Buster Brown shoes, the heavy brown old-fashioned kind. Helene hadn't thought they even made Buster Brown shoes anymore.

The youngster crossed her green-stockinged ankles primly. "No, I'm not brave," she said. "But I'm very grown-up. That," she confided, "means acting like you're brave, even when really you're not."

"I see." Helene checked once more to make sure the blood tubes were all sodium-heparinized green-tops and that she had a few spares in case one didn't pull enough vacuum. Few things were worse than having the tube fail after you'd already stuck a person, especially a child. Finally, still blocking the girl's line of sight, she heparinized a 21-gauge needle.

Kids could be fine until they got a look at the needle. Then they were apt to scream bloody murder, kicking and thrashing their incredibly strong little bodies around while Mom and Dad tried to hold them.

Hitting that small, fragile vein was no cinch any time, but when it belonged to little Miss or Mister Destructo, then you were talking hematoma: a great big purple-green bruise where you'd had to go in twice or even maybe three times to get a single tubeful. Maybe a good-sized shiner on you, too, if a flying fist or sneaker managed to connect.

Helene turned, syringe in hand. This child didn't have Mom or Dad with her, and if a kid was going to pitch a fit, now was when it happened. Still, there was no sense showing you expected it, so Helene merely steadied the child's arm, placing her left hand under the child's elbow and poising the needle with her right. The big brown eyes widened a fraction, but that was all.

"Ready?" Helene asked. "Can you hold real still?"

Catching her bottom lip between her teeth, the child moved her head gravely up and down. "Uh-huh," she said faintly, but by that time Helene had already snicked the 21-gauge through the skin and into the bluish vein beneath.

"Mmmph," the child said, her chin coming up a little, but otherwise she didn't twitch. Dark red blood fountained into the green-stoppered tube.

"Worst part's done," Helene said. "Now we just fill up a few more." Smoothly she slipped the first tube off the needle and socketed a new one onto it. More of the child's blood spurted.

"You are being just fabulous," Helene told her, dropping the first tube into the wire basket behind her. "Who taught you how to be so brave—I mean, so grown-up?"

The child blinked shyly. "My dad. He says I should practice for when I have my scar fixed. It's pretty big," she added, "and ugly when I wear a bathing suit."

"Oh my. How did that happen?"

The child looked embarrassed. "I tipped a kettle over on myself when I was little. But my dad put ice on me and now he's having me save up my blood so the doctor can give it back when he's making the scar better. That," she finished, "is why I'm used to having needles."

"Your father sounds like a smart man. You know this blood I'm taking now isn't for your operation, though, don't you?"

"Uh-huh." The big brown eyes grew somber. "I might not get to have it even. The judge might say I have to wait." The child's brow furrowed. "Can I ask you a question?"

"Sure." Helene slid the final green-top onto the needle.

"Um, when you test them, do you know which is which?"

"Whose blood in which tubes, you mean?" Helene slipped the rubber tourniquet from the child's arm. "Nope. Well, I know which ones are your tubes," she amended. "That's what I'll be matching the others with. But for the rest, I only have numbers. I won't know whose tubes matched yours until I look the numbers up in the book where the names are written."

The child nodded seriously. "Like a game, sort of. Only not a very fun game."

"No," Helene agreed. "I expect none of this has been much fun for you, has it?"

She dropped the final blood tube into the basket. The child watched as Helene withdrew the needle from her arm, then took the cotton ball she was offered and pressed it to the puncture mark.

"Press hard," Helene told her, and the little girl obeyed, frowning with concentration. Then she looked up, her brown eyes filled with tears.

"Oh, honey, what's wrong? Did I hurt you? I'm sorry."

The child pressed her lips together and shook her head. The green-ribboned braids swung back and forth.

"But," she appealed, "couldn't you just cheat a little bit? Find out which tubes are which and match them up the way I ask you?" She thought a moment. "I could pay you," she offered. "I save most of my allowance."

Helene was shocked. A nice kid like this, one in a million, smart and polite and sweet—offering a bribe. Why did they all have to fight over her this way and put the poor thing through such a circus?

But of course she knew why. If you read the newspaper or watched TV, you could hardly miss finding out. Helene hoped that wasn't how the child learned what these tests were for.

"No, honey," she said, "I'm afraid I couldn't do that. You see, people have to be able to believe in the results of tests like these. They're very important. Even you have to be able to believe in them, so whatever the answer turns out to be you'll know for sure it's the truth."

"I already know the truth." The child's soft pink lip thrust out mutinously. "I know who my mom and dad are, and even if you take out *all* my blood and test it, they'll *still* be my mom and dad."

And to that there didn't seem to be any good answer, so Helene just took back the blood-dotted cotton and tossed it into the wastebasket. The bluish puncture on the child's arm was barely visible.

"Okay, honey, that's it. All done."

The little girl nodded, slid from the chair, and to Helene's surprise held out her hand to be shaken. Her tears had gone, but the small fingers were still damp and chilly with anxiety.

"Thank you for being so nice to me," she said. "It really didn't hurt a bit. And I'm sorry I asked you to do something wrong. I wouldn't want you to get in trouble or anything."

"I know, honey. It's all right, don't worry about it." You poor little thing, Helene added silently.

Taking back her hand, the child tried to smile and nearly managed. "Good-bye," she said.

She went out through the door to the waiting area. She had told her father that she would be all right alone, so he had been waiting for her out there, reading old issues of *The Immunology Review* and *Lab Management Quarterly*.

If in fact he really was her father, which was what Helene was about to discover. Good luck, honey, she thought as the door closed quietly; I hope it all turns out OK for you.

Taking the three green-topped tubes from the wire basket, Helene dropped them in the pocket of her lab coat and walked through the door to the tissue-typing laboratory.

Inside, the lab smelled faintly of burnt gas, formalin, and Cidex sterilizing solution. Overhead fluorescents gave off a bright white light and a barely audible hum. Floor-to-ceiling wooden cupboards and a black Formica counter ran along three sides of the room; a central freestanding bench held a sink with nozzles labeled Gas, Air, O_2 and Vacuum in addition to the usual Hot and Cold.

Beside the sink stood a rack of clean Pyrex flasks, a Bunsen burner with a red rubber hose running to a gas nozzle, and a squat centrifuge that resembled a pressure cooker. Against the fourth wall stood a counter covered by an exhaust hood, for working with fumes or contaminated aerosols.

Half-blocked by the hood was the laboratory's only window, an ancient double-hung affair: spotless on the inside, grimy on the outside, it afforded a narrow view of a small square of sky. On summer days Helene would have liked to open this window, but its lock was frozen and the frame had been painted shut years ago.

Now Helene ignored the window in favor of the thermostat, fiddling with it in hopes of coaxing up some heat. Her attentions produced a small clicking from the mechanism and a series of protesting thumps from the ventilator, but no warm air.

Shrugging, she buttoned her lab coat, under which she wore jeans and sweater, sneakers, and a Timex digital wristwatch that also functioned as a stopwatch, alarm clock, and programmable calculator. As she readied a Hamilton syringe and a set of microtitre plates at the lab bench, the watch read 9:25 A.M.

Turning to her clipboard she began filling in another tissue-typing worksheet, her fifth of the morning. Copying from the labels on the blood tubes, she listed the child's name, date of birth, when the samples had been obtained and by whom, and the child's recent transfusion history. On this line, as on the other four worksheets she had filled out this morning, Helene wrote "None."

To record the chain of custody under which the samples were secured between drawing and testing, she wrote "Does not apply—proc. immed. p̄ venipunct." and initialed this. On the line asking how the client had been identified, she listed "Photo ID #4525667-S, State of Connecticut," thinking as she did so that no nine-year-old girl should have to prove her identity to anyone, much less to some stranger getting ready to stick a needle in her arm.

Then, having completed the appropriate paperwork, she turned her attention to the procedure at hand. It was picky work and time-consuming, but not particularly difficult, first separating red cells from white cells and serum with a specific-gravity solution, then spinning the white cells into a pellet in the centrifuge.

Next, the white cells were tricked into separating further; the T-cells would adhere to a column of nylon wool suspended in fetal calf serum, while the B-cells would not. Then the T-cells were washed off with warm solutions and the B-cells aggregated with cool. Finally the microtitre plates were prepared.

With an auto-pipette calibrated to millionths of a liter, Helene dropped a microliter of T-cell solution into each of the plastic plate's seventy-two small wells. Each well already contained a microliter of antiserum, a different type for each well, so that when the careful task of pipetting was done she had only to cover all the plates with glass slides, set them in the incubator, and wait: an hour for T-cells, three for B-cells.

If her luck ran right she would be finished by five and out of here on time, for once; with organ transplants running at the rate of two a day in the state—a hundred a day nationwide—she'd been busy as hell lately, matching available organs with people who needed new kidneys, livers, lungs, or hearts.

Cold weather slowed things for a time, as motorcycle season ended and the pool of organ donors dried up temporarily. But soon snowmobiling and icy-road accidents would begin, treating the demand for healthy tissue to a renewed supply of harvestable cadavers.

So tonight, dinner and to bed—unless, of course, this first set of tests proved inconclusive.

The tests could be simple: look through the microscope, count cells killed by the antiserum in each of the plate's wells, score each field from one to eight by consulting a printed chart, and read down the chart for your genotypes.

And they might be simple: Mendelian law being what it was, each of a child's antigens was directly traceable to one or the other of its parents.

Best would be a classic Mendelian cross: four unique antigens from father, four from mother, while the other tested adults bore no antigens common to the child's, ruling out blood kinship as perfectly as examples from a genetics text.

If Helene's luck didn't run right, though, she would have to go on to track the chromosomal cross-overs, antigen cross-reactivities, and gene-recombination frequencies. Worst case, she'd have to check out four sets of grandparents and who knew how many aunts and uncles, and end up swinging through four different family trees like a monkey in the jungle.

Helene sighed as she closed the incubator door. While these possibilities were troublesome, she knew they were also the basis for her place as chief technician in the immunology lab, so she could not entirely resent them.

Gregor Mendel hadn't had a clue about human immune response, which Helene sometimes suspected of generating new antigens just out of spite. Half the human tissue antigens—probably more—had not yet even been identified, and most techs didn't understand how to handle these unknowns when they showed up in a potential tissue match.

But Helene did. She couldn't explain just how she knew which immune system proteins, lurking on the white-cell surfaces, waited like shrapnel bombs to explode in a transplant patient's immune system. Still, she knew which serum reactions looked bad but were little more than saber-rattlings, which looked good yet were in truth murders waiting to be committed. Tissue matchings endorsed by herself had acceptance rates approaching 95 percent; the best other labs could do—on good days—was 75.

Questioned, Helene only laughed and said she could smell a white cell getting ready to pick a fight. Privately, though, she sometimes wondered if it happened to anyone else, the looking and looking, day in and day out, until she was no longer seeing cells but seeing into them. Human blood cells, stained, fixed in formalin: Helene saw them and felt, simply, a pricking in her thumbs.

Now, with the microtitre plates incubating and no others waiting to be processed, she set her watch timer for an hour, locked the lab, and headed downstairs to the hospital cafeteria. After lunching on a carton of blueberry yogurt and a bran muffin, she strolled to the credit union office, deposited a paycheck of $532.07, and took a flyer advertising low rates on loans for new or used cars.

Then she headed back past the pharmacy and the diagnostic-imaging departments, the clinical chemistry lab and the medical records room and the mail room, until she reached the basement of the building where her own lab was, twelve stories up.

Stepping from the elevator on the twelfth floor, she picked her way among coils of cable, stepladders, power tools, and dumpsters filled with torn-down sections of drywall, walking under yellow utility lamps strung haphazardly from dropcords. There was no sign of workmen, only a clutter of open toolboxes and an imperfectly swept-up mess of plaster dust with footprints tracked through it.

Helene wished they would hurry. On this floor, her lab alone had escaped the uproar of remodeling; with the others moved elsewhere until the job was done, working up here was a bit like working on the moon: isolated, and too silent.

Her watch beeped its one-hour reminder as she unlocked the lab and let herself in. Good, she thought, swinging the door shut behind her; a watched incubator never boiled.

Removing the warm T-cell plates and carrying them to the lab bench, she added five microliters of sticky tan rabbit-complement fluid to each well and set the plates aside. The rabbit serum would cause the killed cells to absorb stain so they could be seen and counted.

Next, she began the patient task of staining and fixing the wells from plates she had prepared earlier, first adding five microliters of eosin, then an equal amount of formaldehyde fixative. Finally she relaid the glass slides over the rows of wells to flatten the seventy-two convex droplets in each typing plate.

Sixty minutes later she laid the first plate into the clips of the Leitz inverted microscope's heavy black viewing stage, adjusted the rheostat on the illuminator, and peered into the instrument's binocular eyepiece, adjusting the fine-focus knob as she did. Swiftly she began counting the killed cells in each viewing field, hardly glancing up as she noted the results on the first worksheet.

By a little after 3:00 P.M., all the T-cells had been counted. On the five worksheets, only columns labeled *Dr* remained unfilled.

These columns were for the results of B-cell plates, the antigens occupying the fourth loci in each blood sample's immune-system fingerprint.

Staring at the letters and numbers in the grids already filled in, Helene felt the pricking of her thumbs spread into her wrists and begin shooting ominously toward her elbows. Bending to the eyepiece of the Leitz, she pronounced to herself the numbers of cells killed by the antisera in each well of the first B-cell plate, then made a note on the worksheet.

Filling in the *Dr* loci was like getting the final letters in a crossword puzzle or making visible a message written in invisible ink. Slowly, what had been hidden began to appear, each new symbol confirming a meaning that to Helene had already become obvious.

Really, she thought, how very unlikely and astonishing. And completely unarguable, for she had drawn all the samples herself and was sure there had been no mistake.

Bending for a last squint at the final field, she heard a small clicking sound behind her, almost like the sound of the thermostat she had been fiddling with earlier.

Only not quite like that.

Frowning, she raised her eyes from the microscope. Someone stood framed in the open doorway of the lab. Helene had an instant to know the face, but before she could put a name to it the clicking sound came again, then exploded in a bright white thunderclap.

Reaching out blindly, she found the worksheets and clutched at them, feeling them crumple wetly in her hand as she fell.

Good luck, honey, she thought as the explosion faded and the white light grew brighter.

Wondrously, unimaginably brighter.

The crack of two rocks rapped sharply together underwater startled the small bright fish drifting in schools like neon clouds over the coral landscape. In a flashing instant they vanished into the waving green fields of turtlegrass and forests of sea cucumber.

Edwina Crusoe kicked once and ascended toward the wavery surface. Breaking through, she spat out the snorkel's mouthpiece and dragged her goggles back.

"What?" Above her loomed the *Bertram*'s white fiberglass hull. Tami had thrown the rope ladder over the side.

His lean, toast-brown face appeared at the rail. "Sorry," he said. In his hand was something that looked like a pocket radio with an aerial sticking up from one end. "Mainland."

"Blast." She kicked off her flippers, caught them before they could sink, and scrambled up the hemp rungs.

"Rough being indispensible," he agreed. Hauling the ladder up, he stowed it in the footlocker with the cushions and life preservers. "Catch your breath, I told them it'd be a few."

She dropped her gear on the canvas tarp and toweled her hair briefly with the coarse length of terry cloth he handed her. The warm Caribbean sun dried the droplets on her body, leaving small white salt circles that she brushed away.

"You should have told them I'd drowned."

Fastening the locker hasp, he grinned at her. "They'd never believe it." He picked up the can of polish and the cloth with which he had been lustering the aft bulkheads and gazed with sudden interest over the gunwale at the blank blue horizon.

"Go on, take it below before the sun fries you." He tossed the wireless phone at her. A moment later came the distant growl of diesel inboards, a white dot of spray appearing just outside the line of breakers at the lagoon's mouth.

The approaching craft found its way through the barrier reef and cut its engine as it drew alongside. It was an old Chris-Craft cruiser with dark-tinted windows, its foredecks and cabin trunk weathered to a pewterish teak-gray.

Edwina fished an icy bottle in Tsing Tao from the cockpit cooler and went below, pulling the sliding door shut behind her. Tami liked privacy for his business dealings, some of which came on abruptly and not all of which, she felt sure, involved being handsomely paid for a couple of days' worth of easy skippering.

The aft cabin bristled with navigation gear: radar devices, sextants and compasses, weather gadgets, and a library of charts. Not for the first time, Edwina wondered what sort of contraband Tami made his living running.

It could hardly be drugs; in the many trips she had made here she had always chartered with Tami and had never seen him with so much as a single joint. But that didn't mean he was necessarily a stranger to other exotic transportables: rare shells, for instance or the jewel-like chrysalises of tropical butterflies, whose prices were skyrocketing as their species edged steadily nearer to extinction.

In her own small cabin she sat cross-legged on the narrow bunk, drawing the curtain over the porthole, which at this time of day resembled a hot, staring eye. After several long swallows of the scouringly cold beer, she leaned the bottle on her bare leg and pressed the button on the wireless phone.

A brief electronic sputter was followed by the voice of the AT&T international operator, the satellite dish on the flying bridge overhead drawing the signal in as if it came from the island and not from two thousand miles away.

You can run but you can't hide, Edwina thought sourly, as a familiar voice came through the handset.

♦ ♦ ♦

Returning to the above deck, she found the Chris-Craft gone and Tami locking the hatch on the aft hold.

"You look like you just stepped on a spiny urchin," he observed.

The beer had gone warm; she poured the rest over the lee rail. "Friend of mine's been hurt at home. Anyone flying out of Port Caribe that you know of? I have to go back."

Tami straightened. With his fierce white teeth and his hair blue-black in the sun, he looked like a modern-day pirate.

"Not unless you want to fly a powder-puff run."

It was local slang for a cocaine trip. The small planes took off from Panamanian carriers, skimmed in low, then island-hopped until they reached Port-au-Prince or one of the other distribution centers. From there the drug was muled a few kilos at a time into Miami—or, increasingly, along the less closely watched supply lines like the Marina Key-West Palm Beach route.

"They're fast," Tami said, "but sometimes they get shot down."

She shook her head. "I'll find a charter. If I make it fast, I can get the night flight direct out of Kingston."

Tami considered, "Vinnie Cusano runs a milk and vegetable haul off Madrigal. We could call him."

"Uh-huh." she stared at the waves. "But first I'd have to get to Madrigal."

Tami's boat worked out of the island of San Jiralomo, a small mountainous atoll often uncharted and almost unknown to any but hard-bitten diving enthusiasts. Its only settlement boasted saloons, a dive shop, a ramshackle wooden hotel, and very little else. Getting on and off San Jiralomo took ingenuity, which was fine with Edwina except in emergencies.

"Vinnie can't fly in here, and if he did he couldn't fly out again," she said.

Frowning, Tami pretended to consider this, then vanished below. An instant later came the clatter of the anchor being raised, its chain reeling smoothly onto the power capstan, and the gurgly grumble of the *Bertram*'s 350-horse MerCruisers coming to life.

A sudden gust of diesel fumes reminded her why power boats were called stinkpots. Still, the *Bertram* was faster than any sailboat. Strapped into the companion benchseat with the banners snapping and the outriggers screaming overhead, she watched the water's surface drop away as the boat's stem nosed up.

"Not bad," she shouted. "What's she do, fifty?"

Tami shook his head, pushing forward in the throttle, which seemed—although of course that was ridiculous—to be up only about halfway.

Fifty knots was pretty good for a cruiser. Tami's mouth moved, but she couldn't hear what he said. He throttled up once more and the forty-foot *Bertram* seemed to gather itself in response, bunching its muscles for a lunge forward.

Then came a faint electronic whine, a whisper of resistance, and an amazing thing happened: the craft lifted onto the water and *skimmed* across it.

Hydroplane wings, Edwina realized: the smooth, tightly folded structures she had seen below the waterline but had been unable to identify. Now the *Bertram* was flying, just kissing the waves. Sixty-five knots, seventy.

Tami cut hard to starboard and spray flew up in a series of cold, brisk slaps. Green waters deepened to purple-black.

"What?" she shouted, cupping her ears.

"I said," he bellowed, "her top's around ninety. Never had her up that far though. Want to try?"

What the hell. You could live an adventurous life and die having fun.

Or you could play it safe and get shot in the head in broad daylight, while supposedly secure inside Chelsea Memorial Hospital in New Haven, Connecticut.

She would be there, she calculated, in a little under twelve hours. "Let'er rip!"

Behind and below, the MerCruisers howled like beasts out of their cages. Tami, his eyes and his grin stretched wide as they could go, throttled up a final time.

A *lot* faster.

◆ ◆ ◆

In the gray predawn the Boeing 737 banked over the Hudson River, buzzed Manhattan from Times Square to its leg-turn over High Bridge Park, cleared the Triborough with, apparently, inches to spare, and dropped like a stone toward the East River.

Reminding herself that the pilot no doubt did this every morning, that he must be well trained and extremely experienced, Edwina studiously unclenched her stiff, white fingers from the armrests and began gathering her belongings.

Hours earlier she had taken off from an oiled-dirt runway, out of a soup bowl crater surrounded by mountains and jungles of lush, sinister-looking greenery. The lurching ascent, accompanied by protests from the Cessna two-seater and curses from the hung-over pilot, had in no way resembled anything envisioned by Orville and Wilbur.

Nevertheless she preferred it to this landing at La Guardia, where the black waves rose up so fast she was sure she could read the labels on the bits of garbage bobbing in them in the long moments before the 737's wheels bumped reassuringly down.

In the terminal the wait for once was not interminable: she stood for just a few minutes while her papers were examined and her duffel rooted through by a sleepy customs clerk who blinked only at the line on her visa listing her occupation as "registered nurse."

Dressed in dark Levi's and boots, a black leather bomber jacket over a white silk shirt and a rope of turquoise and beaten-silver lumps at her throat, Edwina knew she must not look like a nurse to him. She apparently also didn't resemble someone who hid cocaine and marijuana among her underthings, for after a cursory check and a final puzzled glance he waved her on through.

Feeling the mild euphoria of someone who has, in rapid succession, descended safely from 37,000 feet and been declared street-legal by a U.S. government official, she hoisted her duffel and proceeded to the long-term parking lot. There she found the Fiat Spider just as she had left it: black canvas top unslit, apricot paint unmarred, head and tail lights all present and intact.

This seemed a miracle until she spotted the seven buff tags stuck under the driver's side windshield wiper. It appeared that she had parked the Spider in a spot that was For Official Use Only—an offense carrying a fifty-dollar-a-day fine.

Ticketing her for this offense was clearly unreasonable. Of course she was using the space officially. She was parked in it wasn't she? Stacking the summonses neatly one atop the other, she tore the entire pile into twenty-eight eminently satisfying pieces and dropped them into a trash bin marked Fine For Littering $25.

Gratified at having saved $375 instead of only $350—by not spitting in the subway, she calculated, she could raise the total to $400—she fired up the Fiat and roared down the concrete ramp, heading for the lane marked 678—Whitestone Bridge—New England.

By the time she got onto the bridge, however, her pleasure was extinguished by the memory of why she was returning to New Haven. Also she lacked exact change for the toll. Sighing, she edged the Fiat into the line backed up from the booth marked Attendant On Duty, hoping as she did so that this wasn't an omen for the day.

But it was, as she discovered a few moments later when the little car began listing gently but irrevocably to the left, a signal generally employed by the Fiat to let her know that one of its Michelins was flattening. She could change the tire here in the middle of the Whitestone or limp on through the toll to the shoulder, a process that would inevitably warp the rim.

Slamming out of the car, she yanked the jack and lug wrench from behind the driver's seat and stomped around to the trunk. As she removed the spare, the honking began: first brief nudging toots, then long earsplitting blares.

Which was how she knew, aside from a clear mental picture of a seventeen-year-old girl with a bullet in her brain—

Which was how she knew, the marrow-shriveling blasts of an eighteen-wheeler's air horn now confirming this utterly and completely—

Which was how Edwina Crusoe knew that she was no longer in paradise.

BANTAM MYSTERY COLLECTION

____57204-0 **KILLER PANCAKE** Davidson • • • • • • • • • • • • • • $5.50

____56859-0 **A FAR AND DEADLY CRY** Peitso • • • • • • • • • $4.99

____57235-0 **MURDER AT MONTICELLO** Brown • • • • • • • • • $5.99

____29484-9 **RUFFLY SPEAKING** Conant • • • • • • • • • • • $4.99

____29684-1 **FEMMES FATAL** Cannell • • • • • • • • • • • • • $4.99

____56936-8 **BLEEDING HEARTS** Haddam • • • • • • • • • • $5.50

____57192-3 **BREAKHEART HILL** Cook • • • • • • • • • • • • $5.99

____56020-4 **THE LESSON OF HER DEATH** Deaver • • • • • • $5.99

____56239-8 **REST IN PIECES** Brown • • • • • • • • • • • • • $5.50

____56976-7 **THESE BONES WERE MADE FOR DANCIN'** Meyers • • $5.50

____56272-X **ONE LAST KISS** Kelman • • • • • • • • • • • • $5.99

____57455-8 **TO PLAY THE FOOL** King • • • • • • • • • • • • $5.50

____57251-2 **PLAYING FOR THE ASHES** George • • • • • • • • $6.50

____57172-9 **THE RED SCREAM** Walker • • • • • • • • • • • $5.99

____56793-4 **THE LAST HOUSEWIFE** Katz • • • • • • • • • • $5.99

____56805-1 **THE CURIOUS EAT THEMSELVES** Straley • • • • • • $5.50

____56840-X **THE SEDUCTION** Wallace • • • • • • • • • • • • $5.50

____56969-4 **THE KILLING OF MONDAY BROWN** Prowell • • • • • $5.99

____56931-7 **DEATH IN THE COUNTRY** Green • • • • • • • • • • $4.99

____56172-3 **BURNING TIME** Glass • • • • • • • • • • • • • • • $3.99

- -

Ask for these books at your local bookstore or use this page to order.

Please send me the books I have checked above. I am enclosing $_____ (add $2.50 to cover postage and handling). Send check or money order, no cash or C.O.D.'s, please.

Name _____

Address_____

City/State/Zip_____

Send order to: Bantam Books, Dept. MC, 2451 S. Wolf Rd., Des Plaines, IL 60018
Allow four to six weeks for delivery.
Prices and availability subject to change without notice.   MC 8/96

SUE GRAFTON'S

KINSEY MILLHONE IS

"A refreshing heroine!" —The Washington Post Book World

"The best new private eye!" —The Detroit News

"A stand-out specimen of the new female operatives!"
—The Philadelphia Inquirer

"The gutsiest, grittiest female operative going!"
—Daily News, *New York*

___27991-2	**"A"** IS FOR ALIBI	$6.99/$8.99 in Canada	
___28034-1	**"B"** IS FOR BURGLAR	$6.99/$8.99	
___28036-8	**"C"** IS FOR CORPSE	$6.99/$8.99	
___27163-6	**"D"** IS FOR DEADBEAT	$6.99/$8.99	
___27955-6	**"E"** IS FOR EVIDENCE	$6.99/$8.99	
___28478-9	**"F"** IS FOR FUGITIVE	$6.99/$8.99	

*"Once a fan reads one of Grafton's alphabetically titled
detective novels, he or she will not rest until
all the others are found."*
—Los Angeles Herald Examiner

RITA MAE BROWN
& SNEAKY PIE BROWN

"Charming . . . Ms. Brown writes with wise, disarming wit."
— *The New York Times Book Review*

Sneaky Pie Brown has a sharp feline eye for human foibles. She and her human co-author, Rita Mae Brown, offer wise and witty mysteries featuring small-town postmistress Mary Minor Haristeen (known to all as Harry) and her crime-solving tiger cat, Mrs. Murphy.

WISH YOU WERE HERE ___28753-2 $5.99/$7.99 Canada

The recipients of mysterious postcards start turning up murdered and Harry may be the only one able to link the victims. Mrs. Murphy and Harry's Welsh corgi, Tee Tucker, begin to scent out clues to the murderer before Harry finds herself on the killer's mailing list.

REST IN PIECES ___56239-8 $5.99/$7.50

When pieces of a dismembered corpse begin turning up around town, the primary suspect is the new drop-dead-gorgeous romantic interest in Harry's life. Mrs. Murphy decides to investigate and has a hair-raising encounter with the dark side of human nature.

MURDER AT MONTICELLO ___57235-0 $5.99/$7.99

Mrs. Murphy and Tee Tucker are helped out by Pewter, the corpulent cat from a nearby grocery, in solving a two-hundred-year-old murder that someone in Crozet wants left undiscovered.

Ask for these books at your local bookstore or use this page to order.

Please send me the books I have checked above. I am enclosing $____ (add $2.50 to cover postage and handling). Send check or money order, no cash or C.O.D.'s, please.

Name _____

Address _____

City/State/Zip _____

Send order to: Bantam Books, Dept. MC 43, 2451 S. Wolf Rd., Des Plaines, IL 60018
Allow four to six weeks for delivery.
Prices and availability subject to change without notice. · MC 43 8/95

Enthralling tales of deception, detection, and murder from

DOROTHY CANNELL

 ## THE WIDOWS CLUB

____27794-4 $5.50/$7.50 Canada

MUM'S THE WORD

____28686-2 $4.99/$5.99 Canada

THE THIN WOMAN

____29195-5 $5.50/$7.50 Canada

HOW TO MURDER
YOUR MOTHER-IN-LAW

____56951-1 $5.50/$7.50 Canada

HOW TO MURDER
THE MAN OF YOUR DREAMS

____07494-6 $19.95/$27.95 Canada

FEMMES FATAL

____29684-1 $4.99/$5.99 Canada

Ask for these books at your local bookstore or use this page to order.

Please send me the books I have checked above. I am enclosing $____ (add $2.50 to cover postage and handling). Send check or money order, no cash or C.O.D.'s, please.

Name _____

Address _____

City/State/Zip _____

Send order to: Bantam Books, Dept. MC 34, 2451 S. Wolf Rd., Des Plaines, IL 60018
Allow four to six weeks for delivery.

Prices and availability subject to change without notice.   MC 34 2/96